HEAD
SHOT

also by OTHO ESKIN

The Reflecting Pool

HEAD SHOT

A MARKO ZORN NOVEL

OTHO ESKIN

OCEANVIEW PUBLISHING

SARASOTA, FLORIDA

4367

ISBN 978-1-60809-520-9

Published in the United States of America by Oceanview Publishing

Sarasota, Florida

www.oceanviewpub.com

10 9 8 7 6 5 4 3 2

PRINTED IN THE UNITED STATES OF AMERICA

For Neal, Edward, Katherine, and David

ACKNOWLEDGEMENTS

I would like to thank my literary agent, Judith Ehrlich, for her invaluable advice and creative guidance during the course of writing this novel; the late Richard Merek for his insightful suggestions on an early draft; and Ed Stackler for his careful review of a later draft. Thanks also to Erica Ferguson for her excellent proofing suggestions; my personal support team—Judith Ehrlich, Erin Bradford, and Ludovica Villar Hauser—who ably assisted with pre-publication work; and my publishers, Pat and Bob Gussin and the rest of the Oceanview team for their fine support. A belated thanks to Ludovica Villar-Hauser and the staff at Parity Productions for producing a wonderful Zoom launch for the first Marko Zorn novel. And, finally, my heartfelt gratitude to Therese, who kept me going throughout the writing of this book.

HEAD
SHOT

CHAPTER ONE

THE WOOD PANEL explodes above my head, and I drop to the ground and lie pressed against the wet stone steps, sucking in oxygen, my heart pounding, my arteries pumped with adrenaline. I want to scramble to my feet and make a run for it, but I force myself to stay motionless. Here, I'm hidden by the yew trees and shrubs in my front yard. Standing, I'm an easy target.

My face is a few inches from my copy of *The Washington Post* in its plastic wrapper to protect it from the rain. Another giveaway I hadn't yet returned home from police headquarters. I must do something about that problem in the future.

Assuming I have a future.

I'd parked my car in front of my house rather than in my garage, where it would normally be tucked away. It's a 1964, fire-engine-red Corvette convertible. That might as well be a billboard advertisement: This is where Marko Zorn lives. Come and get me. I'm an idiot.

This is a quiet neighborhood of single-family homes, most built in the 1920s, with large yards and wide front porches where people once sat and drank iced tea on warm days. It's a typical Friday early-spring evening and my neighbors are at home from work, drinking martinis, and watching the evening news. The TV screens flicker dimly behind drawn curtains. It's twilight and beginning to rain. No one was on the porches or in the street when I arrived. No one is watching my house.

Except, of course, someone is watching.

He must be hidden behind one of the cars parked across the street or maybe he's in Mrs. Euler's garden, crouched among the red rambler roses, waiting for me, waiting for me to open my front door, waiting for me to give him a clear shot. How could I have not spotted him? I must be getting sloppy.

The shooter now has a problem: Did he see me duck to pick up my newspaper just as he pulled the trigger? He has to be certain he's made a kill; otherwise he won't be paid. That means he must leave his hiding place and cross the street and, to do that, he must show himself.

I figure I have maybe twenty seconds before my killer walks up the path to my house to finish me off. I grope in my pocket for my cell phone—the only weapon I have on me. In the dimness, I can't make out the buttons that control my home security system, so I punch randomly and the lights in the house are suddenly ablaze. The light in one of the bedrooms flashes on, then off; the exterior security lights flood my front lawn illuminating me as well. I kill the floodlights and push more buttons until one activates the shrieking burglar alarm. I think I may even have turned on my kitchen toaster oven. I switch the lights off, then on, then off again, turning my street into a kind of demented amusement park filled with the sound of barking dogs.

I hit the panic alarm on the ignition key fob of my Corvette, and the air shivers with a blaring new siren that harmonizes with the burglar alarm. I remotely key the Corvette's ignition and activate the car's entertainment system. Mozart's *Queen of the Night* aria bursts into the twilight: very pretty but not quite the effect I was hoping for, so I switch to another channel and land on a rock station and pump the volume up to maximum.

Perfect.

I call 911 and report a "disturbance in progress" on my street, having to yell to make myself heard above the noise. I identify myself as a police officer and give my address.

In minutes, my crankier neighbors switch on their porch lights and emerge from their homes to find out what's happened to their peaceful neighborhood. They stand on their porches and stare in awe at my house as it flashes on and off to the sound of what seems to be mariachi hip-hop.

The sound of a new siren shatters what's left of the neighborhood peace. A police cruiser, lights flashing, swings around the corner at the end of my block, stops in front of my house, and two uniformed cops emerge. Time, I decide, to end the sound-and-light show. The street goes dark: the rock and roll stops; the barking dogs fall silent.

My phone rings, and when I pick up, a gravelly baritone announces: "We must talk. Ten o'clock. The usual place."

"I'm kind of in the middle of something just now," I say. "Can it wait until tomorrow?"

"It can't wait." The phone connection is cut. He never stays on the line more than a few seconds in case his phone calls are being traced. Which they certainly must be by any number of hostile organizations—public and private.

Two uniformed DC police officers appear from behind my azalea bushes and look down at me.

"Show us your ID," says one cop.

"Marko Zorn, Metropolitan Police, Homicide." I get to my feet, slipping the phone into my pocket. I move as nonchalantly and as inconspicuously as I can to stand between the two cops and my front door. I don't want them to see the hole in the wood panel and ask questions about what happened. I'm not sure why I'm doing this, but for the moment I don't want to have to explain that a few minutes ago somebody tried to kill me using a high-powered rifle. I don't need that event showing up in the official incident report drawing the attention of the chief of police and maybe even Internal Affairs. I don't know what happened this evening, but I'm sure I need to find out who's trying to kill me before it becomes part of my record.

My name must mean something to one of the cops. I don't recognize him, but I can tell he sort of recognizes me but is unsure from where—maybe from some police department holiday party, maybe from a photo array.

"Is this your house?" the other cop asks.

"Sure is." I hand him my ID.

The second cop examines my police shield and ID in the dim light and writes my name and police ID number in his notebook. "Are you responsible for this disturbance?"

"I just had a new home-security system installed, and it must have blown out."

The cops look skeptical. "You better have that system checked," one says. "You don't want this to happen again."

When the cops return to their police cruiser, I examine my front door. There's a hole the size of my fist in one of its wooden panels. If it weren't for the steel plates I'd installed, the round would have gone clean through the door.

My neighbors give me dirty looks as I cross the street and walk along the opposite sidewalk, searching among the wet leaves. I stand for a moment, looking across the street at my house, trying to imagine just how the shooter must have seen me, parking my Corvette, walking up the path, stooping down to pick up *The Washington Post* newspaper the delivery guy left this morning after I'd gone to work.

How long, I wonder, had the shooter been waiting for me to show up? It can't have been long. A man with a rifle, almost certainly equipped with a silencer, would draw a lot of attention in our bucolic neighborhood. That means the shooter must have arrived just before

I did and taken up his position, and that means he must have been following me. I change my times and routes day to day for just this reason: to avoid unpleasant surprises. Somebody is tracking me. I decide that speculating about this any further is a pointless waste of my time, and I continue my search.

Using my handkerchief, I pick up a large brass shell casing I find in the gutter among the wet leaves—a rifle round. This I slip into my pocket.

The neighborhood has returned to its normal peacefulness; a single dog a few blocks away is still barking: it hasn't gotten the message the party's over. When I finally go into my house, I make sure that all security systems, including the multiple motion sensors, are operating as they should. They are, but I retrieve my .45 automatic I keep in my bedside table. Just in case.

I pour myself a glass of Elijah Craig bourbon to calm my nerves, turn on a recording of Miles Davis's *Kind of Blue,* and try not to think about the man with a rifle waiting for me across the street.

I consider not going to the meeting I was summoned to. But that would only provoke Cyprian Voss into sending some of his goons to drag me there across town. I've already had enough adventure for one day, and that would injure my dignity. I decide to go peaceably.

* * *

At that moment, as I'm soon to learn, the great actress takes a revolver from its bracket on the wall strides across the stage to the drawing room door, where she stops, turns, and says, her voice in a trembling rage: "You are evil and your evil will be exposed this night." She steps into the drawing room, closing the door behind her. At 9:42, someone puts a bullet through her head.

CHAPTER TWO

WHEN WE MEET it's always at the same place: a small, slightly seedy, Thai restaurant. Cyprian Voss has a weakness for Thai food; someone once told me this goes back to when Voss was involved in a covert action in some war. I don't know which war or on which side: probably both.

A sign on the restaurant door reads "CLOSED". Two men stand on either side: one is Raul; the other, Horst. There will be two more like them guarding the back door, and a fifth one in the kitchen, testing the food.

The dining room is deserted. A pale light from behind the bar shows me the way to a door at the back of the room. I step inside.

A huge man sits at a table. He wears a dark, double-breasted suit, partially covered this evening by a napkin tucked into his collar. His snow-white hair hangs to his shoulders. He raises his large head and smiles at me. At least I think it's me he smiles at; Cyprian Voss is wall-eyed, so he seems to be looking at two things at once. We do not shake hands: he detests being touched.

"Mr. Zorn," the man booms jovially. "Good of you to join me. Forgive me for not getting up. It's hard for me to stand; it's the humidity; it affects my joints."

"You can't stand up because you're too fat."

"That's uncalled for, my boy." He smiles and wipes his wet, pink lips with his napkin. I try to gauge the man's mood. He can be friendly, or he can be deadly. I look for a tell but can't read him.

The table is covered with dishes of food. I smell spiced shrimp soup and pad thai fried noodles. The man eats a large spoonful of fried rice, some of the grains falling to the table.

"You look distracted, dear boy."

"Someone just tried to kill me. I want to know who."

"I'm afraid I can't help you there." He laughs mirthlessly. Something he does when he's lying. He scoops a large helping of khao phat kai onto his plate.

I have to be careful: like all wild animals, if Voss senses fear or weakness, he'll attack.

"If you go on eating like this," I say, "it will kill you."

"Or one of my many enemies will kill me. Or maybe one of my friends: it might even be you, Mr. Zorn." He smiles at me. "We have an assignment for you."

I've worked on the side for Cyprian Voss for several years but I know nothing about who he really is, who he works for, or who controls the large sums of money he pays me and others like me. I'm pretty sure he represents a consortium of wealthy men involved in banking, manufacturing, and mining. As far as I can tell, their immediate political aim is to stop Russia from reclaiming the power and territories it lost at the end of the Cold War. What other aims they may have, I don't want to know.

"Do I have to remind you," I say, "that in addition to dealing with whoever tried to kill me tonight, I have a full-time job as a homicide detective in the Washington, DC, police? At the moment I have half a dozen open cases."

"This entire assignment will take only a few days."

"I need to get rid of the man who tried to shoot me, whoever he is."

Voss waves away my protest. "You are capable of doing two things at once, as you recently demonstrated when you prevented the assassination of the President of the United States, neutralized a domestic terrorist group, and, at the same time, managed to rid Washington of some of its worst gangsters. Very neatly done, sir: I compliment you. I won't ask how you managed that."

Good. Some things are better left unexplained. Voss knows I'm a senior detective with contacts and sources among law enforcement and intelligence agencies and among those on the other side of the law. Voss is happy to take advantage of these sources, not to mention my unorthodox way of getting results. But we have an unspoken understanding: Voss knows I have a strict personal ethical code, and he never asks me to do a job that violates that code. He has others on his payroll for that kind of thing.

"Did you not hear me?" I say. "Somebody tried to put a bullet through my head."

"I did, but this assignment is important."

"So is my head."

"Nina Voychek is the prime minister of the Republic of Montenegro," Voss goes on as if I'd said nothing. "She's arriving in the United States this Sunday evening. Someone plans to kill the lady. Your assignment: see that doesn't happen. I am informed the lady in question is young and quite beautiful. That should appeal to you."

This makes no sense. Why is Voss asking me to babysit some visiting dignitary from somewhere in the Balkans? I'm not a trained bodyguard. That's not my business. This woman will have her own security team plus whatever security the US government provides. This doesn't add up.

"I'm not a bodyguard," I say.

"You have other talents."

What is he not telling me? I've worked long enough for Voss to know when he's lying. I feel sure there's a lot more to this assignment than he's telling me.

"You could hire any number of professionals; there are plenty of former Special Forces types around DC looking for a paycheck and some action."

"This assignment requires nimbleness and a certain delicacy." Voss shovels a heaping spoonful of fried rice and chicken into his mouth and chews reflectively for a moment. "For years, Nina Voychek was the leader of the democratic opposition to the Russian-backed gangsters running her country," he says at last.

"Good for her. I don't know the lady; I'm not sure I know how to pronounce her name. Get someone else."

Voss ignores my protest. "Mykhayl Drach was, until recently, the ruler of Montenegro and on the payroll of Vladimir Putin."

The name Mykhayl Drach gets my full attention.

"Drach's government was recently overthrown in a popular uprising led by Nina Voychek. Mykhayl Drach escaped from Montenegro," Voss continues. "Two weeks ago he was located in Chicago."

"I know: I located him."

Voss dabs his lips with his napkin. "I sent you to Chicago to carry out a routine extraction with instructions to turn the man over to the International Court of Justice for a trial for crimes against humanity. You were not supposed to instigate an international, high-profile riot."

I don't like to be reminded about that Chicago business; what happened there still gives me nightmares. "I can't take this assignment."

"I'm afraid I must insist. If you refuse, that would leave me no choice but to take drastic action."

I feel my pulse speed up. "Are you threatening me?"

"Threatening? Of course not."

"I don't care to be threatened: By you; by anybody. Threats to me usually end badly. For everybody."

Voss pushes himself slowly to his feet. "If you'll forgive me, I must excuse myself for a moment. My bladder isn't what it used to be. Take time to consider your answer, Mr. Zorn. Consider most carefully."

I hate to admit it, but Voss is right about one thing: I did screw up in Chicago. I should have known what would happen when I met those three old men from the émigré organization who told me how they'd lost their parents, brothers, and sisters—children even—slaughtered by Drach's militias: whole villages razed and burned. I should have known what would happen when I saw the rage in their eyes.

That doesn't answer my question: why me? I figure I have a couple of minutes before Voss returns, so I do a search on my cell phone for Nina Voychek. According to a potted biography, she was born in a small mountain village in Montenegro, studied law at the university in the country's capital, and spent three years in the United States at Columbia to study international relations. On her return to Montenegro, she became a political activist in the resistance movement in opposition to the Drach regime.

There are a dozen pictures, mostly from media archives: Nina Voychek appearing at political rallies; Nina giving speeches. One is obviously a police mug shot and is identified as taken when she was arrested for treason by the former regime. One shows her with a group of young men and women who look like college kids. I can make out the lower Manhattan skyline. In that picture, her hair is cut short and she's laughing with her friends. She has a long, slender neck; a charming smile; and large, intelligent eyes. Another picture shows her on what the text says is the day of her release from prison. She looks worn and older, and there is no smile; her throat is concealed by a thick woolen sweater. There are brief references to several recent attempts on her life, including a Reuters report that someone planted a bomb in her official car just a few weeks ago.

Voss is right about one thing: Nina Voychek is beautiful. This assignment might not be as arduous as I feared. Spending a few days with this lady might turn out to be quite agreeable.

I search, looking for a sign of a husband or significant person in her life. All I find is a passing mention of someone named Sasha who seems to have been executed by the Drach regime a year or so ago. There's a picture of her looking at a polished stone in what appears to be a park or cemetery. The scene is described in the accompanying text as a memorial for the martyrs in the struggle against tyranny.

* * *

That brings me back with a jolt to that Chicago street and the three old men. Montenegro means Black Mountain: the men on that street were from the Black Mountain, as were Mykhayl Drach and his brother and also the lady prime minister herself. These people and their ancestors have lived in the hills and deep valleys of the Black Mountain for a thousand years, and they honor the old ways. The families of murder victims do not rest until revenge has been exacted. A death for a death: that's the mountain way. I should have known.

The street had been empty when General Drach left the building where he'd been hiding: he wore a tailored gray suit and sunglasses with gold frames. As soon as he was alone in the street, heading for his car, a crowd appeared as if from nowhere, flooding the street and sidewalks until the area was densely crowded: mostly old men and women, some with canes, some on walkers. I recognized the three old men I'd met that morning. The crowd surged around the general, pressing close in—some shouting curses and others weeping—until they formed an impenetrable knot. The general stared at me for a second, wild-eyed, before he disappeared under the unstoppable tide of raging men and women.

The crowd dissolved as quickly as it had appeared, leaving the street empty. Mykhayl Drach's broken body lay on the pavement: his sunglasses torn from his battered face; blood poured from deep knife wounds in his chest and abdomen and onto his nice Savile Row suit.

*   *   *

There are sounds from down the hall. Voss is returning, and he'll expect my answer. Of course I'll agree to take the assignment. I have already had one dangerous enemy tonight. I don't need Voss to be another. I'd kind of like to get to know this lady prime minister. Plus, I need the money.

Voss sits at the table and looks at me sharply with one of his eyes. "I trust you have reconsidered your decision." He heaps a mound of shrimp and rice onto his plate.

"I'll take on the assignment."

"Good man."

"On one condition. That I'm free to dispose of my enemy at the same time I'm babysitting your prime minister."

"Very well but don't lose your focus. Do not repeat your failure in Chicago."

"I saved the cost of an international tribunal," I protest. "Everybody should be grateful."

Voss scrapes the last remaining bits of shrimp from his plate. "I can't say I personally regret Mykhayl Drach's violent death. He deserved every slash and blow he received."

"It sounds as if you had a personal stake in the general's execution."

"My family comes from Montenegro, and members of my family were among Drach's victims."

I don't know whether to believe him or not.

"I'm so pleased you've seen reason and will do the job. You will, of course, be paid your usual fee of $250,000, plus expenses."

This job can't be what Voss says it is. Nothing in his world is what he says it is. There's always something hidden.

"Are there risks you've forgotten to mention to me?"

Voss makes a dismissive gesture. "Nothing that you can't handle, my boy."

"What will I be facing?"

"The *bratva* is involved."

"What do the Russian Mafia have to do with a visiting head of state from Montenegro? Is Putin outsourcing his thugs from Moscow to kill the lady?"

"Not thugs from Moscow. They're local talent: most likely from Brighton Beach in Brooklyn. They're just backup. The main job will be carried out by a professional assassin. But these *bratva* boys are tough and dangerous and may cause trouble for you. Watch your back."

I'm not too worried about the *bratva*. It was probably one of them who took a shot at me this evening. That was a close thing, but now I'm warned. I've dealt with more dangerous opponents than a bunch of thugs from Brooklyn. I can take care of myself.

"How am I supposed to get close to the prime minister?" I ask.

"You will receive full instructions tomorrow morning." Voss looks forlornly at the empty plates arrayed in front of him.

What is he not telling me?

CHAPTER THREE

My CELL PHONE rings, and Voss looks annoyed at the interruption. The caller ID tells me it's my partner, Detective Lucy Tanaka.

"Hey," Lucy says. "I have a situation."

"So do I."

"You'd better come to the Capitol Theater. There's been a murder."

"I'm a bit occupied just now," I say. "Can't you cover it?"

"This is a very unusual situation. The victim is a world-famous actress, and she was murdered on stage during the performance of a play."

A world-famous actress. My throat constricts.

"I was called in as duty officer," Lucy continues, "but I need a senior officer for this situation. This is anything but routine."

"I'll get to the theater as soon as I can." I cut the phone connection and turn toward Voss. "I must go. I have a police emergency."

I stride out of the restaurant before Voss can protest, and I drive as quickly as I can to the crime scene. I use the Corvette I took from home even though I know it's a mistake. Whoever shot at me has certainly identified my car, and he's going to try again. I'll have to arrange alternate transportation, but that will have to wait until tomorrow morning.

The Capitol Theater is located in an old building dating from the 1930s used these days for roadshows and pre-Broadway tryouts.

It's tucked in among commercial office buildings, and all that distinguishes it from its anonymous neighbors is a large marquee stretching over the sidewalk, tonight glittering with hundreds of electric lights announcing a "Major Theatrical Event" and a "World-Famous Star."

Lucy Tanaka stands in the theater lobby beneath a poster featuring a beautiful woman with coal-black hair, high cheekbones, and large, dark eyes. My heart breaks.

Lucy's an experienced homicide detective and has been my partner for almost five months now, and she knows what she's doing. She will have secured the crime scene, called in the medical examiner and forensics, and, with any luck, solved the case so I can go home and finish my bourbon and remember a woman I once loved.

I push through the noisy, anxious crowd, their faces flushed, eyes bright. They've experienced something exciting this evening: the stark nearness of death. Many are on their cell phones, some doubtlessly talking to their pet reporters. Most are middle-aged and well dressed. There are a lot of balding heads and sparse gray hairs among the men who look like they've come directly from work, some still clutching expensive briefcases with nice brass fittings.

The women are in heels, some wear fur stoles, and many wear pearls: single strands, not multiple strands, of course. They look like they had their hair and nails done this very afternoon at an expensive salon.

A hand touches my arm. "How long are we going to be held here, Detective?"

"We'll let you go as soon as we can, Your Honor."

"Who's the victim?" I ask Lucy, although I know the answer.

Lucy is a small woman, attractive, in her early thirties. She looks fragile—almost birdlike—but I know she's tough, determined, and resourceful—and always ready to challenge anybody who gets in her way, including our bosses. Including me. That's one of many things I admire about her.

"Victoria West: the famous actress." Lucy nods toward the lobby wall where the posters promoting the current production are displayed. "Winner of six Tony Awards," and "Winner of two Oscars," the banners proclaim. The figure in the posters does not come close to capturing Vickie West's stunning beauty.

"She's the star of tonight's play," Lucy says. "Does the name Victoria West mean anything to you?"

"It means everything to me," I say. "What happened here tonight?"

"Ms. West was shot at the end of her performance in front of several hundred people in the audience as well as the cast and crew. She was in a small room just offstage at the time. It must be suicide."

"It wasn't suicide."

Lucy blinks, puzzled at my abrupt reply, then resumes. "We're getting names and contact information from the audience. Some very important people are here tonight, or so they say. So far I've identified a deputy attorney general, an undersecretary of defense, and two Supreme Court justices; they're getting restless."

"As soon as you've collected names and addresses, let the audience go. They look harmless. Let's see the victim." I cringe inwardly when I say the word.

Lucy leads me through a pair of double doors, guarded by a uniformed policeman, and into the theater auditorium itself. The house lights are up; the seats are empty. Just a few crumpled programs on the floor indicate the room was recently filled with life. The atmosphere is now desolate.

At the far end of the auditorium is the stage, lights bright. The set appears to be an old-fashioned living room of some kind, with dark wainscoting, velvet drapes, and heavy oak furniture. A couple of large

armchairs and a chaise longue are placed around the stage. Two doors
lead off the stage set. A painting of a man in an old-fashioned military uniform with an intimidating mustache hangs above a marble
fireplace. Beneath the picture hangs a curved cavalry saber in a silver
scabbard; a long, gold cord hangs from the hilt.

Now that I'm on stage, I see that the fireplace is actually made of
plywood, painted to look like marble. The wainscoting and everything else is fake. I'm not sure why but this unsettles me. I can't tell
what's real and what's pretend in this world.

A man paces center stage dressed in a suit and jacket, shirt collar
unbuttoned: he's short and wiry, with close-cropped, blond hair,
thinning at the top. He wears yellow loafers and, as he paces, speaks
urgently into his cell phone. He's wearing a lurid silk tie sporting the
image, in bright pink and orange, of Keith Richards.

"Marko," Lucy tells me, "this is Garland Taylor. Mr. Taylor is the
director of tonight's play."

"My name is Marko Zorn. I'm with the Metropolitan DC police.
Homicide."

"Is this going to take long?" the man demands.

"It's going to take as long as it takes."

"I will not tolerate some city employee wasting my time: I have
important things to do."

"This city employee has important things to do and will not tolerate anybody wasting his time."

"I don't think I like your attitude, Officer."

"If you don't like my attitude stop acting like an asshole."

Garland Taylor opens his mouth to say something I expect is offensive. I don't wait to hear it. "Lucy, show me the crime scene."

I follow Lucy to a single door, stage left, and we stop at the entrance
to a small room where somebody has set up temporary floodlights.

"Booties!" Hanna Forbes yells at us fiercely. "No booty, no snoopy."

Lucy and I slip on latex gloves and shoe coverings. I take a deep breath and enter the room, steeling myself.

Although I know what to expect and think I'm prepared, the sight of Victoria West hits me like a hammer blow. She lies crumpled on the floor. She's thirty-five, but her stage makeup makes her look older; her face is white, but her beauty is undiminished by what was done to her tonight.

"A single head shot to her left temple," Hanna announces.

To me, Vickie is still the girl I saw run onto a stage a long time ago. I still hear her first words: "All hail, great master, great sir, hail. I come." There must have been other actors performing that night, but I remember no one but Vickie. I was enchanted by this beautiful sprite, so full of life. I guess maybe I still am.

I knew from that first moment at the theater years ago I had to meet this woman—had to know her. I was obsessed. I was a young police officer with the NYPD at the time, working out of a lower Manhattan precinct, and it wasn't hard to locate an address and telephone number for her. She hung up on me the first few times I called, but I was persistent, and finally I talked her into having dinner.

We had an electric connection over a meal at a Chinese place on Houston.

She asked me about my work as people always do when they meet a cop: what's it like? Is it dangerous? Do you carry a gun? I replied with vague answers until she gave up and realized I didn't want to talk about my work, and she stopped cross-examining me.

She told me she was living in a walk-up apartment in the East Village, barely getting by on a few acting jobs but starting to have some success. She'd found a hot-shot agent named Cynthia Fletcher, who'd gotten her into small parts in some prestige productions.

We couldn't get enough of each other. I don't think we even got to the Peking duck; instead we ended our dinner date in her apartment in bed. That was the beginning of what I thought would be a life-changing relationship.

It lasted for a little over three months. During that time, we made plans for the rest of our lives. We talked about finding an apartment to share. Then she was cast in a Broadway production of *Hedda Gabler* and my life fell to pieces. She became distracted and often nervous and upset. She spent long hours in rehearsals. When I complained she said I didn't understand the theater. She told me I didn't understand her, didn't understand what she needed.

It was about three months after our first meeting, and I'd been investigating an assault on Mott Street. It had been a bad day, and I needed to talk to Vickie. We'd been having some ugly arguments, and I decided to go to her place unannounced to sort things out between us. I'd prepared a kind of speech apologizing for whatever it was I'd done. I even bought some flowers. Roses. Roses were her favorite, although she didn't have the money to buy roses for herself.

When I got to her door, I found it locked. I knocked, gently at first. I knew she was home: this was not one of her rehearsal nights, and I could see a light under her door. I became frustrated, which is to say, pissed off, and banged on the door loudly. Neighbors came out and told me to pipe down. Which only made me madder.

When Vickie opened the door, she was wrapped in a bathrobe. And nothing else, as far as I could see.

"This is not a good time, Marko. We'll talk tomorrow."

The bad day and my desperate need for her—everything just boiled up. I said things I shouldn't have said. I think I threw the flowers on the floor of the landing. She let me have it. This would have gone on except we were interrupted by a voice from the bedroom: a deep, resonant baritone.

"Who the fuck is it, Vickie? Tell whoever it is to get the fuck out of here. I'm getting cold."

Vickie's face drained of color. "Please, Marko. I'm so sorry. Just go."

In those days I used to carry a service weapon and, for one second—for one brief second only—I almost lost it: I wasn't sure what I was capable of. This was the woman I loved, the woman I'd planned to spend my life with, and all I could feel for her now was blinding rage. Without a word, I turned and left, kicking the flowers out of my way.

That was the last time I saw Vickie West. The last time until tonight.

Vickie wears old-fashioned clothing appropriate for her role as a young Norwegian bride in the late 19th century—black with touches of white lace around her throat and wrist, velvet trim, white blouse, and a silver-and-ivory brooch.

I crouch down and examine the body, careful not to touch her. There's a bloody wound in her left temple. I see no exit wound. She grasps a small, pearl-handled revolver in her right hand. For a moment I think I'm going to be sick.

Her eyes are sightless, her skin bloodless white, but nothing can take away my memory of Vickie's large dark eyes and warm smile. I won't let this grotesque imitation make me forget that.

"That is Victoria West," Lucy says, standing just behind me, her voice subdued. She must sense my pain. "She was an actress."

"Dead. Shot once in the left temple," Hanna Forbes announces. "Nine minutes past ten, according to dozens of witnesses who heard the shot. May I take the body away?"

Hanna Forbes, in charge of the crime scene, is a tall, lanky woman and tonight wears cargo pants, accessorized with plastic shoe covers and gloves, and a grungy ball cap with the word "Orioles" printed on it.

"Use the stage door. The lobby is full of people, and I don't want them to see this."

Hanna nods and starts to prepare the body for transfer to the Medical Examiner's lab.

"What's this room we're in?" I ask Lucy.

"It's supposed to be some kind of drawing room."

"Doors? Windows?"

"No windows. There are two doors. It seems the victim was alone in this room at the time of death."

"Weapon?" I ask.

Hanna points to the revolver in the dead woman's hand. "A .38 Smith and Wesson Special, I think."

"You *think*? You just *think*? That's not like you. Is there any doubt about the weapon?"

"There are three, possibly four, guns around here." Hanna points to the far side of the small room. Lying on the floor is a large black revolver. "Fake," Hanna announces. "I can tell you it's not a real gun. I'm assuming it's a prop for this play."

"You say there are other guns?"

"There's another gun just like this one somewhere: also a prop. Lucy has secured it. The fourth gun is real enough; it's a starter pistol. The stage manager uses it at the end of the play for some kind of sound effect."

This is all wrong, I think. I deal with murder all the time. There are a limited number of reasons why people kill: money, sudden anger, sometimes jealousy. None seem to fit here. Vickie was a person people wanted to love.

The director, Garland Taylor, is on his cell phone when Lucy and I return to the stage set.

"Mr. Taylor," I say. "Put that phone away."

"This is an important conversation."

"So is the conversation we're about to have. Where were you when Miss West entered the drawing room?"

"Backstage." His voice is high-pitched with barely suppressed impatience.

"Tell me what happened."

"My leading lady committed suicide." Taylor clutches his phone to his chest as if it were a talisman.

"Why would she do that?" Lucy asks.

"How the hell should I know? Why does anyone commit suicide?"

"Did she have a bad experience during this evening's performance?"

"Everything went fine until the end of the last scene."

"Did you get along with Miss West?"

"Absolutely. I'd directed her in several earlier productions. I'm a huge admirer. And Ariel and I were close friends."

"Ariel?"

"Ariel was a name her intimate friends always used for her."

"Take us through the last few minutes of the performance," I say.

Taylor's phone rings. "Can we talk some other time? I've got to take this call."

"No, you don't." My initial dislike of this man is beginning to evolve into active aversion.

"For God's sake. This is Solly calling from LA. Solly is Creative Management," Taylor pleads, as if I had a clue who Solly is. Or cared. "It takes weeks to get through to him, and this is the man himself. No one refuses to take a call from Solly."

"Now's your chance to make history. Tell Solly to be patient and wait his turn. Tell me what happened tonight."

Taylor takes a deep breath and looks at his phone forlornly. "This was opening night. The performance went fine; Vickie was absolutely fabulous as usual—up until the very last minute. I was on the other side of those double doors waiting to take my curtain call with the cast. Vickie was going to make some kind of important announcement, and she insisted I be there with her."

The director's cell phone rings, and Taylor glances at it.

"Don't even think about it," I say. "What happened that last minute?"

"Vickie took the gun from where it hangs over the fireplace as we'd rehearsed a hundred times. She crossed from stage right to stage left to the door to the drawing room, then said something to Arthur Cantwell and stepped through the door there." He points to the door to the small room. "She shut the door, and a moment later, she killed herself."

"What did you mean Victoria West was absolutely fabulous until the last minute?"

"What's this got to do with her death? She shot herself. End of story."

"The story ends when I say it ends. Did something happen?"

"She forgot her last line."

"What did she say?"

"I don't know. Arthur Cantwell was on stage just a few feet away from her, and she was speaking directly to him. Ask him."

"I'm asking you. What did she say?"

"I'm not accustomed to being spoken to in this manner by a city employee."

"Get used to it. Why did she forget her line?"

"What is the name of your superior officer?"

"Wrong answer. Why did she forget her last line?"

"I don't know. All I know is she blew it, recovered, and made her final exit. If actors forget their lines and there's silence, it totally fucks up the scene, so they say something, anything, even nonsense, instead. The audience never knows the difference."

"What did she say instead of her scripted lines?"

"I told you, I don't know."

He's lying: of course he knows what she said.

"Were you surprised when you heard the gunshot?"

"We're performing Ibsen's *Hedda Gabler*. In the play, Hedda kills herself at the end of the play, and the script calls for a gunshot just at that moment."

"What was Miss West supposed to do when she went into that small room?"

"She would shut the door and wait for the starter gun to fire. After a few minutes she would return to the stage and take her curtain call."

"What happened when the shot was fired?"

"The other actors on stage thought it was their cue to rush to the drawing room door, as called for in the script. Even though it was quite dark in the drawing room, they knew immediately something had gone wrong."

"What did you do?"

"I ran onto the stage and told our stage manager to kill the stage and house lights. I looked into the drawing room and saw Victoria was dead."

"Then what?"

"I told the cast to leave the stage immediately and told our stage manager to call 911. I said something to the audience—there'd been some kind of accident and asked them to remain in their seats. The audience, of course, was completely mystified. Some probably thought this was part of the production—some postmodern shit. The medical people came. Somebody must have called the police; then you lot showed up."

The door to the small drawing room opens, and the medical examiners wheel the body of Victoria West out on a gurney—covered now by a heavy black cloth—and across the stage. We watch in silence as Victoria West makes her final exit.

I think of her last words she said on the stage when I saw her that first night: "Merrily shall I live now, under the blossom that hangs by the bough."

I'm heartsick ... now that the initial shock has passed I feel nothing but anguish. I know I can't rest until whoever did this to Vickie is made to pay.

I pull myself together and focus on my job. "Do you have an understudy to take over the part?"

"You think some ambitious, young starlet killed Vickie West to get the part? Some *All About Eve* crap?"

"Something like that."

"There's no understudy. We close the show tonight."

"Show me what the stage looks like when you turn the lights off."

"Why is that necessary?"

"It's necessary because I say it's necessary."

Taylor shrugs. "Michael! Douse stage and house lights."

There's a second's pause, and then we're plunged into total darkness except for a little light from the auditorium exit signs.

"What the hell's going on?" Hanna yells from her crime scene perch. "I can't see a damn thing."

"Sorry, Hanna. Mr. Taylor, bring up the lights."

Taylor shouts orders, and the stage and house lights come back on.

"That room Miss West was in: it's closed on all sides," I say. "Why is that?"

"Maybe you should talk with our set designer."

"Maybe you should answer my questions."

"Partly to block the view so the audience can't see the backstage area when the door is opened."

"And the second door?"

"Vickie used it to enter and leave the drawing room from the backstage area."

"Let's look at the victim's dressing room," I say to Lucy. As we leave, Taylor whips out his phone and speed-dials someone.

Victoria West's dressing room is one floor above the stage and is filled with roses, the air heavy with their fragrance. There are several wreaths with pink and blue ribbons expressing cheerful good wishes. The walls are adorned with head shot photographs, mostly professional studio portraits of beautiful people who, I assume, are actors who have performed in this theater in the past. Many are posed at odd, unnatural angles with dramatic side lighting, which, I guess, people in the theater world find arty.

The walls are painted pale lavender, Vickie's favorite color. Lying on the dressing table is a charger cable not plugged into anything. "This is for some kind of electronic device," I say to Lucy. "Where is the device it's supposed to charge?"

"We haven't found one yet."

"Keep looking. It may be important."

Suddenly, I can't stay in this room any longer; it breathes Vickie's presence, and I need to escape. Lucy can supervise the search.

"Garland Taylor said we should talk to some actor named Arthur Cantwell," I say as we return to the stage. "Tell him to meet us here."

Hanna is still in the small drawing room.

"Hanna," I say, taking from my pocket the shell casing I picked up in the gutter across the street from my house. "I want you to check this for me."

Hanna takes the shell in her gloved hand. "It's from a rifle round. Not a common rifle round. I'll take a look when I get back to the shop. You know our victim this evening was shot with a handgun, not a rifle."

"This has nothing to do with the investigation into the murder of Vickie West. It's a different case."

CHAPTER FOUR

A MAN WEARING a casual, elegant pair of Italian chinos, sneakers, and a yellow shirt opened halfway over his suntanned chest steps onto the stage. A long, raffish, white silk scarf is wrapped around his shoulders.

"I'm Marko Zorn. I'm with the police."

"Arthur Cantwell," the man replies.

Cantwell is around forty: tall with strong, handsome features. But it's the voice that's riveting—a plumy, deep baritone with some kind of accent found nowhere naturally on this planet. It reminds me of old movie stars like Ronald Colman or James Mason. It's also a voice from my past, a voice I'll never forget.

"We need to talk," I say.

"I live to serve."

"Leave the sarcasm to me, Mr. Cantwell."

"It was inevitable, you know," Cantwell continues, pretending I'd said nothing. "This death was inevitable. The immutable laws of the theater dictate that someone be shot here tonight."

"I don't believe I've seen those laws in the criminal code."

"Anton Chekov once said, 'if in the first act you have hung a pistol on the wall, then in the following act, it should be fired.'"

"This is no joke," I tell him.

"If you say so."

"I say so. And Chekov said rifle, not pistol."

Cantwell shrugs and settles onto the chaise, stretching out full length, making himself comfortable. I can see now he's had serious work done on his neck and chin and around his eyes: He's as fake as the plywood marble fireplace. It must have cost him a fortune.

"What did you see this evening at the end of the last scene?" I ask.

"Vickie went into the drawing room and closed the door and shot herself." He sighs. "Vickie was always looking for a dramatic exit . . . I suppose she hit this one out of the ballpark this evening."

I consider punching this guy's lights out, but I know I'm not supposed to do that sort of thing. It would achieve nothing and would mean a lot of paperwork. Besides, he's not worth it. "Was there anything different about her performance tonight?" I ask.

"She forgot her exit line."

"What was she supposed to say? I understand she was addressing that line to you."

Cantwell closes his eyes for a moment, concentrating, or pretending to concentrate. "She was supposed to say: 'I'm sure you flatter yourself that we will, Judge. Now that you are the only cock on the walk.'"

"You being the 'cock' she's referring to?"

"Obviously."

"What did Vickie say instead?"

"I have no idea."

"You have no idea? She was speaking to you directly."

"I wasn't really paying attention."

I don't believe Cantwell for a moment. But, for some reason, he doesn't want to repeat Vickie's words. I'll have to get back to him and find out what he's hiding. And why.

"Did she seem distressed or anxious when she said that last line?" I ask instead.

"No more than usual. She was always nervous and very insecure."

That's not the Vickie I knew. She was volatile but never insecure and never nervous. Why would Cantwell say that when we both know he's lying?

"I didn't notice anything out of the ordinary about her performance," Cantwell continues after a moment's reflection.

"Except that she forgot her last line."

"Except for that."

"Did you know Miss West before rehearsals started?"

"Our paths have crossed from time to time."

"How did you become involved with this production?"

"God knows why Garland wanted to revive this old warhorse. But when he decided to do it, naturally he thought of me. He needed a big name. I starred in *Hedda* years ago in New York. That New York production was a sensation. Garland approached me, and I made myself available and the rest is history: at least it was until tonight. Now history has fucked me, and I'm back to doing voiceovers for Pixar."

"And Miss West's connection?"

"Garland needed someone to play Hedda and Vickie was available. Vickie played Hedda in my New York production. She was a little old for the part now. Hedda's supposed to be a bride just back from her honeymoon. I mean, give me a break. Vickie's great, but it's been a long time since she's been a young bride."

"Mr. Cantwell, you're annoying me, and I do not care to be annoyed. And I think you're hiding something."

"Are you calling me a liar?" Cantwell demands. "Do you have any idea who you're talking to?"

"I'm talking to someone who's making an ass of himself in a criminal investigation. It's late and I've had a very bad day and you're giving me a headache."

"You should know that the district attorney of the Southern District of New York and I are close friends."

"You should know I'm deeply unimpressed with that information." Cantwell turns away in a huff.

"We're not done yet. Were you and Miss West on good terms?"

"We're professionals. We would not allow any ancient history to get in the way of our art."

"I understand she was going to make a speech when she made her curtain call. What was she going to say?"

"It's not important now."

"I'll decide what's important. What was she going to say?"

Cantwell sighs. "She was going to announce that she and I were to be married at the end of the *Hedda Gabler* run."

That takes my breath away. Vickie—beautiful and talented—a woman whose smile could bring any man she wanted to his knees. She was going to marry this weasel?

"You and Miss West were going to marry?" I struggle to find words.

"That's what I just said, didn't I?"

I try to think if there is anything I can arrest Cantwell for, but nothing comes to mind. I know there's something Cantwell just said that bothers me. I know I should ask him about it, but I can't recall what he said. My unasked question nags at me, but it's late. I've had a terrible day—somebody tried to kill me, Voss has pulled me into a job I'd be better off avoiding, and now I'm stuck talking to this jerk who is seriously getting on my nerves. No surprise that I'm losing my concentration.

"One final question. Was Miss West involved romantically with anybody in this production?"

"You mean was Vickie fucking the cast?"

"Mr. Cantwell, I object to you speaking like that about Victoria West. She was somebody I admired. My partner, Detective Tanaka, finds that kind of language distasteful, and I find it juvenile."

"Is that all?"

"For the moment. Don't leave town."

"Don't leave town? Are you kidding me?"

"Do I look like I'm kidding?"

Cantwell turns on his heels and stalks petulantly off the stage, flinging his white silk scarf dramatically over his shoulder.

A woman with long blond hair, dressed in a black turtleneck sweater, and wearing heavy black eye shadow and long artificial eyelashes, sits at a small wooden table in the backstage area. She's pulled her black sweater over her hands so only the tips of her black fingernails show. She has lightly applied lipstick of a kind of orangey color.

"Good evening," I say. "I'm with the police. My name is Marko Zorn. Can you answer some questions for me?"

"I guess so." The voice is soft and so low as to be almost inaudible.

"Who are you?"

"I'm Props, sir."

"When you say you're 'Props', what does that mean?"

"I take care of the props for this show. You know: Props."

She smiles at me. She has a warm, inviting smile. It's hard to make out her features in the dark, but I can see she has large dark brown eyes.

"Did you handle the guns this evening?"

"Yes, sir."

"How many guns did you handle?"

"There are two guns, sir. Just props, you know."

"Could you have given Miss West a real gun by mistake? Maybe a pearl-handled revolver?"

"No, sir. The gun she took from the wall was a prop gun."

"Our investigators have identified three guns used in this production."

"That sounds right. The two guns I placed on stage are props. There's a starter pistol Mr. Toland, the stage manager, uses. I have nothing to do with that. I don't know anything about the pearl-handled revolver you mentioned."

"Is this where you sit during each performance?"

"That's right. I keep an eye on my props."

"So you have a good view of the backstage area?"

"Pretty much."

"Including the door to the small drawing room where Miss West was shot?"

"It's right there in front of me."

"Did anyone go in or out of that door this evening?"

"Only Miss West during the performance. No one else went near the door."

"Was there anyone backstage tonight you didn't know?"

"I don't really know any of the people in this production." She smiles. "I just started working here three days ago."

"What did you mean when you said you take care of the guns?"

"The stage manager—that's Mr. Toland—just before curtain, he hangs the guns on wooden brackets above the fireplace below the saber. I don't know why they're there. I've never read the play."

"Can you see Mr. Toland when he fires the starter pistol?"

"I can't see him do that from where I sit."

"Did you see Miss West during the performance?"

"I saw her when she went into the drawing room just before opening curtain. And later, during intermission, she came out. That's when she and Miss Fletcher went upstairs to Miss West's dressing room."

"Who is Miss Fletcher? Is she part of the cast?"

"I think she's Miss West's agent or something."

"This agent and Victoria West were alone together in Vickie's dressing room? Have I got that right?"

"Yes, sir."

"How do you know they were in the dressing room?"

"I could hear them."

"Miss West's dressing room is one flight up. That's a long way."

"They talked real loud. Like they were having an argument."

"What did they say?"

"I couldn't hear the words. When Miss Fletcher came out of the dressing room, she looked upset. Am I in trouble?" She asks.

"What makes you think you're in trouble?"

"You think I gave Miss West the wrong gun."

"What's your name?"

"Everybody calls me Props."

"What does the Department of Motor Vehicles call you?"

"They call me Lily."

"Just to be clear, Lily," I say, "When you heard Miss West and Miss Fletcher arguing, you didn't know what they were arguing about?"

"I couldn't make out a single word."

"Thank you."

"Except one." She smiles sweetly at me.

"What word was that?"

"When Miss Fletcher left Victoria West's dressing room the door was open, and I heard Miss West yell something that sounded like 'Valerie.'"

"Like a name? 'Valerie'?"

"Something like that."

"Thank you, Lily."

"I always like to help the police when I can."

"Have you helped the police before?"

"Nothing like this. Nothing like murder. I used to date a policeman. He was a sergeant. That was in Cincinnati. His name was Larry. I've always had a weakness for policemen. Larry was nice but wasn't as good-looking as you." She smiles warmly.

I can't help but ask. "What happened to Larry?"

"Larry went away."

Lily's attractive, and she has a way of cocking her head to one side, looking at me with a side-glance from the corner of her eye. A woman with an expressive, animated face is always appealing. Is it the darkness of the room? Is this girl flirting with me?

"Would you like to have a police officer drive you home? It's very late, and it's raining."

"Are you offering to take me home, Detective?"

"Sorry. I have a murder to investigate."

She gives me a pouty look. "I thought Miss West committed suicide."

"It was murder. Definitely murder. I can have one of the officers drive you home."

"No thank you, sir," she whispers. "It's very gallant of you to offer." She collects her coat that hangs from the back of her chair, and picks up her purse. She wears black jeans, ripped at the knees, and scuffed tennis shoes. "Good night, sir."

She makes a small kissing motion with her lips, turns, and disappears into the darkness.

That's when I remember the question I wanted to ask Arthur Cantwell.

"Has Arthur Cantwell left the theater?" I ask Lucy, who's standing at the edge of the stage and looking into the empty auditorium.

"I just saw him walking out the front door."

Lucy and I catch up with Cantwell as he's about to climb into a waiting SUV under the marquee in front of the theater. Beyond, a steady rain falls.

"Mr. Cantwell," I call out, "I have one more question."

Cantwell turns around and faces me; he's not pleased.

"What is it, Detective? I answered your questions."

"You mentioned something about an 'ancient relationship' with Victoria West. What was that relationship?"

He sighs heavily. "If you must know, Vickie and I were once married."

"And you're marrying each other a second time?" I'm having a hard time speaking.

"The triumph of hope over experience, as they say." He smirks.

"That's not funny."

"I suppose I could never get enough of Vickie."

"And you forgot to mention that you and Vickie were once married?"

"It was a long time ago."

"What else did you forget to tell us?" Lucy asks.

"That was about it."

"Tell me about your marriage."

"Here? Standing on the street in the middle of the night? Now? In the rain?"

"Here. Now. In the rain."

"We were both cast in the New York production of *Hedda Gabler*. We were young, and we fell in love. Vickie was a beautiful, passionate young woman, and ours was a very torrid, very public affair. We burned up the stage. Hell, we burned up the city of New York. Vickie had been involved with some loser before being cast in the show, but when she and I connected on stage, she dumped him.

My heart pounds with anger. And now I recognize the voice—the voice I heard long ago from Vickie's bedroom telling Vickie to get rid of her noisy visitor.

"Vickie and I married just after the show closed," Cantwell says. "We stayed married for a little while; got divorced. Both of us remarried later. It was long ago. If you want more details about my private life, you're going to have to ask my publicist. I'm already late for a dinner engagement, although Vickie's death has quite put me off my appetite."

"One more thing," I say. "Did you have a pet name for Victoria West? Something you called each other in your intimate communications? At least one other member of the production has used such a name."

"A pet name? How adolescent. Certainly not! I wouldn't do such a thing."

Cantwell climbs into his SUV.

"Break a leg," I call after him, hoping he'll interpret me literally.

"He doesn't seem like a very nice person," Lucy says to me as he drives off.

"That's just an act."

"Where do we go next in this investigation?" she asks.

"Find out if anybody in the cast or crew knows how to use firearms. Victoria West was shot in a dark room, probably at some distance. That would take a skilled shooter. And find whatever device Vickie was charging in her dressing room."

"How about you?"

"I'm going to find out why Vickie West forgot her last line."

As Lucy goes back into the theater, my cell phone rings. "Detective Zorn? This is Lieutenant Matt Granger of the Chicago Police Department. Sorry to be calling you so late in the evening but something's come up."

"How can I help?"

I guess this must be about the violent death of the former dictator of Montenegro on a street in Chicago, in which case I have no intention of helping. That would lead to him wanting to know why I was in Chicago and who was paying me. Neither subject do I want to share with the Chicago police.

"There were two killings here in Chicago this week," Granger is saying. "We hope you can help us in our investigation."

"The DC police are always happy to help our brothers in Chicago."

There's a brief pause at the other end while Matt Granger of the Chicago police tries to decide whether I'm being a smartass.

"I don't see how I can help," I say.

"I understand that you were in Chicago recently."

"That's right."

"You may have been in contact with at least one of the victims. Does the name Milan Jovanovich mean anything to you?"

I am wrong. This isn't about the murder of the general from Montenegro. This is something else.

"The name Milan Jovanovich doesn't ring a bell," I say.

"I'd like you to think very hard before you answer."

I'm silent for a long moment while I pretend to think very hard. "Sorry. Can't remember that name. If I think of something, I'll get in touch." I cut the connection.

My phone rings as I'm about to go back into the theater. The caller ID indicates it's the US Secretary of State calling me. It's the middle of the night and I've had a terrible day and I want to go home. I consider ignoring the call. But I can't really do that, can I? That would be unpatriotic.

"I'm trying to reach a Detective Zorn," a voice on the phone says.

"This is your lucky day."

"My name is Saxton. I'm the personal assistant to the Secretary of State. I'm calling on his behalf. The Secretary needs to speak with you. Can you come to the State Department tomorrow morning at seven thirty?"

"Seven thirty in the morning?" I ask, trying to hide my shock.

"The Secretary has an opening in his schedule then."

"Good for him."

"I know it's short notice but the matter is urgent: a matter of life or death."

The man at the other end doesn't say whose life or death, but I must assume it involves the visiting prime minister of Montenegro that Cyprian Voss told me about.

"I believe I may have an opening on my calendar at seven thirty tomorrow morning."

"I'll meet you at the Diplomatic Entrance." Saxton doesn't sound like he has much of a sense of humor.

"It's a date," I tell him.

CHAPTER FIVE

"Officer Zorn?" A tall man in a gray suit and tasteful gray tie asks as I get out of the police cruiser that has brought me to the State Department.

"In person," I say.

The clouds above are dark and ominous. I had to get up much too early to make this. I hope the Secretary of State offers me coffee.

"I'm Jason Saxton." The man holds a large umbrella above us so we both get some protection from the rain that's coming down hard. "The Secretary is waiting for you."

I follow Saxton into the Department of State's diplomatic entrance, and we're waved through an array of security checkpoints, across the vast lobby, to a bank of elevators. We ride to the seventh floor. Saxton leads me into a crowded outer office: a dozen young men and women peer at computer screens and speak in hushed tones.

"Mr. Secretary, Detective Zorn from the Metropolitan Police is here," Saxton announces as we step into a large, elegantly furnished office.

The Secretary of State sits at an imposing desk; he's in his shirt-sleeves and wears a blue tie and dark blue suspenders. He looks at me over a pair of half-glasses, rises to his feet, and we shake hands. "I'm

Leland Cross. Thank you for coming, Detective Zorn. I appreciate your taking the time to see me."

I nod and study his face carefully hoping to determine whether this last-minute appointment is a good thing or if I'm in serious trouble. I'm pretty sure I'm not here because the Secretary of State has taken a sudden interest in my health. He looks like what he is: a former senator or governor from somewhere. Probably some place with amber waves of grain where the wind blows free, and therefore I'm pretty sure I don't trust him.

Behind the desk are large windows looking out toward the National Mall and the Lincoln Memorial, although it's hard to make much out. The rain has turned the city into a misty, gray mezzotint.

"Thank you, Jason," Cross tells his assistant. "Ask Janet to wait for us. We'll need to talk to her shortly."

The office walls are hung with artwork, mostly modern American masters. I catch sight of an Edward Hopper called, I seem to remember *Hotel Lobby* an early Joan Mitchell, an inferior Willem de Kooning, and a nice Hans Hofmann. A Frederic Remington bronze statue of what seem to be three troopers shooting into the air, sits on a credenza.

"Please, make yourself comfortable, Detective." Cross gestures to an armchair and we sit, facing each other, separated by a teak coffee table. Cross is tall and has a nice haircut. I must get the name of his barber.

"I know you have a busy schedule," he tells me. "I apologize for taking you away from your duties. The mayor told me you are investigating the tragic suicide of Victoria West. I remember her from her movies, and my wife and I saw her just a few nights ago in a preview performance of *Hedda Gabler*. She was brilliant; such a tragic loss."

"We have a team of experienced officers investigating that case," I say vaguely.

I see no sign the Secretary of State is going to offer me coffee. I'm almost tempted to note the absence and inquire, in a friendly way, whether the State Department's budget has been cut again. I decide against being a smartass this early in our meeting. At least not until I learn for sure why I'm here.

The Secretary places his manicured hands on his knees. "Have you been informed that you've been placed on temporary assignment to the Department's Diplomatic Security division?"

This must be what Cyprian Voss meant when he told me I'd get my instructions in the morning. How does he manage these things? I must ask him next time I see him. Not that he'll tell me.

I did agree to take on Voss's assignment to protect the visiting prime minister, but that was before Vickie's murder. That was before everything changed for me. I'm no longer sure I want to take time out to be somebody's bodyguard. Right now my sole concern is to find Vickie's killer.

"I've heard nothing about that," I say. I don't want the secretary asking where I've heard about this protection gig; I don't want to tell Secretary Cross about Cyprian Voss. Ever. I don't think Cross would approve of Voss. Or vice versa.

"I spoke with your mayor, and she has released you from your regular police duties. For the next few days, you will, technically, be working for me as a 'special consultant.' You will be paid the standard US government per diem. I'm sure you will do your duty. As a good citizen."

It's been a long time since anyone called me a "good citizen." I want to tell Cross that I have something more important on my mind: a murdered woman who once gave meaning to my life. I don't say anything though. From his perspective, Vickie is irrelevant.

"Very well," I say, "I'll do my duty, as you put it."

"Good man."

"What is it exactly I'm supposed to do?" I ask.

"The prime minister of Montenegro is coming to the US on a state visit. Her life has been threatened. You will be assigned to her security detail to help see that no harm comes to her."

"I'm not a professional bodyguard," I protest. "I'm a homicide detective. Why have I been assigned this?"

Leland Cross looks puzzled. "Actually, I was rather hoping you could tell me."

"I haven't a clue."

"Have you ever met Nina Voychek?" Cross asks.

"Never."

"Do you know anybody in the current Montenegrin government?"

"Not a soul."

"I ask," the Secretary of State goes on, "because we would very much like to know why you specifically—by name—were requested by the government of Montenegro to be the liaison with the visiting delegation. That's most unusual."

Maybe it wasn't Cyprian Voss after all. Maybe somebody else has a hand in this. "I'd be happy to turn this assignment over to someone else," I say.

"I'm afraid it has to be you. If we change the liaison officer at the last minute, it will complicate this visit—which is already far too complicated as is." Cross sits back in his chair. "I don't suppose you have top secret security clearance."

"I'm afraid not." I don't tell him I once did have top-secret clearance but it was rather rudely taken away. He'd only want to know why.

"That makes things a bit awkward," he says. "I'm going to share with you some information that is highly sensitive." He pauses. "I'm going to take you into my confidence. You must on no account speak to anyone outside this room about what you learn here today. I rely on your discretion."

"You have my word." I need to know why I've been assigned to protect Nina Voychek even more than the Secretary of State needs to know. If Voss is not behind this, I must know who is.

"Your word will have to do." Leland Cross presses a button on a small console on the table next to his chair. "Send Janet in."

A moment later an African American woman enters the room. She's in her early forties, a little over six feet, slender, and athletic. She carries a thin, black briefcase. "Mr. Secretary," she says, nodding, then looks at me—not in a friendly way.

"Janet, this is Detective Zorn of the DC Police. Janet Cliff is with our Bureau of Diplomatic Security and is in charge of the Nina Voychek visit. Janet, please take a seat while we put Detective Zorn in the picture."

"Good idea, Mr. Secretary." She doesn't sound like she thinks it's a good idea at all. She sits where she can keep an eye on me.

"As you may be aware, Detective Zorn," the Secretary of State says, "there has recently been a major political upheaval in the country of Montenegro. You know about ethnic cleansing? The Oak Forest and other massacres?"

"I've read about them."

"It was a bloody mess and many people were killed, but, in the end, the forces of democracy prevailed. The man most immediately responsible for the ethnic cleansing was a man named Mykhayl Drach. Have you ever had any contact with a man by that name?"

That's an awkward question.

"Mykhayl Drach?" I ask. "I can't say I know the man." It's probably against some law or other to lie to the Secretary of State, but I have other, more serious things to worry about. And being lied to is part of his job, isn't it?

"Janet, please fill Detective Zorn in on why we think there may be a connection."

"We've received reports from the Chicago police that Mykhayl Drach was recently located in Chicago. Your name has come up in that connection."

"I can't imagine why," I say.

"We were wondering if that could have anything to do with why you were requested as liaison by the new prime minister's government," the Secretary says. He pauses, hoping I will jump in with something helpful to say. I don't. Does Leland Cross know more about the Chicago business and is he lying to me? I suppose lying is part of the Secretary of State's job description, too.

I'm tempted to ask how my name came up with the Chicago business. I decide not to pursue that line. Who knows where it might lead.

"Mykhayl Drach was, to put it bluntly, a mass murderer," Secretary Cross says. "Nina Voychek was his principal political opponent, and Drach had her arrested several times and brought before a special political tribunal where she was sentenced to death. The sentence was canceled each time at the last minute. When Drach's regime fell, Nina Voychek was sworn in as the new prime minister of a democratic government. Mykhayl Drach escaped at the last minute from Montenegro and was, until recently, in hiding.

"We have reliable intelligence that Goran Drach, Mykhayl Drach's brother, plans a coup d'état that is to begin with Nina Voychek's assassination. Drach is acting, we believe, as the surrogate of the Russian Federation. Nina Voychek's assassination while she is a guest of our country would not only be a major embarrassment to the US government, it would also be a significant setback to US interests in the region as it would open the doors to Russian influence in that country."

"Do you know how the assassination is to be carried out?" I ask.

The Secretary looks at Janet Cliff. "Unfortunately, no. I've asked the CIA to keep me informed. In the meantime, all we know is that the attack is supposed to take place here in Washington in the next few days. We believe Goran Drach has recruited a professional assassin to carry out the . . ." He pauses while he tries to find the right word.

"Assassination," Janet volunteers.

"Thank you, Janet. Please fill in Detective Zorn on your security arrangements."

"The delegation arrives tomorrow evening at Dulles Airport," she says. "While traveling to the US, the prime minister's security is the responsibility of her own people. The moment she steps off that plane, she's my headache. Our people have already secured the arrival site. Officials from the State Department and the Departments of Defense and Treasury will be there to meet her as will the Ambassador of Montenegro. Arriving with Voychek will be a small delegation."

"What's the drill when she arrives?" I ask.

"There will be a few moments of protocol to meet and greet, after which the prime minister and her entourage will be taken by convoy to the residence of the embassy of Montenegro here in DC, where she'll be staying. While she's inside the residence her security is the responsibility of her own people. The US government is responsible for the embassy perimeter and for her travel in and around the city and to and from Dulles Airport. Your role is limited—stand by and stay inconspicuous until called upon."

"I'm good at being inconspicuous."

"Try real hard." Janet takes a single sheet of paper from her briefcase. "This is the prime minister's movements schedule."

The paper is marked "Secret" in red at the top and at the bottom. I consider taking out my reading glasses but decide against it; there's no point in adding to the list of my inadequacies I'm sure Janet Cliff is compiling mentally. It's dated today, Saturday. The delegation from Montenegro arrives tomorrow, early Sunday evening. I skim briefly through the appointments: the State Department; the White House, with photo op; the Pentagon; appointments on Capitol Hill with members of Congress; several press interviews at the Montenegro embassy. She's scheduled to depart on Friday. One item toward the end of the visit schedule means serious trouble. On Thursday, her last official day in Washington and the day before she leaves the US to return home, a large reception is scheduled to take place at the Lincoln Memorial. I don't like that at all.

"I'm going to Dulles Airport tomorrow evening to meet the delegation," Janet Cliff tells me. "Come with me and I'll give you any last-minute information about the arrangements. Meet me at the diplomatic entrance at five." She speaks to the Secretary of State. "With your permission, sir."

"Yes, Janet. Go ahead."

Janet gets quickly to her feet and looks at me intently. "Don't be late."

"I can't emphasize how important this visit is," Cross says after Janet Cliff leaves. "It's vital that Nina Voychek be unharmed. Perhaps you should familiarize yourself with Montenegro and its history: It might give you some perspective."

I'm really sorry the Secretary of State said that last bit. Montenegro has been a nation, sort of, for three thousand or more years. It's been the victim of war, revolution, and invasion: the Hittites, Scythians, the Egyptians, Alexander the Great, the Greeks, the Romans, the Crusaders, the Turks, Napoleon, and the Nazis have all stormed in and out of that tiny country.

Now it's Russia's turn; the latest chapter in the country's sorry history. And I'm supposed to prevent it?

Changing the course of human history is not part of my job description.

CHAPTER SIX

THE HOMICIDE DIVISION'S conference room is dreary and dispiriting this morning. The rainstorm that swept into the city last night shows no sign of abating and the streets glisten as cars and buses run with their headlights on bright. Rain spits against the dirty windows, and the room still smells of tobacco, although no one's been allowed to smoke in here for years.

I call a car rental agency and arrange for them to drop off an inexpensive vehicle for me near police headquarters.

"Good morning," I say as Lucy enters the conference room.

"Good morning," Lucy says, sitting opposite me at the conference table. "Were you and Victoria West in love?"

She must have picked up on my reaction when I first saw Vickie's body last night and must sense that Vickie once meant a great deal to me. Just the same, I'm startled by her question. Lucy and I have an unspoken understanding: we don't ask about each other's private lives. When she first joined homicide, I asked her whether she was married; she said no and told me her parents didn't approve of the men she was seeing. But we never pry into matters unrelated to police business.

"Vickie and I were once very close," I tell her. "We were both young. She wasn't much more than twenty when we met; I was twenty-five. It didn't last long and didn't end well."

"What do you mean, it didn't end well?"

"Vickie was a force of nature: passionate and wild and fervent and she never did anything by half. Whatever captured her attention, she did with full force. That included falling in love. And falling out of love."

"Since then?"

"We've had no contact in years. I haven't even thought about her." That part is not entirely true, but Lucy doesn't need to know that. That's a very personal thing.

"When Miss West was here in Washington, did you meet with her?"

Why is Lucy asking me these things?

"No," I say.

"You've had no contact at all?"

I don't think Lucy believes me.

"Vickie did send me a note about a week ago. I never replied."

"I'll need to see that note."

"Okay."

"Did you see her perform at the theater?"

"After our breakup, I never saw her in any performance: on stage or in her movies."

Lucy looks skeptical but says nothing as Frank Townsend, chief of homicide, arrives. He looks unusually cheerful this morning, despite the weather. He's followed by a dozen men and women homicide detectives, most clutching coffee containers, some carrying the sports section of *The Post*. They take their seats, nurse their coffees, and look up sports scores.

"I better let you all know," I say. "I'll be away for the next few days. I've been put on a special assignment to the State Department as police liaison with a VIP mission."

"Like hell you are," Frank says.

"I've just come from the Department of State. The Secretary of State said he cleared this with the mayor."

Frank mutters something rude into his coffee mug.

"What kind of temporary duty?" Roy Hunt asks. Roy is a recent transfer from burglary to homicide and is out to make a name for himself. He's good-looking and wears an annoying, pencil-thin black mustache and has a big, manly chin. His dark hair is slicked back, and I'm sure he uses product although he hotly denies this. He has an objectionable habit of smoothing his thin mustache with the little finger of his right hand. I'm almost sure he dyes his mustache. I know he's after my job.

The secretaries think he's adorable.

"I trust your performance will not reflect poorly on the police department," Frank says to me.

"No more than usual."

"I should take over the Victoria West case," Roy Hunt announces eagerly. "What with Marko off flitting around with the elite."

"Lucy can handle the investigation just fine," I cut him off before the discussion gets out of hand.

Frank turns to Lucy. "It's open and shut: a suicide. Right?"

"I guess," Lucy replies.

"We don't guess in homicide: this isn't vice."

Hanna, the police forensics expert, enters the room clutching a thick file folder. "Good morning, buckaroos." She's not smiling as she takes a seat at the table, opens her file, and pulls out a fistful of glossy photographs. "I'm afraid I must spoil your morning."

The photographs show Victoria, lying crumpled on the floor of the small drawing room just as I'd seen her last night. It still pains me to look.

"Victoria West did not commit suicide," Hanna announces. "There's no gunshot residue on her head, hands, arms, or clothing. She was shot from a distance: a minimum of ten feet. Miss West's fingerprints were not on the weapon."

"Anybody else's prints?" Lucy asks.

"Nothing. The weapon was wiped clean. She was murdered."

"Which gun was used?" I ask.

"The Smith & Wesson .38 Special. A single shot fired."

"The one she was holding in her hand?" Lucy asks.

"That's right."

"But she was alone in that room," Lucy says. "No one went into that room except Victoria West. No one came out."

"You know what this means, fellas," Frank Townsend announces. "Instead of a tragic but simple suicide, we have a major, high-profile murder case. The victim was a world-famous celebrity. The violent death of a beautiful woman always gives the media a hard-on, so we'll have every news organization in the country covering this story. Until something worse comes along, this murder will dominate the news cycle. I'm going to speak with the chief now." Townsend rises to his feet. "I'm assigning every available detective to this case. Detective Tanaka is in charge of the Victoria West investigation. Until we have enough evidence for an indictment, all leave is canceled."

A muffled groan goes around the table.

Townsend scoops up his files and notes and leaves the room, followed by the detectives crowding through the door after him, clutching their coffee containers, leaving Lucy, Hanna, and me alone.

"Tell me about the rifle round I gave you last night," I ask Hanna.

"It's from a high-velocity round; probably 338 Lapua Magnum cartridge."

"The kind of ammunition used in a SAKO TRG 42 sniper rifle?"

"Among others. Where did you get it?"

"I found it lying in a gutter in my neighborhood."

"I don't think I'd care for your neighborhood. Anything else you need me for?"

"Not this morning."

"Then I'll get back to the lab." Hanna picks up her photos and notes and leaves.

"What was that shell casing Hanna was talking about?" Lucy asks.

"Nothing to do with the Victoria West case. It's something else I'm working on."

Lucy looks at me with concern. This has happened before. She knows I get involved in activities not strictly called for in my police duties—sometimes I'm out of the office for several days at a time—but she doesn't pry. And she suspects Frank Townsend and I have some kind of understanding about this, but she doesn't ask. Which doesn't mean she's not curious and doesn't mean she's happy with the situation.

I'm about to get up and leave when Lucy gestures for me to stay.

"Last night," she says, "Arthur Cantwell told us Victoria West was seeing someone when they met in the New York production of *Hedda Gabler*. He said that she dumped some 'loser.'" Lucy takes a deep breath. "Were you, by any chance, that 'loser'?"

"Is it relevant?"

"Of course it's relevant. A spurned lover, bitter and angry, seeking revenge. That person always goes right to the top of our suspect list. That's what you taught me."

"That breakup was years ago. I'm not bitter nor angry."

"I think you are angry, Marko."

"Am I a suspect?"

"Naturally you're a suspect. I go by the book, you know that. That's what you trained me to do from the first day when I became your partner." Left unsaid is: I never go by the book despite what I preach. I make up my own rules as I go along.

"Where were you at ten minutes after nine last night?" Lucy asks. I can tell she's uncomfortable asking me these questions, but she's a good cop and she'll go by the book.

"At home."

"Do you have any witnesses?"

"I was alone." I can't really tell Lucy about my meeting with Cyprian Voss: she would not understand Cyprian. "You're going to have to trust me."

I know what must be going through Lucy's mind. For the first time since we became partners, she's asking herself: can I trust Marko? Do I really know who Marko is?

CHAPTER SEVEN

As I'm about to leave the conference room, my cell phone rings and the caller ID reads "Embassy of Montenegro."

"I wish to speak to Detective Marko Zorn," a voice says in a pompous, irritating tone.

"That is I," I say, trying to sound more pompous and irritating than the other guy.

"Ambassador Lukshich wishes to speak to you."

"And who may I ask is Ambassador Lukshich?"

"Ambassador Lukshich is the Ambassador Plenipotentiary of the Republic of Montenegro," the voice at the other end replies, offended. "It is in regard to the delegation that arrives this evening. The Ambassador is expecting you at the embassy now."

"Would you be so gracious as to inform me where the hell your embassy is?"

The voice on the phone grudgingly gives me an address on Sixteenth Street.

Lucy catches up with me as I'm about to leave police headquarters. "It's raining hard," she says. "Do you want to borrow my umbrella?"

I decline. Male homicide detectives do not carry umbrellas. Maybe in England they do, but not in this country. Certainly not an umbrella with pictures of fish in pastel colors. I thank her warmly. Lucy is obviously trying to take the sting out of the questions she asked me earlier.

As I leave police headquarters, a cab is pulling up to the main entrance to pick up a man holding a folded newspaper over his head to keep the rain off.

"We can share the cab," the man calls out to me, gesturing for me to join him.

The man is about thirty, tall and lean, with a narrow face and small eyes set close together. He has sandy close-cropped hair. You don't often run into this kind of goodwill on the streets of Washington, particularly in the rain.

"Thanks," I say. "I've got my own wheels."

He shrugs, climbs into his cab, and disappears. I find the car the rental company left for me, and I head for my appointment.

The embassy of Montenegro is housed in a modest building compared to its grand and stately diplomatic neighbors. Above the front door flies a flag with a red field featuring a double eagle under a crown. To one side of the front door is a plaque that reads: "Embassy of the Republic of Montenegro." An inscription in Cyrillic lettering that says the same thing is on the other side of the front door. Two CCTV cameras are placed above the entrance.

The outer door is glass and is protected inside by a heavy iron gate. There's a small canopy above the door that gives me some shelter from the rain while I press the brass doorbell. A small man wearing steel-rimmed glasses unlocks the outer gate.

"Detective Zorn?" He smiles a pretend smile.

"At your service."

"Please do come in," his eyes blinking rapidly. "I will take you to the ambassador."

The entry area is adorned with a Ficus tree and a photograph of a woman I recognize from last night's internet search: Nina Voychek.

She's wearing a smart business suit and a white turtleneck sweater. Her clothes are stylish and cut in the European fashion and she's very attractive. She looks to be about thirty and has blond hair worn in a chignon.

"Is that your prime minister?" I ask. I figure it's time I started to do my homework for this job.

My escort stops and looks at the picture, blinking. "That is Madame Voychek."

I shrug off my raincoat, which is dripping on the nice parquet floor. I had to park my rental car almost two blocks away. Parking in this part of the city is a bitch, so I was caught in the rain and I'm pretty well soaked.

I follow the man through a lobby where there are more flags and pictures of mountains.

"We're going to the chancery," my escort explains. "Where our offices are. The chancery is ordinarily off-limits to outsiders."

He seems to think he's given me some special honor by allowing me to visit this part of the embassy. "The other part of the embassy is residential, you understand. And for receptions. That is where our prime minister will be staying."

He leads me up a flight of marble steps into a waiting room. A middle-aged, heavyset woman with white hair sits at a desk to one side of a set of large, ornate double doors. She studies me thoughtfully.

"Inform His Excellency his visitor is here," my guide tells the woman. She presses a button on her desk and says something in a low voice.

"Please take a seat," she tells me. "The ambassador will see you shortly."

The door we'd just came through opens, and a young woman enters. She clutches several file folders and seems timid, even frightened, as she glances nervously at the secretary and at my escort. She can't be more than twenty.

The white-haired secretary says something, and the girl crosses the room anxiously and passes one of the file folders to the secretary who looks through it quickly, then rises. She says something to my escort and, grasping the file tightly, she and my escort disappear through the double doors, leaving me alone with the young woman.

There is a moment of awkward silence while I smile reassuringly at the girl. She stares at me, then abruptly pulls a sheet of paper from her file folder, tears it in half, and scribbles a note on the back. She presses the paper urgently into my hand. She's trembling.

"You are police." She speaks in a whisper. "Your name is Zorn." These are not questions: they're statements. How does this woman know my name? How does she know I'm police?

"Can I help you?" I ask.

"There is danger."

"Are you in trouble?" I ask.

"I must speak to you."

This young woman isn't shy; she's terrified.

"I'm listening."

"Not here. Private. I call you. Your telephone number, please."

I give her one of my cards with my name and cell number. "Do you need help?"

"I call tonight," she whispers, looking over her shoulder at the double doors to the inner office. "At midnight."

"What is your name?" I ask.

She looks as if she doesn't understand my question and walks away quickly. The ornate double doors open, and I slip the paper she's given me into one of the outer pockets of my raincoat. My escort with the glasses returns to the waiting room, followed by the secretary, who studies the young girl intently, then me. The girl bows—as if ducking from a blow—and hurries out of the office, closing the door behind her without looking back at me.

"Excuse the delay, Detective Zorn," my escort announces, his eyes blinking rapidly. "We have important communication from our ministry. His Excellency will see you now."

He knocks on a door, opens it, and I follow him through. The outer doors are of carved oak; a set of inner doors is covered with thick black leather. The leather padding, I assume, is to make the office soundproof. I wonder what kind of secrets the Embassy of Montenegro wants to hide.

Beyond the doors is a large office with more flags and an impressive antique desk decorated with lots of ormolu doodads. Seated at the desk is a distinguished-looking man with a thick black mustache; his hair gray at the temples. He looks like an ambassador from central casting.

"That will be all," the man says, rising from his chair. My escort backs out of the room silently, through the double doors, closing them behind him, leaving the ambassador and me alone.

"I am Vuk Lukshich," the man says, holding out his hand. "Ambassador of the Republic of Montenegro. You must be Detective Zorn."

"I must be."

"Please have a seat." He gestures at a large wingback chair. "May I offer you a slivovitz? Or is it too early in the day for you?"

"It is never too early for a proper slivovitz." I sit in the armchair the ambassador indicates while he goes to a liquor cabinet behind his desk, fills two small glasses with a clear liquid, and brings them across the room. He passes me one of the glasses and takes a seat across from me.

"To the success of our mission." He raises his glass and drains it: I do the same. The slivovitz is good quality, well-aged, and goes down smoothly.

"Our mission?" I ask, trying not to sound stupid.

"I understand you are to be the police liaison with our prime minister's delegation for the next few days," the ambassador says.

"I am."

"That is our mission. That is your mission."

I can't seem to get the frightened young woman out of my mind and I think about asking the ambassador whether something's wrong in the embassy. He seems friendly enough. But then he's a professional diplomat. He's paid to be friendly. I decide against asking about the young woman. There was something that makes me think that asking the ambassador would only make matters worse for her.

"Do you know why you were designated to be police liaison?" the ambassador asks.

"I have no idea."

"Do you have any connections in Montenegro?"

The Secretary of State asked me the same question. What is going on here?

"None I know of," I answer.

"You are a man of mystery then."

"I'm just a simple policeman."

The ambassador raises a skeptical eyebrow. "I doubt you are a simple policeman."

The ambassador somehow looks a little less friendly now.

"As you know," the ambassador goes on, "our prime minister arrives tomorrow evening for a state visit to the United States."

"So I've been told."

"You should know there are people deeply opposed to Nina Voychek and to her new democratic regime. There are those from the former regime who will stop at nothing to remove her from power, including having her assassinated. Our responsibility—yours and mine—is to prevent that from happening. That is my duty and, for the next few days, your duty as well."

"I understand."

"I'm not sure you really do. I want to be clear. The prime minister's enemies are implacable and dangerous."

"Do her enemies include Russia?"

He shakes his head slightly. "Russia? That is only gossip, Detective. Baseless gossip. Leave international politics to us professionals."

"Are Russian gangsters from Brooklyn involved?"

The ambassador laughs softly. "Certainly not. Why would such people be interested in the internal affairs of my country? Would you care for another slivovitz, Detective?"

I would like one but decide I should keep a clear head, and I decline the offer.

"The threat to our prime minister comes from discontents and criminals in our country," the ambassador is saying.

"A domestic affair?" I say.

"Precisely. Your assignment may sound routine; I assure you it is not. You yourself may even be in some danger, Detective Zorn."

The Secretary of State neglected to tell me about that part.

"You are to be in the greeting party at Dulles Airport tomorrow evening," the ambassador says. "I wanted to meet you before the delegation arrives. These events are always chaotic, and there will be no time for polite conversation. I like to get the measure of the man I work with."

"Have you got the measure of the man?"

"I believe I have. I remind you; we are dealing with dangerous and determined opponents. Be most careful."

That was strange, I think, as the twitchy man with the glasses escorts me out of the office, down the marble staircase, and to the front entrance. The ambassador could have told me on the phone about the dangers I'll face and saved himself some slivovitz. There is only one thing the ambassador could want from this meeting: he wanted to see me face-to-face and he wanted to get my photograph. As my escort and I walk through the embassy, I look for cameras but see none. That doesn't mean there aren't any, it just means they're small and well concealed. There are the two CCTV cameras above the front entrance, but those cameras, oriented as they are, would not produce a clear head shot of somebody waiting at the front door and that, I assume, is what they need. By now I'm thoroughly annoyed: I don't like photographs taken of me, particularly by hidden cameras controlled by people I don't know for reasons I can only guess at.

It's still raining as I leave the embassy. I dash for my car, an old Honda Civic. No fun to drive, but it's at least inconspicuous.

Once inside the car and out of the rain, I study the note the young woman gave me and remember the fear in her eyes. The paper is a bit smaller than letter size and is perforated at the side as if torn from a Teletype machine. On one side is a single handwritten word in shaky block letters: "opasnosti".

On the reverse side are a series of numbers.

19602 34978 62974 42379 29374 89762 42981 39576
37465 28051 38964 43865 72861 94275 75429 68452
97531 29465 74531 92640 25431 56241 33217 25196
48371 29432 53428 76194 76154 92137 84316 78164
92865 43298 76417 25487 65318 72491 75319 86534
29178 42694 72985 96435 24765 45018 87326 22913
56920 11813 67897 97451 08596 54832 41697 53219
75321 89147 39741 56318 92541 72615 32937 43812
63592

The bottom of the page has been torn away.

The numbers appear to be random, and I can make no sense of them. I study one side of the paper, with the numbers, then the other, with the single word, "*opasnosti*", turning the page over and over again.

I don't know the language they speak in Montenegro, but I'm pretty sure I know what this word means. It's much the same in Russian. And it means "danger."

CHAPTER EIGHT

A TALL YOUNG man with a stiff military posture is waiting for me at my desk when I return to police headquarters. He has close-cropped blond hair cut in a crew cut, military style.

"Matt Granger," he announces, holding out his hand. "Chicago police. You're Detective Zorn."

"Bingo." We shake hands. Not warmly.

"Didn't we recently talk on the phone?" I ask, in a nice way. I don't want to alienate him. You never know when you'll be in Chicago and might need a friendly cop.

"Correct. We did talk on the phone," he says.

"And you've come all the way from the City of Broad Shoulders to continue our chat. To what do I owe the honor?"

"I didn't think our chat went all that well. May I?"

I indicate he's welcome to sit down.

"To be honest," Granger says, taking a seat stiffly. "I don't think you've been completely honest with us."

"I've told you what I know."

"I'm investigating the murders of two men. I asked you whether you knew the name Milan Jovanovich. You said you knew nothing about him. I find that surprising."

"Life is full of surprises." I've been assuming all along the Chicago police want to talk to me about the mob killing of General Drach. I don't want to go there. This would lead to awkward questions about what I was doing in Chicago and who I was working for. But the murder of two other men: that's different, and I think I'd better find out what's going on.

"We believe whoever killed these men were professional hit men," Granger says.

"What makes you think so?"

"The victims were playing chess in a club on the South Side. Two men walked into the club and shot them. Point-blank. Then the killers walked calmly out. It sounds like the hit was carefully planned and the victims were targeted."

"That sounds like a Chicago mob hit."

"If it was the Chicago mob, we'd know about it. We have well-placed snitches in the organization."

"Who do you think it was, then?"

"We're pretty sure these men were out of New York. We have CCTV films of the killers entering and leaving the chess club. They're not locals; we're sure of that. We sent the tapes to the FBI, and they have one of these guys in their database."

"Do they have names?"

"No names yet. The Bureau identified one man as definitely associated with the Brooklyn branch of the Russian Mafia."

"What has New York got to do with a shooting in Chicago?"

"That's what we'd like to know. We thought maybe you could help us."

"Who are the victims?"

"The two chess club victims were members of an émigré organization of people originally from Montenegro. Milan Jovanovich is secretary of that organization."

"They sound harmless. Why would anyone want to harm a couple of chess players?"

"We believe all three victims were involved in a violent killing that took place a few weeks ago in Chicago. The shooting at the chess club, we think, was some kind of payback. Now the third man, Milan Jovanovich, is on the run. Probably hiding out. We need to question him."

"I wish I could help."

I'm lying to Granger, and he probably senses it, but I have no choice. He's getting into a sensitive area. "Send me the CCTV tapes of the two killers," I say. "And I'll have them thoroughly checked out at this end. If I come up with anything, I'll let you know."

"I appreciate your cooperation." His jaw is tight.

I don't think he really appreciates my cooperation at all.

"Why do you think the Brooklyn Russian mob sent these men to Chicago?" I ask. "I would have thought Chicago had plenty of local talent."

"We have no idea why the Russian Mafia was involved. And we don't like outside organizations sending people to our city to do their dirty work."

"Tell me about this violent killing that took place a few weeks ago," I say. Why am I asking this question? I should be getting rid of this cop, not drawing him out and getting into a discussion about an incident I really don't want to talk about. But I'm curious about how much the Chicago police know about what happened.

"A man named General Mykhayl Drach was brutally murdered on a street in the East Side. In the middle of the day. In broad daylight. He was attacked by an angry mob and almost torn to pieces."

The first time I saw Mykhayl Drach, he was coming out of an Orthodox church called Sveti Stefan, where he'd been hiding for a week or more. He stood, blinking in the bright sun, as if he'd come out of a cave, and was suddenly surrounded by a large, angry crowd: Mostly old people, men and women, some carrying canes, some on crutches, some even on walkers. They shouted curses at him. Some were crying. I recognized Milan Jovanovich and the two other old men I'd met that morning.

"Are you saying the name Mykhayl Drach means nothing to you?" Granger demands.

"I've never met the man."

Drach disappeared under the mob, his face white with terror. Our eyes met for a second as if he were pleading to me for help.

"Chicago's a tough town," I say.

"This man Drach was the former dictator of the country of Monte-negro. Do you know anything about that country?"

"Never been there. I hear it has nice beaches. What was this former dictator doing in Chicago?"

"We think he was hiding out while trying to raise money for his cause. According to our sources, Drach was planning on a coup d'état to overthrow the present government. Jovanovich and his friends were politically opposed to General Drach and his regime and were trying to stop him. They got a tip where he was hiding, and we think they organized the mob that attacked him."

"Some organization."

"We know you were recently in Chicago, Detective."

Oh, oh. Here we go, I think. "That's possible. I may have spent an afternoon at the Art Institute."

Of course I was nowhere near the Art Institute. Instead, I was meeting with three elderly strangers.

Granger's phone rings. "Hello," he says, his voice low. "Yes. Yes."

He covers the speaker with his hand. "It's my commander," he says to me. "I've got to take this call." Granger moves away, his back to me, and continues speaking in a voice so soft I can't hear a word. I think back to that first meeting with the men in Chicago.

It was a little warm for the season and a pleasant breeze was blowing off Lake Michigan. I met with the men in a room in the back of a hardware store, all three smoking Camel cigarettes, their fingers stained by a lifetime of smoking.

The man who was the spokesman was Milan Jovanovich, an emaciated man of about seventy, his sparse white hair slicked over a bare scalp. He and the others all wore dark suits and ties as if they had dressed up for this occasion. Maybe they always dressed that way.

"You're telling us you know nothing about this General Drach. Or Milan Jovanovich?" Granger asks, putting away his phone and returning to me.

"That's what I'm saying."

Jovanovich had contacted Cyprian Voss through a complex network of obscure and nameless intermediaries and contracted with him to find Drach somewhere in Chicago. That's the kind of thing Voss does. For a substantial fee. Voss sent me to Chicago to do the job.

Jovanovich gave me an old business card, bent at the edges and soiled. I suspect he must have carried it in his wallet for years. It read: MILAN JOVANOVICH with a street address and cell phone number.

"We believe you were in Chicago when all this was going on," Granger says.

"I often visit your lovely city. I hit the Lollapalooza Festival only last year."

I may have gone too far this time. Granger gives me a hard look. I'm afraid he's having a hard time controlling his temper.

"What you tell me is very serious," I say, trying to sound sympathetic. "I'll do everything I can to help you find this missing man."

This time I mean it.

Granger gives up and says he has to get back to Chicago. I don't know whether he believes me about what I know or don't know about the Chicago murders. Probably doesn't believe a word I say.

I give him ten minutes, then make my phone call to Jovanovich. The phone rings ten times without an answer. Am I too late? Have the Russian hit men found Jovanovich and already dispatched him as they had the chess players? Maybe Jovanovich is looking at the caller ID and deciding whether to answer. Maybe he doesn't recognize my name. Maybe he's too scared to answer the phone. Too scared to find out who's on the other end of the line. Or worse, maybe it isn't Jovanovich who's looking at the phone right now. Maybe it's one of the *bratva* enforcers, an uninvited stranger who's wondering who's calling and whether this is a loose end that must be attended to.

A voice comes on the line, hoarse and shaky. "Who is this?"

I recognize the voice: from the back room of a hardware store somewhere in Chicago, an old man clutching a bent Camel cigarette.

"Milan?" I ask. I don't use a last name. I don't know who else might be listening.

"My friends have been murdered," the voice at the other end whispers. He must remember my voice because he doesn't ask who I am.

"Where are you, Milan?" I ask.

There's a silence, finally: "They're after me. They killed my friends."

"I know."

"They've been to my home. They want to kill me."

"You never told me what you planned to do when I told you where General Drach was hiding."

"We did what had to be done."

"You should've told me."

"It was better you not know. If I'd told you, you would have been . . . what is it you call it in English?"

"An accessory."

"That is right. An accessory."

He has a good point. I was probably better off not knowing what would happen once I told them where to find General Drach. Would I have gone ahead with my search for Drach if I had known what was in store for him? I don't know.

"Who's looking for you?"

"The men who killed my friends. I don't know their names. They're not from around here."

"The Chicago police believe they're Russians from Brooklyn, New York."

"I hate Russians."

"Why would these Russians kill your friends? Why are they after you?"

"Somebody has paid them."

"Who?"

"I don't know. Somebody who wants revenge for the death of Mykhayl Drach. Somebody holds me responsible."

"You were responsible."

"Will you help me?"

"Are you safe where you are?"

"For a few more hours. Maybe a day. No more. I can't hide with friends or family. They'd be killed. Can you help me?"

"Where are you?"

"Chicago. Will you come to Chicago and help me?"

"I can't go to Chicago. It will be someone else."

"Who is this other person? How can I trust this person?"

"You'll get a call this afternoon. Somebody will ask you where you are. You can trust him. Give him the address where you're calling from. He will come and get you. He'll take you to a safe place."

"I can't give my location to a stranger. To some person I don't know. How do I know he's not one of the Russians?"

"He will use a code word. A word only you and he know. When you hear that word, you'll know you can trust him."

There's a long silence. "Very well. What is the code word?"

"Ostrog."

"Ostrog," he repeats. "Our famous Montenegro monastery. That is good. The Russians will never think of that. Russians are ignorant fools."

CHAPTER NINE

WHEN I HANG up, Lucy comes to my desk.

"Have you made any progress in the Vickie West investigation?" I ask.

"I've interviewed all the cast and crew," Lucy tells me. "Two admit to knowing something about firearms: Arthur Cantwell says he's a skilled shooter and has several high-powered hunting rifles. He says he's a hunter and shoots things on safari in Africa."

"The second?"

"Tim Collins, another of the actors. I've got Mr. Collins in interview room nine right now. I'm about to take his statement. Do you want to join me?"

* * *

Lucy and I meet Collins in one of the nicer interrogation rooms. He's a slender, good-looking young man with longish blond hair.

"Your partner said you had some questions." Collins is not sure which one of us to talk to, shifting his eyes from me to Lucy and back.

"Where were you at the time Miss West was killed?" Lucy asks Collins, trying to take charge of the conversation.

"I was backstage waiting to take my curtain call."

"Who else did you see backstage?"

"Michael Tolland, the stage manager. Cynthia Fletcher, she's Vickie's agent. And Natalie Esmond. Arthur Cantwell must have been there, but he would have been on stage. And that creepy props girl."

"How did you get involved in this production?" Lucy asks.

"Through a casting agent. I mostly work in television these days. You've probably seen me."

"What might I have seen you in?" Lucy asks.

"My first TV gig was a corpse on *CSI*. I've been in dozens of shows since."

"You told Detective Tanaka you know about guns," I say.

"Not real guns. Pretend guns."

"What do you mean 'pretend' guns?"

"For three seasons I appeared on a TV series called *The Phantom*."

"I remember that show," Lucy exclaims. "I loved it. Which part did you play?"

"I was Eliot Flynt the most dangerous international assassin in the world, and he used all kinds of special weapons."

"You played the part of an international assassin?" I ask, curious, despite myself. "I'm sorry I missed it. Is it still on?"

"My contract wasn't renewed at the end of season three. The show's not worth watching since my character was written out. There were artistic differences between me and the showrunner. He was a douchebag."

"I mean, what happened to the character you played," I ask. "The international assassin?"

"He was flying over San Francisco in his personal helicopter, planning to kill the king of somewhere or other who's riding in a cable car on Powell Street. Flynt has some kind of super rocket aimed right at the cable car. The so-called star of the series, Harry Something, who can't act for shit but earned five times what I got and plays a CIA agent, is standing on the Golden Gate Bridge. He has this pistol and he shoots the assassin's helicopter so it blows up over Alcatraz Island and crashes in flames into San Francisco Bay. End of Eliot Flynt. End of contract. The show's been crap since."

"You know it's not possible to shoot down a helicopter with a handgun," I say.

"Who cares?"

"Did you use firearms as part of that show?" Lucy asks, becoming a bit impatient as the questioning drifts off course.

"Lots of guns. And all kinds of other weapons. All fake, of course. We had a police sergeant on set at all times to be sure the guns were harmless and we didn't kill each other."

"Do you own any real guns?" Lucy asks.

"I won't allow guns in my house. I have two small kids at home, and I don't want them playing with guns. Know what I mean?"

"But you know how guns work?" I say. "In your work on that show, you became familiar with various weapons. How they were armed? That sort of thing?"

"I guess. I used them all. In one episode I was supposed to set off a neutron bomb."

"I'm not concerned with neutron bombs today," I say. "What about more conventional weapons?"

"You mean like a pearl-handled revolver? Sure, but I've never fired a real gun; in fact, I'm afraid of guns."

"Very wise," I say.

"Do you have any idea why someone would want to kill Victoria West?" Lucy asks.

"I have no idea why anyone would want to kill anyone. Unless they're killing bad actors who get all the good contracts and agents who don't return phone calls."

"Did you get along with other members of the cast?"

"There were no serious problems; maybe some friction during the rehearsals early on. The former props manager was fired a few days before opening night. Artistic differences, according to rumor. The director found a replacement right away. Cantwell was his usual asshole self."

"How was Victoria West during the performance last night?" Lucy asks. "Anything unusual in her behavior?"

Collins reflects for a moment. "Her performance was brilliant. Absolutely brilliant. She'd found Hedda's anger—her fury. It was kind of scary, actually."

"Did anything strike you about what Collins said?" I ask Lucy after Collins leaves.

Lucy reflects. "He said he was a corpse on CSI. How do they do that? Do they just hold their breath, you think?"

"He also said the previous props person was fired over artistic differences. How in hell do you have artistic differences over props?"

CHAPTER TEN

A POLICE OFFICER opens the door to the interview room. "Detective Zorn, there's a man who says he needs to speak to you. He says he has information in connection with some murder case."

"Can you take this?" Lucy asks. "I'm supposed to attend a press conference with the chief on the Victoria West case."

The man waiting for me is short with a round face and thinning white hair partially covering a pink scalp; he wears a pale gray shirt, a gray suit, a black bow tie, and loafers with leather tassels. He's about sixty.

"Aubrey Sands," he announces cheerfully with a bright smile. "You must be Detective Marko Zorn."

"I must be. I understand you want to speak to us about a murder investigation."

"That's right. The Victoria West case." He removes a business card from a small, leather holder and gives it to me. The card reads:

Aubrey Sands, Penny Lane Murders

This is followed by a telephone number, an email address, and a website address.

"You're the lead investigator in the Victoria West murder case?" the man asks.

"My partner, Detective Tanaka, is now in charge of that investigation. She's at a news conference right now. How can I help you?"

"It is I who can help you. I can help you solve the Victoria West murder mystery."

"We always welcome the public's cooperation. Do you have information you would like to share? I can pass it along to my partner."

"Not information. Advice. I write mystery novels, you see. Maybe you're familiar with the Penny Lane murder series."

"I'm afraid not."

"These are what are called cozy mysteries. Maybe you've heard of *The Christmas Pageant Murder* or *The Carousel Murder*."

"I can't say I have."

"You don't read mystery novels?" The man seems genuinely astonished.

"I have enough real crime in my life as is. I don't need fantasy crime."

Maybe mystery fiction is too close to home. I don't say it though. Sands seems a decent guy who's only trying to help. I don't want to be rude by disparaging his profession.

"You should read mysteries, you know," Sands is telling me. "You could get a lot of tips on solving crimes."

"I'll try to remember that."

"I've written nine Penny Lane books," Aubrey Sands says. "The events take place in a small town on Maryland's Eastern Shore."

"I'm afraid I don't see the appeal of fictional murder mysteries."

I'm not sure why people read these books. Violent death is a terrible thing. Not just for the victims and families. But for those of us who deal with violent death every day as a profession. We learn to live with it, I guess. What do we lose in learning to do that? Too much, I sometimes think.

"Think of these mystery books as intellectual puzzles. A brutal crime is committed. Who is the culprit? The author leaves clues. Sometimes they are false and misleading. Sometimes they're real. It's kind of a contest between author and reader. Who's smarter? Who can solve the mystery first?"

"Who wins that game?" I ask.

"Usually it's the author. The character the author creates who seems like the obvious villain turns out to be innocent. And the one the reader least suspects is the criminal. And the reader always gets the motive wrong. It's never what one thinks; it's usually something quite different."

"I'll try to remember that."

"I'll make a little confession, Detective—as one professional to another—we writers sometimes cheat a little."

"So do I. I'll stick with the Sunday *New York Times* crossword."

"My principal sleuth is Mrs. Peregrine Partridge, the local librarian. Peregrine is a widow and lives alone with her cat."

"And she solves your mysteries, I suppose."

"She's very observant, and she solves many murders that confound the local police."

"It's true," I say, "the police are frequently confounded."

"I'm certain I could help solve this murder. All I need is the opportunity to examine the crime scene."

"I can't permit that, Mr. Sands. The crime scene is off-limits to everyone except official police investigators."

"My sleuth often visits the crime scenes, and she always finds a clue the police have overlooked. Peregrine must frequently remind Sheriff Rogers—he's the local constable—don't look so hard. Look obliquely and you will see more."

"And does he?"

"I'm afraid not. But Peregrine does."

"I'll try to look more obliquely next time."

"You haven't made any progress, have you?"

"It's early days."

"You see but you do not observe, Detective."

"I think I've heard that advice before."

"I don't wish to sound disrespectful. I'm sure you and your men are highly competent."

"Like the police in your small town," I say.

"Exactly. And, like you, they are suspicious of meddling amateurs. But you have a very special problem."

"Meaning?"

"You have a classic 'locked room' murder."

"I've been in this business many years, Mr. Sands," I say. "And I've investigated dozens of murders. I've never seen a real 'locked room' murder. Never even heard of a real one. They don't exist; they're figments of the imagination of crime-story writers. No offense, but they're only good for entertainment."

"But you have one right now. According to the press, Victoria West was alone in a small room when she was killed. There were no windows. The only doors were closed and in view of hundreds of people. At the beginning of the performance there was no one in that room. At the end of the play, somebody shot her. The gun that was used to kill her was found clutched in her hand. Nobody entered that room except the victim; nobody left that room. How was it done, Detective Zorn? How was it done?"

"My partner will figure it out."

"I think you need my help. I've written two books involving 'locked room' murders: *The Harvest Festival Murder* and *The Case of the Missing Bicycle*. Read them; they might give you some insight."

"Thank you, Mr. Sands. I'll pass along your suggestions to my partner."

"You're not going to let me look at the murder room, are you?" Sands looks disconsolate. "Not even a peek?"

"Sorry. It's not possible. But thank you for your offer."

"That's it?" Sands asks.

I give Sands my business card. "Please call me or Detective Tanaka if you have any real information."

He stops and turns back to me. "You are, of course, quite right, Detective. There's no such thing as a real 'locked-room' murder. Not even in genre fiction. The mystery always turns out to be a matter of misdirection."

CHAPTER ELEVEN

THE TEXT MESSAGE on my phone comes at two in the morning and reads: *I have a message for you from Vickie that will explain everything. Meet me at the Capitol Theater stage door at 2:30 a.m. This message is for you alone. Bring no one with you. Oliver will join us.* There's no indication who sent it.

I am by temperament and experience deeply suspicious and, under normal circumstances, I'd go back to the theater only with armed backup. But this is different; "Oliver" has invited me. I know I have to go. And I must be alone.

I pick up my rental car I parked a block from my house and drive to the theater. When I arrive, I find the stage door located in an alley alongside the theater. As I get out of my car, I receive a second text message: *Stage door unlocked. Come right on in.*

The alley is dark and deserted, but I know somebody is watching me.

This is really stupid. I know I shouldn't do this. Walk into a commercial building in the middle of a murder investigation, at night, alone, with no backup. I'd never tolerate such behavior in an officer working under me. So I am extra careful.

I can't help myself. Oliver is waiting for me.

Inside the stage door is a long, brightly lit corridor; the only furniture is a battered, metal folding chair leaning against one wall.

Shouldn't there be a security guard on duty here? Maybe at night they just lock the doors. Just the same, I'm careful.

My phone vibrates and a new message appears. *Very good, Marko. I like punctuality in a man. Go to the end of the hall and look for a door with a sign reading Staff Only.*

I move slowly along the hallway until I find the door marked STAFF ONLY, and a new text appears on my phone. *Happy to see you are being cautious. So very wise of you. Open the door and go down the stairs. Oliver is waiting for you in the carpentry shop.*

The door opens onto a narrow flight of steep, wooden stairs. I turn off the overhead stair light so I do not make myself a target, then cautiously work my way down, bracing myself on the walls.

The step next to the bottom is loose and creaks under my weight. In front of me is a door with a sign that reads SHOP.

I step into a large room brightly lit by fluorescent lights and filled with carpentry machine tools. There's a sweet smell of sawdust in the air—plywood and cedar—and glue and oil paint. In the center of the room is a worktable on the center of which lies a small object that was once a cheap, green plastic turtle named Oliver.

Oliver is now a pile of crushed plastic.

I've just walked into a trap.

I lunge to one side and grab for the light switch next to the door. I'm lucky: my fingers find the switch, and I turn off the lights, plunging the room into darkness just as a shot is fired at me from across the room.

For the moment I'm blind: so is the shooter.

I hold my breath, crouching behind what I think is a workstation, and reconstruct in my mind the layout of the room from my brief glimpse before it went dark. The shot was from a small-caliber hand-gun fired from about twenty feet away so the shooter was probably standing with his back to the far wall. Did I stumble onto a burglary? Who burgles a carpentry shop?

This was carefully planned. Someone has lured me here, waiting for me to walk through the door. In the brief instant before I killed the lights, I saw nobody, so the shooter must have been hiding behind a tall drill press waiting for me to open that door. The staircase behind me was dark, and I made a poor target. Had I left the stair lights on, I would be dead.

Now the shooter has missed me, and he's lost his best chance. He has to figure out where I'm hiding. He can't risk turning on the lights; he doesn't know I'm unarmed and I can't shoot back. To my far left, I remember seeing a table saw. To my far right, as near as I can reconstruct the room, there is a band saw or maybe a table-mounted router.

I wait and listen in the darkness. I try to remember to breathe.

The killer must be moving silently through the room toward me, listening for any sound that will give away my location.

There's another shot. I see the muzzle flash, closer this time and to my left, from somewhere near the drill press. I hear the round strike metal.

The shooter takes two more wild shots in the dark, but he isn't aiming to hit me because he can't know where I am. He's trying to force me to stay motionless and hide until he can get between me and the door I entered and trap me inside the workshop, blocking my escape back up the stairs. The shooter is doing the smart thing. That makes this a game of nerves, and I don't plan to play his mind game.

I dash through the open door I just entered, stop at the bottom of the wooden staircase, remember which is the loose step—second from the bottom, I think. I reach down into the black void of the stairwell and smash my fist onto the wooden step, making a loud creak, then step as far away from the stairs as quickly as I can.

My killer fires twice more. He thinks I'm escaping up the stairs and am trapped in the narrow, confined stairwell—an easy target. He's not trying to hide now. He thinks he's got me trapped, and he dashes up the stairs in search of what's left of me.

I wait at the bottom of the stairs half expecting the killer to come back down when he discovers he's missed me, but no one appears, and after two minutes, I go up the stairs, being careful to avoid the creaking step. The air is thick with the smell of gunpowder.

There are loud voices when I get to the top and the corridor flickers with flashlight beams. Somebody switches on the corridor lights, and two nervous cops, both with guns drawn, stand at the stage door.

"We heard gunshots," one of the cops says nervously.

I identify myself while one of the cops goes downstairs to search the workshop. It's pointless: he'll find out soon enough. My attacker has long gone.

"Nobody in sight," the cop announces when he returns. "Looks like you flushed a burglar. All I could find was a broken plastic toy on one of the tables. Does this belong to you?" He holds in his hand the crushed remains of Oliver.

"Nothing to do with me," I say.

I explain to one of the cops this was not a burglary but a planned attack—on me. The cop listens politely but is unconvinced while his partner prowls the area around the stage door. I show the cop the texts on my cell phone. He looks more perplexed than convinced but records the texts in his notebook

"Oh, Sweet Jesus," the prowling cop yells. He's looking into a small utility closet cluttered with brooms and mops. Huddled in a fetal position on the closet floor is a man wearing some kind of uniform with a shoulder badge reading "Special Police."

I've found the missing guard. A thin black cord is wrapped tight around the man's throat, cutting deep into his flesh.

I now have two murder victims to deal with: Vickie and this poor son of a bitch.

I call Lucy and fill her in on what has happened in the theater shop. The two cops have already called in their murder report, and it's only a matter of minutes before this part of the building will be swarming with police investigators.

"Are you okay?" Lucy asks as soon as she arrives at the stage door.

"I'm fine." I can see she's unconvinced.

"Somebody tried to kill you? That's not fine. Who did this?"

"I have no idea."

"What are you doing here?" she asks.

"I got a text message on my phone telling me to come here. It indicated that I might get important information about Victoria West's murder."

"You came by yourself? Without backup? That was stupid."

What can I say?

"Why didn't you call me?" She's mad now. "You should have called for backup."

"I know. I just thought this might be personal."

"What do you mean *personal*?"

I show Lucy the text messages.

"Who's Oliver?"

"Oliver is a cheap plastic toy turtle. The kind you buy at souvenir stores. Oliver has a little spring inside that made him hop. That cop has what's left of Oliver."

"You're losing me."

"Vickie bought it for me years ago. After one of our arguments. It was a kind of peace offering. We swore on a stack of paper napkins that if she was ever in trouble, she'd send Oliver to me as a sign she needed help."

Lucy looks slightly disgusted. "Who knew about this Oliver turtle?"

"It wasn't a secret exactly. It was just a private thing between me and Vickie. When I got the text, I thought . . ."

"You thought Vickie was communicating from the next world?" Lucy is exasperated.

"Not at all. I just thought that somebody Vickie knew well; somebody she might have trusted—maybe she told him about Oliver . . . I don't know what I was thinking."

"You weren't thinking, Marko. That's the plain truth."

"Have our IT people check these text messages. See if they can find out who sent them."

She takes my cell phone. "I'll assign this case to Roy Hunt. He'll jump at the chance to run his own murder investigation."

I'm sure Roy will be overjoyed. I'm also pretty sure he'll get nowhere. This was too carefully planned, and Roy is a fool.

While Lucy calls Roy and gets her troops in order, I review the events of the last few days to see if I can make sense of what's happened. I now understand two things: this attempt on my life is connected to the murder of Vickie West and may be connected to the attempt in front of my house. I'm now a target as well. Whoever is after me knows a great deal about me, including my private cell number. Even worse, he knows about Oliver.

CHAPTER TWELVE

"SOMEBODY TRIED TO kill you last night," Frank Townsend says. He's at his desk, clutching the morning crime report. I can tell, even at a distance, it contains information on the shooting in the theater basement.

"You were in the theater?" Frank demands. "Why were you there?"

"I was investigating the Victoria West murder case."

"That's no longer your case, remember? Who tried to shoot you?"

"Assailant unknown."

"Somebody's trying to kill you, Marko. I won't have it."

I don't remind Frank this is hardly the first time that's happened.

"I don't need babysitting, Frank."

"I say you do. I can't have my officers being shot at by person or persons unknown. Flitting around the city like you usually do— you're an easy target."

This is going to get sticky. I really can't have a record of everyone I see.

"Are you using your own car to get to work?" Frank asks.

"I'm driving a rental car." I sigh. "Okay. For the next few days, until we nail the man who attacked me, I'll keep my Corvette safely tucked away in my garage and I'll use rental cars."

"Not good enough. You're an easy target any time you're on the street."

"Do you want me to hide out in the men's room for the rest of my career?"

"I don't think you're taking this situation seriously."

He's wrong about that. I do take this seriously. Deadly seriously. Frank doesn't even know about the attack on me the other evening when I was going into my house.

"I'm assigning an armed police officer to accompany you when you're away from police headquarters," Frank announces. "He'll pick you up in the morning at your home and drop you off at night until we clear up this shooting mess."

"I don't think . . ."

"Don't argue. That's an order."

"I'm going to be traveling all around the city in connection with my duties with the State Department."

That's a desperate ploy on my part. I know it won't work.

"Go ahead with that assignment. Your armed escort will take you wherever you need to go."

"You're overreacting . . ."

"And you'll be driven in a marked police cruiser. That way, if there's an attack on you or there's a roadblock or someone tries to force you off the road, your escort can use his flashers and siren and can get away fast."

"Is that all?"

"No. I'll instruct your escort to use a different route when he picks you up in the morning and brings you back to your house at night—a different route each day."

This is going to get complicated. I'll just have to work around the problem and hope for the best.

"I've selected a very special police officer for your escort," Frank Townsend is saying. "He's a splendid young officer with an outstanding record. He's a trained marksman and has won national championship competitions in handgun and carbine shooting. You'll be safe with him."

Why is Frank doing this? Why is he authorizing the cost of a police officer just to keep me company? He knows I can handle this situation. I always have in the past.

"What's going on here?" I ask. "I've been in tight spots before, but you've never assigned someone to act as my bodyguard."

"If you must know, the Chief called me into his office first thing this morning. He read about the attack on you and said it would be intolerable if you were attacked again, maybe injured, maybe even killed. The press and TV would spin a scandal out of this. They'd say it was gross negligence if the police couldn't protect one of their own after we knew he was already a target of a prior attack. And you were personally requested by the Secretary of State to provide security for a visiting head of state. The Mayor doesn't want the Secretary of State to get on her case. If I allowed you to be harmed after what we know, I could lose my job. So just do it."

I give up.

"I have a lunch date across town. Can my bodyguard give me a lift?"

*   *   *

I'm at the main doors of police headquarters when a police officer in a smart-looking uniform stops me. He wears a crisp white shirt, dark navy-blue trousers with sharp pleats, a gold shield. Under his arm he holds a standard-issue eight-point service hat and at his waist he wears a Glock service weapon in a holster.

"Detective Zorn?" he asks. He speaks in a soft, courteous voice. He's maybe thirty and has handsome features. His skin is olive.

I wonder for a moment whether I'm about to be arrested for something. The insignia on his collar tells me he's a lieutenant, and the tag on his immaculate white shirt tells me his name is Bonifacio. I've never met him before.

"That's me," I say brightly, trying to exude innocence.

"I am to be your escort," the lieutenant tells me. "I will drive you whenever you are obliged to leave police headquarters."

"That's not necessary, Lieutenant. I can take care of myself."

He sort of smiles. "Those are my orders, sir. From Captain Townsend. I'm sure you understand."

"Good to meet you, Officer Bonifacio. Do you know where the Isle of Capri restaurant is?"

"Yes, sir."

"Then it sounds like we're good to go."

"We climb into a police cruiser parked in the police pool lot. It's a standard Ford Crown Victoria, less scratched and dented than most. Bonifacio must have pulled strings to get a cruiser this nice.

Tucked just above the front windshield is a 12-gauge pump-action shotgun.

"Expecting trouble, Lieutenant?" I ask, pointing to the shotgun.

"You never know. I thought, seeing as how you are my passenger, I better be prepared."

* * *

The Isle of Capri went out of style sometime in the late nineties, as did its menu, so I was touched when Carla Lowry left a message telling me to meet here for a late lunch. Has she decided to forgive and forget?

That would be so out of character.

The Isle of Capri was once where the rich and powerful came to play and admire one another. No rich or powerful people come here anymore. The carpeting is worn. The once-bright upholstery is shabby. The old photos of scenic views of Italy are faded. The waitstaff is from Honduras.

Carla Lowry looks up from a stained menu with a photograph of the Roman Forum on its cover. "You're late."

"And a good afternoon to you, Carla."

"I've had a terrible day. Don't say anything to annoy me."

In the old days, Carla and I used to come here for dinner. The food was no better then than it is now, but the carpet and upholstery were cleaner and brighter. There were candles on the tables: battery-powered electric lights have replaced the candles.

A waiter brings a wicker basket of bread, and Carla orders spaghetti Bolognese and snatches a piece of bread from the basket.

"A cappuccino for me," I tell the waiter. Even the Isle of Capri can't ruin a cappuccino, I figure.

"Somebody tried to kill you last night," Carla announces between bites. "According to my morning crime report, you were in the basement of the Capitol Theater and somebody shot at you."

As head of the Criminal Investigation Division at the FBI, Carla makes it her business to know everything.

"That's about right."

"Do you have any idea who that person was? Or why he has it in for you?"

"I have no idea."

"What are you up to, Marko?"

"Nothing special."

She looks unconvinced. "I hope you're making progress on the murder of that actress," Carla says, between bites of bread. "I seem to remember you once knew the lady."

"That was a long time ago. I am now a person of interest in the case."

"Of course you are."

Carla takes a second piece of bread from the basket and tears it ferociously to pieces. "I understand you were in Chicago recently."

"It was just for one day."

"A lot can happen in one day. I believe Leland Cross has briefed you on the planned assassination of Nina Voychek."

"The Secretary of State gave me a sketchy outline."

"Leland can be obscure when he wants to be." She dips her bread into a saucer of olive oil. "You understand, it's critically important that Nina Voychek come to no harm."

"So I've been told."

"I have the same assignment for you," she tells me. "Keep Prime Minister Voychek alive and well at all costs. You'll get your standard fee from the Bureau."

I see no point in telling her about the substantial fee I'll get from Cyprian Voss for the same thing. Carla doesn't know about Cyprian Voss and I intend to keep it that way.

Why is the Bureau paying me when the State Department is already doing so? Carla isn't saying, but I suspect she wants me to be a little more proactive than does the Secretary of State.

"You're telling me to take a bullet for the lady?" I ask.

Carla shakes her head impatiently. "I'm not telling *you* to take a bullet. I want the *assassin* to take a bullet."

"Why is the FBI asking me to do this? I'm not a trained security guard. Why don't you hire a professional bodyguard? Or use one of your own agents?"

"Because you have already been assigned by the State Department to the minister's security detail. Because you are resourceful as you recently demonstrated when you foiled a plot to assassinate the President. Because you're a badass."

Carla never seems bothered about hiring me from time to time for special services. It's strictly against police department rules and I'm pretty sure it's probably against FBI rules as well. Neither of us is disturbed by breaking rules if that's what it takes to get the job done.

"What can you tell me about this assassin?" I ask.

"All we know is that somebody has paid a huge amount of money to hire someone to off the prime minister. The payment's been traced to a bank in Macao, and funds have been transferred to a local bank here in the States. The principals are operating through cutouts— standard trade practice. Names unknown."

"Who's behind the assassination?" I ask.

"The CIA believes Russia is financing the operation, but Goran Drach is doing the operational planning and execution."

"Tell me about this Goran Drach."

"He's Mykhayl Drach's brother, or was before Mykhayl was murdered by an angry mob in Chicago. Goran Drach hasn't gotten over his brother's death and the loss of power, and he's determined to regain that power with Russian help. Putin, we think, wants to maintain control of Montenegro, using Drach as a pawn, but wants to keep his hands clean."

"His hands clean from what?"

"The murder of Nina Voychek. This was supposed to be followed by a coup back in Montenegro and the installment of a pro-Russian regime with Mykhayl Drach as Supreme Leader. Now, with Mykhayl's death, Goran plans to succeed his brother as Leader. Your job is to see that none of this happens. There have already been two attempts on Nina Voychek's life; one just a few weeks ago. Her enemies are deadly serious."

A waiter brings a plate heaped with pasta drenched with some sauce. A second waiter appears with a pepper grinder the size of a mortar that Carla impatiently waves away. A third waiter serves me my cappuccino. I was wrong about it being impossible to ruin a cappuccino.

"How do you know all this?" I ask.

"It's naughty of you to ask, Marko, but seeing as how you are personally involved, I'll share some information with you. The CIA has recruited one of Goran Drach's lieutenants in Montenegro, and he's been persuaded, in return for receiving a large amount of your taxpayer dollars, to share what he knows about Drach's plans."

"I get the picture."

"Not quite. I'm afraid it's a bit more complicated than that. In addition to Montenegro politics, a personal element has been added to the stew: Goran Drach is determined to avenge the death of his brother, Mykhayl. These are the traditions of the Black Mountain. Apparently, Goran has a very personal score to settle."

"If I take on this assignment, there's something I need in return," I say as I push away my worthless cappuccino. I decide not to mention that I've already agreed twice to take on this same assignment. She doesn't need to know all the little details.

Carla looks at me suspiciously, a fork full of pasta suspended in the air. "What do you want in return?"

"There's a man whose life is in danger," I say. "In serious danger. I want the FBI to provide full protection for him. At least for a week or so."

"Why don't you provide this fellow protection yourself?"

"Because he is, for the moment, in Chicago. And I am, for the moment, in Washington."

"Who is this man and why is he in danger and why should I care?"

"His name is Milan Jovanovich."

"So?"

"He's originally from Montenegro and is now a US citizen and a resident of Chicago. He and an émigré group were involved in organizing that angry mob you mentioned that killed Mykhayl Drach in Chicago. Since then, two of his colleagues have been murdered. The Chicago police have CCTV pictures of their killers, and the FBI has identified one of the killers, as associated with the Russian Mafia in Brooklyn. Jovanovich is in hiding somewhere in the Chicago area. The same thugs who killed his associates are almost certainly searching for him now. When they find him, he's a dead man."

"That's a problem for the Chicago police. Not the FBI."

"I'm pretty sure the Chicago authorities have been penetrated by people responsible for these crimes. Carla, I really need your help."

She eats some pasta. "And I should do this for what reason?"

"Because I'm helping you with Nina Voychek?"

She shakes her head. "You're getting paid for that."

"How about for old time's sake?"

She rolls her eyes. "You can do better than that."

"How about because the people who are after Milan Jovanovich are probably the same people Goran Drach is using to hunt Nina Voychek and are ultimately agents of the Russian intelligence service?"

"You're sure about that?"

"Absolutely." Of course, I'm not sure about anything. I'm just guessing.

"I will not tolerate foreign governments committing crimes in our country," Carla says. "I prefer to keep our crime in-house."

"Does that mean you'll give Milan Jovanovich protection?"

"Give me a name and telephone number. I'll have our Chicago field office take him in and hold him in a secure place."

"My man, Milan, is scared out of his mind and he won't cooperate with just anybody who shows up at his door. He and I have agreed he'll only answer to a coded name."

'You've been reading too many spy novels. What's the code word my people will use?"

"Ostrog."

"Never heard of him."

I scribble Milan Jovanovich's name, cell number, and the word *Ostrog* on a page from my notebook, tear it out, and hand it to Carla, who places it carefully in her purse.

"Thanks. I owe you one," I tell her.

"I know. And I won't forget to collect."

Carla looks at her watch. "I've got to run. I have an appointment on the Hill." She stands, clasping her purse. "Would you mind taking care of the bill?" She leans over and gives me a very quick, very chaste kiss on my cheek. "Do be careful, dear. Try not to die."

CHAPTER THIRTEEN

OFFICER BONIFACIO DRIVES me to the State Department, where I tell him I'll be traveling with an armed security team for the rest of the day and he's free until late this evening.

Within minutes after he leaves, two black SUVs pull up in front of the State Department diplomatic entrance. One of the back doors of the first SUV swings open, and Janet Cliff, the African American woman who is running security for the state visit, gestures impatiently for me to get in. A light rain is falling and I dash across the driveway area and jump in the car. In seconds we're in motion, heading for Virginia. In addition to the driver, another man sits in the front passenger seat.

"Your crew?" I ask.

"Of course not," Janet answers testily. "My crew's already on site. This is my deputy, Rick Talbot." A redheaded man in the driver's seat gives me a friendly wave. "And that's Marty." Janet gestures at the older man in the front passenger seat. "Marty's communications."

We ride in silence for ten minutes until Janet turns to look at me. "Are you armed?" she demands.

"No."

"Good. I don't need any cowboys at this rodeo."

We drive another few minutes in silence. "We better get something straight from the fucking get-go," Janet announces as we cross the bridge over the Potomac River. "I didn't ask for you. I don't want you. I don't think I trust you. Do I make myself clear, Officer? Be invisible and we'll get along."

"I get the—"

"Don't bother to answer. I'm not interested in your thoughts on this or any other subject."

We drive in silence through the Virginia countryside. Finally, I ask: "You ex-military?"

"What's it to you?"

"Just curious."

"Ten years in the Marines. Last four at Parris Island."

"Drill instructor?"

"Damn straight."

"I'll bet you were good."

"I was damn good."

"Was it hard?"

"You mean for me or for the fucking recruits in my care?"

"I mean for you."

"When new recruits arrived for basic training, they'd pile off the bus in their civvies, with their civvie attitudes, mostly young punks who'd spent their growing-up years getting drunk, getting high on drugs, hanging out in malls and parking lots, getting girls pregnant, barely staying out of jail. They'd be taken to their barracks: their new home. And then I'd show up. That was always a dramatic moment. They were angry and scared and ready for a fight and they weren't prepared to be ordered around by some . . ." She stops, searching for the right words.

"By some woman?" I suggest.

"By some fucking woman who looks like me. We sometimes had a difficult transition period but eventually we came to a meeting of minds."

"How long did that transition period last?"

"About fifteen minutes. Then they were mine. These were fucking punk kids—pieces of shit—but by the time the Corps was done with them, they were men."

"Why'd you leave the Corps?"

"I wanted combat. I didn't want to spend the rest of my life babysitting a bunch of crackers. Besides, the Corps' training philosophy was changing. We were told to be nice to the trainees: I don't do nice. It's only a matter of time before these boys would demand fucking milk and cookies at bedtime."

"Thank you."

"Let's get this straight. I have a job to do; I know how to do my job. Let me fucking do it. If I need your help, I'll let you know. Otherwise, stay out of my way."

We drive for a while in more tense silence.

"You know this assassination plot makes no sense, don't you?" I observe.

"I told you, I didn't ask for your opinions."

"Why would the prime minister's enemies plan an assassination here in Washington? Why not in Montenegro, where they have resources and know the territory? Why in Washington, DC, where she'll have massive protection?"

Janet doesn't answer, but I sense I've hit a nerve.

"I've heard of you, Detective Zorn," she says at last. "You have a reputation."

"Thank you."

"That was not a compliment. No more questions. Keep your nose clean and you'll be okay."

"Do you want my thoughts on the movement schedule you gave me?"

"Negative."

"According to that schedule, there's a reception at the Lincoln Memorial. That's a serious mistake."

"I know that. It's crazy shit. It seems the lady's a big deal. A reception for four hundred people—give me a break. Bars, an orchestra for God's sake, and caterers. There'll be Hollywood celebrities and people from human rights organizations from all over the world, members of the diplomatic corps and from Congress. I'd need the National Fucking Guard to provide adequate security and they won't give me the National Fucking Guard. On top of all that, somebody has hired a professional assassin. Now, if you wouldn't mind, just shut up."

Fifteen minutes later, we arrive at the environs of Dulles International Airport. Instead of going to the main terminal, we drive via circuitous back streets to one of the satellite general aviation terminals and stop in front of a set of large doors guarded by two Virginia police cruisers. Several Virginia state troopers carrying submachine guns recognize Janet Cliff, raise the doors, and wave our SUVs into a large airplane hangar. We pile out and Janet joins her waiting crew. I stay back, out of the way, so I can study the security arrangements and look for trouble.

I watch how Janet organizes her people. She's quick and efficient and it looks like her people respect her. I count fifteen people—ten men, five women. In addition to Janet and her redhead deputy, Rick Talbot, and the communications guy, Marty, that leaves twelve men and women who will provide the actual hour-to-hour protective services. I will get to know each one of them personally: which ones have been trained, which ones are new to the job, which ones are observant and have initiative, which ones just go by the numbers.

Standing in the middle of the terminal are two identical, gleaming, black stretch limousines: both the same year with the same trim. One limousine has two flags held in place by brackets on the front fenders: an American flag and a flag with the double eagle of Montenegro.

Vuk Lukshich, the Montenegro ambassador, stands next to one of the limousines, speaking to the man in the steel-rimmed glasses and a couple of others I assume are embassy staff. Janet talks briefly with Lukshich then disappears somewhere.

There are three men and two women who, judging by their outfits, are US government types.

I'm not wanted. Fine with me.

After ten minutes, there is nervous activity among those waiting in the hangar. The massive doors leading to the tarmac slide slowly up, and the US government types straighten their neckties, at least the men do. The women check lipstick and hair in pocket mirrors.

The deafening sound of jet engines shatters the night air as an aircraft approaches our terminal. The sound of the jet engines suddenly stops, and the welcome party disappears through the doors out onto the tarmac.

A few minutes later, nine men and one woman enter the terminal; somebody closes the doors to the tarmac and it's quiet again. There are four in the arriving party who are clearly security types; others, I guess, are government officials accompanying their prime minister. I concentrate on two figures.

One stands apart from the others and is carefully examining the hangar and the people in it. He's doing what I'm doing—studying the security arrangements. He's obviously protection.

I can't see the second figure well—a petite woman partially hidden by the crowd of the greeting party surrounding her.

"You are a police officer, I believe," a voice just behind me says. He's one of the security men who arrived with the delegation.

"That's right," I say.

"I am Viktor Savich. I have come with Minister Voychek. I am told you will assist in providing security."

Savich is a short, muscular man with close-cropped gray hair and pale blue eyes. His face has bruise marks.

"I'll do what I can," I say. "Janet Cliff is responsible for overall security."

"She seems competent."

"She is. You are in good hands. You have nothing to fear."

"Do you really think so?"

"Are you the prime minister's bodyguard?" I ask.

"I am her driver."

"You're more than that, I think."

"I try to look after her. But here I am not allowed to carry a weapon. None of my team are armed and that makes me nervous."

"If it's any comfort, I carry no weapon either."

"That makes me even more nervous."

There is activity within the greeting party. A State Department type gets into one of the limousines. The ambassador heads to the limousine flying the two flags. The security types fan out, ready for departure.

The woman I've been trying to observe separates herself from the others, crosses the terminal floor, and heads toward me. Janet hurries after her.

The woman stops directly in front of me and holds out her hand. "Nina Voychek." She looks up and studies me steadily, no shifting in her gaze as she carefully evaluates me. "I think I've met everyone here this evening," she says. "Except you. I like to know who the people around me are."

She speaks with a slight accent but in perfect English. She is shorter than I'd expected from her photographs I saw on my cell phone—she's maybe five feet six—and slender. She wears a white silk turtleneck sweater, a long, black lambskin coat and flats. Her hair is strawberry-blond and she has lovely, intelligent green eyes. Her warm, infectious smile reminds me of the pictures of the young student I saw on my cell phone.

What Cyprian Voss said is true: She's extraordinarily beautiful.

"It's an honor to meet you," I say. "Welcome to the United States."

Janet approaches. "Madame Prime Minister, it's time we left for the residence." Janet gestures toward the waiting convoy, obviously anxious to get away.

"Of course," the prime minister says. She turns back to me. "What is your name?"

"Marko Zorn. I'm with the DC police."

"Zorn," she repeats as if to secure my name in her memory. "I will want to speak to you again soon."

CHAPTER FOURTEEN

"COME WITH ME," Savich says and we walk quickly to the limousine stationed immediately behind the ambassador's and we climb into the back. A member of Janet's team takes the wheel, and within seconds we're in motion, moving smoothly and quietly out of the terminal, a Virginia State police cruiser is in front, another is picking up the rear. It's raining hard and the wipers struggle to clear the windshield.

"Have you served on a security detail?" Savich asks me.

In the dark his face is almost invisible, appearing only briefly in the light of the headlights from oncoming cars.

"I've never been a bodyguard before," I answer.

"Why were you given this assignment?"

"Your government asked for me."

"Don't you think that strange?"

"I think that damn strange."

"Have you reviewed the security plans for the prime minister's visit?"

"Just the movement schedule. I haven't seen the actual plans. Janet Cliff knows what she's doing."

"I'm sure she does, but I would feel better if you looked over the plans and gave me your personal assessment."

We drive in silence. "Have you been in a fight?" I ask. Even in the darkness of the car I can see his nose is swollen. But not the large nose typical of many Slavs.

He smiles and touches the bruises on his face. "You are a cop. You know how things are. I had to break up a bar fight two nights ago. It could have been worse. At least they didn't break my nose. If you think I look bad, you should see the other guys."

"I don't think you're a regular cop. Like me."

"Are you really a regular cop?" he asks.

I ignore his question. "Are you the prime minister's bodyguard?"

He shakes his head. "Until a few days ago I was a 'normal cop'—just like you. But there have been certain developments that required a change of plans."

"You mean the plot to assassinate Madame Voychek?"

He nods, seemingly surprised. "You know about that? Our ambassador here decided the prime minister needed additional protection."

"Have you known Nina Voychek long?"

"We met for the first time on the flight coming here. I'm a last-minute addition to the delegation."

"Why you?"

"I was for many years a non-com in our army, and I know how to use weapons. And maybe because I speak some passable English."

"You're a cop but today you're carrying luggage and opening car doors."

"Today I'm trying to save my country."

Forty minutes later, our convoy pulls up to the Montenegrin embassy in downtown Washington. The two stretch limousines are guided into a two-car garage, its entrance flooded with brilliant lights; the remaining convoy cars park on the street.

"Come to our suite," Savich tells me. "The prime minister wants to talk to you."

Janet, surrounded closely by her security team, hustles the prime
minister quickly through a door at the back of the garage and into
the embassy residence.

I follow the entourage to the third floor and into a sitting room
crowded with delegation officials, security types, and embassy staff.
The prime minister has disappeared into her private quarters.

I mix among the embassy staff, Janet's security team, and the security group who came with the prime minister. I learn names and
attach names to faces and faces to functions. Marty, the communications man, has disappeared. I guess his job is done for the night. I
learn that Janet's security team is broken up into three teams of four,
each who will work eight-hour shifts while Nina Voychek is in the
country. Janet and her deputy, Rick Talbot, will supervise and coordinate with police, the White House, and the State Department in
twelve-hour shifts. They have all worked together before and appear
to be a smoothly functioning team.

There are four security men from Montenegro. I can't really assess
them. Most speak no English. I look for Viktor Savich but am told
he's with the ambassador and the prime minister. I try to get a fix on
the embassy personnel, but they're cautious and circumspect.

Viktor Savich takes a seat in the chair next to me. "What have you
concluded about security?"

"How sure are you of your own people?" I ask.

Savich studies my face intently. "They all work for the Ministry
of the Interior."

"I'll bet none of them is paid much."

"Very little, of course. Ours is a poor country."

"Be careful then."

"You mean our people can be bought?"

"I mean anybody can be bought. Trust no one."

"Anything else?"

"Where is the prime minister's car kept?"

"In the garage attached to the residence. Both official limousines will be parked there at all times. The doors to the street are kept locked. No one can get in."

"What about the keys to the cars?"

"They are kept in a lockbox secured by a cyber lock. It's located just inside the door to the garage."

"Who has the access code to that lockbox?"

"The State Department security team."

"Will you have access?"

"Of course."

"I'll need to have the access code myself."

"You think that's really necessary?"

"It's really necessary."

Savich hesitates, then takes a notebook from his pocket, scribbles some numbers on a page, and passes the notebook to me. "I ask that you commit this to memory. We don't want this piece of paper to fall into the wrong hands."

Savich has written the numbers: 821914. I study the note long enough to memorize the code. I've had a lot of practice memorizing this kind of thing, and it's not as hard as it looks. Unless the code has been generated by a computer, these codes are often based on some real world events or object: a birthday, an address, something easy to remember. You just have to figure out the mnemonic clue the creator used.

"The day Archduke Franz Ferdinand and his wife, Sofia, were assassinated in Sarajevo," I say.

"Very good, Detective, you know your Balkan history well."

"Nineteen fourteen was the giveaway."

Savich tucks the notebook back into an inside jacket pocket. "The day that launched World War I and led to the collapse of the great empires of Europe. The end of our old Europe."

Why is it, I wonder, that people in that part of the world always seem to celebrate dates marking tragic events and national catastrophes? Maybe it's the slivovitz.

"Have you inspected the cars the prime minister will be using?" I ask.

"You are concerned about a bomb?"

"I'm concerned about a bomb, about someone tampering with the brakes, about gas tank leaks. I recommend that you post a security guard with the prime minister's car twenty-four hours a day, and I'd have the car inspected thoroughly before she uses it."

"I will attend to that myself."

"Next item. According to the movement schedule, there's to be a large reception for the prime minister at the Lincoln Memorial: Cancel it."

"I would love to," Savich replies. "It's a security nightmare. The embassy arranged the reception weeks ago. Invitations to very important people have been sent, and the ambassador says it's too late to cancel."

The door to the inner suite opens and the prime minister enters in casual clothes, a towel wrapped around her head. She crosses to us, pulls up an ottoman, and sits facing us. She wears a soft silk scarf around her neck—pale yellow with a delicate pattern of spring leaves.

"Excuse my appearance," the prime minister says to me. "But I had to take a shower and wash my hair. I feel almost human now." She has a bright, cheerful smile. She is still young and I can easily imagine her as a student going out for a beer after classes.

"It's time I left," I say. "I don't want to prevent you from relaxing."

"Please stay," she says.

"Where did you learn English so well, Madame Prime Minister?"

"I attended college at Columbia but bailed before I got my degree. And please don't call me Madame Prime Minister, it's pompous and stuffy. Please call me Nina."

"Does Janet Cliff call you Nina?"

"I asked her to call me Nina, but she refuses. Everyone on my staff calls me Nina."

"Nina it is. Then you must call me Marko. Why did you leave college?" I ask.

"You've heard about the ethnic cleansing in my country? The Oak Forest Massacre, the atrocities perpetrated against my people by Mykhayl Drach and his brother, Goran?"

"I've heard something about that. I believe you may have lost someone close to you," I say, remembering what I'd seen about Sasha in her bio.

Something about her manner suddenly changes. She no longer looks like a carefree college kid. Her smile vanishes. Her face becomes hard. She reminds me a little of the dangerous men I met in Chicago.

"How could I stay away and do nothing?" she says. "I returned and became involved in the pro-democracy movement—taking part in demonstrations, handing out protest leaflets, printing underground newspapers. One thing led to another."

"Including the attacks on your life."

"The last one was just six weeks ago when a bomb was placed in my car. It failed to explode, but I'm told it was a powerful bomb and had it gone off it would have destroyed my car and everyone in it." She clenches her jaw, all hints of a smile gone. She's no longer the young and innocent college student. I see hatred flash in her eyes. She pauses, takes a deep breath, and regains her composure. "I tell you this so you understand: my enemies are dangerous. If you are anywhere near me, you are in danger. I can face these threats. I am prepared to pay that price for the survival of my country. The same is true for my staff who have come with me." She nods toward Viktor Savich. "The future of my country is at stake. But it's not your country. It's not worth you dying for. I'd understand if you withdrew from your duties."

"Thank you, but I'm committed to seeing that you're protected."

"Even at the risk of your own life?"

"Whatever it takes."

"This time, you'll face more dangerous opponents than you have in the past." Again, I see that flash of anger and hatred in her eyes. She's a dangerous woman when she has to be. I wouldn't want to get in her way.

She shakes her head as if to clear her mind. "Do you carry a weapon, Detective?"

"Only if necessary."

"What happens if you face a deadly, ruthless opponent without a weapon?"

"I can usually manage."

My cell phone rings, and the caller ID reads: "Baltimore Homicide."

"Excuse me, Nina, but I must take this."

"Of course. Go right ahead."

I move away from Nina and Savich to take the call.

"Detective Marko Zorn?" the voice on the line says. "This is Lieutenant Marvin Price, Maryland Criminal Investigations Command. There's been a murder you may be involved with. A woman's body has been found in a culvert just off Route 95 North. We're pretty certain it's a homicide."

"Can you tell when the homicide took place?"

"We can't be sure yet, but our best guess is between nine and midnight."

"What's the victim's name?"

"We don't know; she has no identification. But she had your business card in her pocket."

This murder victim might be anybody, but my instinct tells me it's the frightened young woman I saw in the embassy just yesterday afternoon. "Where are you?" I ask.

Lieutenant Price gives me a location on Interstate 95 North just beyond the Beltway.

I return to Nina. "I seem to have an emergency, Nina. Something I must attend to. I'd like your permission to leave."

"Of course," she says. "I'm quite safe here inside the embassy. I hope nothing is wrong."

"I'm afraid something is very wrong."

* * *

Lieutenant Bonifacio drives me to the crime scene. When we arrive, I tell him to wait for me in the car. There's no point in him getting wet. The highway is clogged with police cars and emergency vehicles, their bright lights flashing in the heavy rain. Ambulances are parked diagonally across the highway blocking two lanes of traffic, and the Maryland State Police have set up flares and closed down part of Interstate 95 North. Glaring floodlights illuminate the east side of the road while a dozen Maryland highway patrol officers swathed in dripping rain gear try to control the congestion of trucks, busses, and cars.

"I'm looking for Officer Price," I call out through the dark rain to a uniformed officer. He points to a man in civilian clothes standing at the edge of a steep ravine a dozen feet from the highway. The grass and vegetation are soaking wet and I slip and slide down the embankment.

"I'm Marko Zorn. DC Homicide," I say. I show the man my police badge.

"Marvin Price," the man says, wiping rainwater from his face. "Sorry to bring you out in crap weather like this, but we need your help."

I pull my raincoat tight around me and adjust the collar, but I can feel cold water trickling down the back of my neck. Price leads me through a wet thicket of bushes and vines to the edge of a culvert where the body of a young woman lies at the bottom.

Price is young and badly shaken. He'll not forget what he's seen here tonight.

"Do you recognize the victim?" he asks.

"I saw this woman for a few minutes earlier yesterday," I say.

"What did she tell you?" Price asks.

"She said she needed to talk to me, and I gave her my number. She was going to call me but she never did."

Price gives me a heavy plastic envelope. Inside is a single business card. Even through the semi-opaque, rain-soaked plastic, there's no doubt it's the card I gave the girl at the embassy.

Three men and two women are lifting the body onto drier ground. Someone focuses a bright light onto the girl's face and I almost gag. The face is swollen, covered with blood. Even in the dark and rain I can see the deep cut left by a rope or wire around the girl's throat. The same wound I'd seen around the throat of the security guard at the theater.

CHAPTER FIFTEEN

THE PICTURE OF the girl appears on my cell phone at six thirty in the morning. Somebody at the Maryland Criminal Investigations Command has tried to clean her up, but there isn't much anybody can do to repair what was done to her. Her face has been battered, her tongue extended through her broken teeth, a black band cuts into her throat.

"God, that's awful," Lucy says as she studies the photo on my phone.

I tell Lucy about the girl I spoke with in the embassy, about the phone call from the Maryland police, and my visit to the crime scene late last night. I don't tell her about the attempt on my own life. It's too soon for that. And I don't mention the paper with the mysterious numbers the girl gave me. Some things Lucy doesn't need to know yet. Some things are too dangerous to know.

"She was beaten before she was killed, wasn't she?" Lucy says, holding the phone at arm's length as if the picture were poisonous. "I'd guess there was more than one person involved. Maybe two to hold the girl—a third to do the killing. Are they going to find the people who did this?" Lucy asks. "Are the killers going to pay for what they did to her?"

"I'll find them. And they'll pay." I wish I were as confident as I sound.

"I don't mean to badger, but I have to see the note you said Victoria West sent you."

I take the letter from my desk drawer and slide it across the desk to Lucy. The page is covered by a neat script written in purple ink.

Dearest Marko,

I hope this voice from the past does not cause you pain. I would understand if you threw this note away without reading it. I did not intend to contact you while I was in Washington but something has come up I think you should know about. It may not be important but it bothers me.

I'm in Washington for out-of-town tryouts for Hedda Gabler. *A week ago, while in the middle of rehearsals, a man contacted me. He said his name was Jonathan Drew and he claimed he was a freelancer working on a profile of me for* The New York Times. *He insisted he interview me at the theater and during rehearsals. To get atmosphere, he said. You remember, I'm a sucker for free publicity. So I agreed. He followed me around the set during the interview and asked questions about the production. He wanted to see the drawing room I use for my entrances and exits; he took photographs of me and the set and of some members of the cast and crew. The strange thing was he asked very few questions about me or my preparation for the Hedda role the way reporters usually do. He did ask questions about you. About our relationship. I told him that was none of his business, but he kept pressing me for insight into our relationship, about why we broke up, and whether we were planning to see each other while in Washington. He even asked whether I knew where you lived and how he could reach you. I became suspicious and I closed down the interview. I called Harry Moll at* The Times—*he handles most theater assignments—and he said* The Times *had never hired a freelancer to do a story on me and if they wanted pictures, they would have sent their own photographer.*

The next day one of the guys hanging lights told me he knew the man who'd interviewed me. They both live in Williamsburg in Brooklyn and he told me my visitor's name was not Jonathan Drew. His real name is Oleg Kamrof. He warned me that Kamrof was dangerous and had a criminal record and he advised me to avoid the man. I've not heard from him since.

Now that I write this all out it seems trivial but at the time I was freaked out and I thought you should know. Probably it's nothing.

With All My Love,

P.S. I almost tore up this note. It seemed such an abrupt way to reconnect with you after all these years. I certainly never intended it to be like this. I almost asked you to forgive me a bit, but you know I never ask for forgiveness. There, I have done just that, haven't I? Am I getting soft and sentimental? Maybe we could get together for coffee. I would like that. I have some wonderful news I'd like to share.

The letter ends with an illegible scrawl: Vickie's signature. Lucy reads it through twice. "Did you reply?"

"No."

"Not even a phone call? A text message?"

"Nothing."

Lucy studies me and tries to figure out whether I'm lying. I can see she finds it hard to believe I made no effort to contact Vickie. But then she knows she's never been able to understand me.

"I'll see that you get this back," Lucy says.

"I'd appreciate that."

"I'll speak with the Maryland police," she says, "and offer what help we can in their investigation."

After Lucy leaves, I consider telling the Maryland police about the message the young woman gave me: I assume it may be related to her murder and is therefore evidence and, by not informing the Maryland police, I'm withholding evidence, which is probably a crime. But I'm pretty sure I have more serious things to worry about than an infraction of the rules. Besides, I'm not big on rules.

CHAPTER SIXTEEN

I CLIMB INTO a police cruiser and Lieutenant Bonifacio drives the cruiser smoothly out of the police department garage and onto the street.

"Take the first right," I say. "Then speed up so we can lose anyone who might try to follow us. Then take the next left."

"You think we're being followed?"

"I don't want to find out the hard way."

The lieutenant almost laughs.

"What do I call you, Lieutenant?"

"My name is Santiago Bonifacio. My friends call me Sandy. Lieutenant Bonifacio is fine."

The lieutenant seems a bit stiff and formal, and I suppose he wants to keep our relationship strictly professional. I can live with that.

We arrive at the embassy in good time. I see no sign of a tail.

"For the remainder of the day I'll be embedded with an armed escort of US government agents," I say. "I'll be quite safe and you can return to headquarters. I'll call you when I need you."

The lieutenant seems like a decent guy trying to do a thankless job. I hate to lie to him, but there's a place I have to go to and people I must see I don't want recorded. For that trip, I'll use a rental car.

"I guess you must have got the short straw for this assignment," I say, trying to be friendly.

"No, sir. I volunteered."

"Why on earth would you do that?"

"I wanted to meet you. You're something of a legend in the Metropolitan Police Department. I wanted to see how you do it. Is it true you rarely carry a gun?"

"I don't like guns." I get out of the car.

When I enter the embassy, I tell the receptionist, the overweight young man with a pimply face, that I must speak with the ambassador. The young man tells me His Excellency is not available. I don't believe that for a minute but don't argue the point. I'm not here for slivovitz and polite conversation. I'm here for information. Anyone will do.

"Who was the man who met me here yesterday afternoon? A short man with steel-rimmed glasses. Nervous. Blinks a lot."

The receptionist smiles broadly. "Ah, yes, sir. That would be Mr. Radich. I'll see if he is available."

"Make him available. At once."

The receptionist anxiously punches buttons on a telephone console and speaks in a language I don't understand. "He will be here directly," the receptionist tells me when he hangs up.

Within two minutes the man with the steel-rimmed glasses bustles up to the reception counter. "Detective? You wish to speak to me?"

"Can we talk somewhere in private?"

He looks confused and a little annoyed. "Follow me." He leads me into the ground-floor reception area.

"First," I ask, "who are you?"

He stiffens slightly and looks miffed. His eyes blink rapidly. "I am Boris Radich."

"You work here?"

"Of course, I work here."

"What do you do in this outfit?"

"I am the Deputy Chief of Mission."

I take my cell phone from my pocket and show Radich the photograph of the dead girl. "Who is this woman?" I make no effort to be gentle with this guy. I'm running out of time and patience and I don't think he deserves gentle.

Radich's face goes white and his eyes blink rapidly as he stares at the screen. "What is this?" he chokes.

"You tell me."

"That's . . . that's Yulia."

"Who is Yulia?"

"Yulia Orlyk. She is an employee of the embassy. What happened to her? Where did you get this picture? We've been looking for her for hours."

"Miss Orlyk was found dead last night."

Radich's knees seem to give way and he collapses onto the edge of a nearby chair. A vein at his temple is throbbing. I don't think it's shock; I think it's fear. There's something about his eyes.

"That's not possible," Radich says, breathing rapidly. "What happened to her?"

"Miss Orlyk was murdered."

"How?" Radich's voice is strained, his face drained of blood as he studies the photo again. "Was she strangled?"

Now, how would he know that? "I never said she was strangled. Why did you think she was strangled?"

He hunches over. "I don't know. I just assumed."

I hand Radich my notebook. "Write down Miss Orlyk's full name and her address and her telephone number."

His hands shaking, Radich scribbles onto the notebook page and passes it back to me, almost dropping the notebook on the floor.

"The investigating office will need someone from the embassy to identify the body."

"Of course." He almost chokes.

"What did Miss Orlyk do here in the embassy?" I ask.

"I can't talk to you about our internal arrangements. They are confidential matters." His eyes blink.

"You can tell me, Mr. Radich, and you will, or I'll have to arrest you and take you to the police station, where you will be interviewed. All of which will be an enormous inconvenience for both of us,"

"That's illegal," Radich protests.

"I'm sure it is, and the police will eventually be obliged to make profound and heartfelt apologies, but by that time, your day would be ruined. My boss might even insist that I be the one who must come here and make a personal apology. That would be embarrassing to me. Save us both heaps of trouble, Radich, and tell me what exactly Miss Orlyk did in the embassy."

"Oh, my God, I must inform Ambassador Lukshich at once." Radich jumps to his feet. He's trembling. "This is just awful. Awful."

"Sit down, Radich. What did Yulia Orlyk do here?"

He sits uneasily. "She was a clerk."

"I'm running out of patience. What kind of clerk?"

"A communications clerk. She was the embassy cipher clerk."

"Do you mean she was the embassy's code clerk? Is that what you're saying?"

"That's right." He's having a hard time breathing.

It comes back to me—the scrap of paper Yulia Orlyk pressed urgently into my hand—the paper with what seemed a meaningless series of numbers. I realize now what I was looking at was a five-digit code. Almost certainly the embassy's diplomatic code.

When I first studied it, I could make no sense of it. But I know someone who can read it. With a little encouragement.

"What exactly did she do here as a code clerk?" I demand.

Radich looks around the room anxiously as if for help, but there's no one there to help. No one but me. "We give her the text of messages we need to send to our home office in Podgorica..."

"Podgorica is the capital of Montenegro?" I ask.

"That's right. When we have confidential and secret messages, she puts the text through our coding system and cables the encrypted text to our home office."

"And if the embassy receives a message in code from your home office in Podgorica, what happens then?"

"Yulia Orlyk would put the coded message through our system and print it out and deliver it by hand to the ambassador. Really, I must inform His Excellency."

"What time did she leave the embassy yesterday?" I stand above Radich so he can't slip away from my clutches.

"She left at eleven eighteen precisely."

"Kind of late."

"There has been a lot of cable traffic these days, what with the visit of the prime minister, you understand. Last night at around ten forty-five, we received an administrative communication from Podgorica informing us there would be no further cable traffic that night. We closed our communications link and I told Yulia to go home."

"What time would that have been?"

"About ten fifty or so."

"And she went home after she logged out?"

"According to the reception desk log she called for a taxi around eleven. That's standard procedure at that late hour for our female employees."

"When did you learn she was missing?"

"The woman Yulia lives with, Mrs. Kostenko, called the embassy last night, around midnight. She said Yulia never got home. May I go now?"

"Not just yet."

Radich is terribly unhappy.

"You have two CCTV cameras installed above your front entrance," I say.

Radich nods cautiously.

"I want the tapes from those cameras from last night."

"That's not possible. They are the property of the embassy."

"You're beginning to seriously annoy me, Radich. Here I thought we were getting along so well. You don't want to annoy me, do you?"

"You are on the soil of the Republic of Montenegro. The cameras are the property of the embassy," Radich announces. "That means they and their contents are the property of the Republic of Montenegro and they are therefore beyond the jurisdiction of the Government of United States and its agents." He sounds like he's reciting something he vaguely remembers from some long-ago course in international law.

"The cameras are outside the embassy building and therefore not on the soil of the Republic of Montenegro," I say, as officiously as I can. As if I knew what I was talking about.

"But they are physically attached to the embassy structure. According to international law, they are therefore on the territory of Montenegro."

"According to the international law relating to diplomatic immunity, an object outside of an embassy even though attached to the embassy is not subject to diplomatic immunity protection, unless it's an integral part of the embassy structure. The courts have clearly ruled that CCTV cameras, even if attached to a diplomatic structure, are not integral. Therefore I, as a representative of the US Government, have the right to seize the films."

He's pretty sure I'm bullshitting but he can't be certain and he's desperate to get away and tell his ambassador about the murder of Yulia Orlyk. "Very well, you may have them. May I go now?"

"You can go when I have the CCTV tapes."

"I'll send them to your office."

"Bring them to me now—then you can inform your ambassador."

Radich slumps in defeat and calls the receptionist. "Alexi, bring the CCTV tapes from last night."

A couple of minutes later the pimply receptionist bustles in, clutching two film canisters. I snatch them from him before Radich can touch them. "Send Yulia's roommate—Mrs. Kostenko—to me. I will speak with her here."

Radich hurries anxiously off. I call Lieutenant Price of the Maryland State Police. "I have the name of the victim. Her name is Yulia Orlyk. She worked for the embassy of Montenegro and was last seen last night when she left the embassy a little after eleven. You can get biographic info on her from the State Department or Immigration Service. They'll have her visa application on file."

A middle-aged woman dressed in black appears in the reception area. "Mrs. Kostenko?" I ask as I stand to greet her. I decide, given the lady's age, she deserves special courtesy.

She nods suspiciously. "That's right."

"My name is Marko Zorn. I'm a policeman. Please have a seat, Mrs. Kostenko."

We both sit, facing one another. She is tense and suspicious.

"What happened to Yulia?" the woman demands. "Has something happened to the girl?"

"I'm sorry to have to tell you, Miss Orlyk is dead."

"No. How could that happen?"

"It looks as though she was murdered." I don't know how to say this in a nice way. There is no way to make murder sound nice.

The woman bends over, her hands over her eyes, and sobs uncontrollably. I never know what to do with sobbing women. They always make me feel uncomfortable and inadequate. I briefly consider

putting my arm around her shoulder, but this is a woman who's probably spent her life in a police state and will see any policemen as the
enemy and not to be trusted. I'm pretty sure a hug from me would
not be welcome, so I sit silently and try to look sympathetic until she
regains control of herself.

Finally, she takes a deep, ragged breath, snatches a handkerchief
from a pocket and dabs at her eyes.

"When did you last see Yulia?" I ask.

"Sometime yesterday afternoon. We work on different floors. She's
in the secure area. She called me around eleven last night and said
she was leaving the embassy and was waiting for her taxi. When Yulia
didn't arrive by midnight, I worry. I call her cell phone. No answer. I
call the embassy. My God, what happened? Do you think it was your
Washington hooligans who did this?"

"No, Mrs. Kostenko, I don't. I don't know what happened to Miss
Orlyk, but it wasn't hooligans. At least not *our* hooligans. I'm sure
of that."

CHAPTER SEVENTEEN

JANET CLIFF ENTERS the waiting room and announces: "Show time, everybody."

Nina emerges from her private suite, accompanied by her ambassador and members of her staff. Nina is dressed in a tailored, teal-colored pantsuit and wears a dark green scarf around her neck. She manages to look both formal and professional and, at the same time, quite sexy. Or maybe that's me.

Nina gestures for the others to stay at a distance as she steps close to me, close enough I can smell her perfume. It's some light floral scent.

"The ambassador has just informed me of the death of the young clerk from our embassy," Nina says. "What can you tell me about this terrible event?"

"Her body was found last night on the side of a highway outside the city of Washington."

"How did she die?"

"It appears she was murdered. I don't have any details yet."

"I must telephone the girl's parents as soon as I return from my meeting with the Secretary of State. Please keep Ambassador Lukshich informed."

She turns and leaves with her ambassador hovering at her side, whispering into her ear. The rest of us follow them to the garage. Nina and the ambassador, along with Janet, get into the car with the flags. Savich and I get in the follow car, and in seconds, we're out of the garage and into the street on the short trip to the State Department.

"Tell me about the girl," Viktor Savich asks.

"One of your embassy clerks, a young woman named Yulia Orlyk, was murdered last night."

"Who killed her?"

"I have no idea. The Maryland police are investigating her murder. I'll keep you informed."

"I must know all the details."

"Did you know the woman?"

"I never met Miss Orlyk."

"I must tell you," I tell Savich, "I met with Yulia Orlyk for maybe a minute yesterday afternoon. We were in the ambassador's outer office."

He turns in his seat to face me. "What did she say?"

"Nothing really. She seemed frightened but wouldn't tell me why."

"That's all?"

"She warned me of danger and promised to call me that night. I never heard from her."

Our caravan arrives at the State Department diplomatic entrance, where Nina is greeted by a group of men and women, all beaming with goodwill. Media people and photographers swarm around her, hoping for a quote and a good picture. After a few minutes, Nina is escorted through security and into the Secretary's personal elevator along with her ambassador. The rest of us follow in less distinguished elevators.

I catch sight of the Secretary of State, Leland Cross, at a distance as he greets Nina and escorts her and her entourage into what seems to be a conference room. The rest of us peons are asked to make ourselves comfortable while the talks take place.

We're in the State Department reception area furnished with what look like elegant—and expensive—antiques, which Benjamin Franklin might have admired. I find a chair that doesn't look too fragile and has a cushion and I wait until I'm needed.

An hour and a half later the doors to the conference room are opened and the diplomats emerge looking tired but happy. And mostly hungry. Secretary Cross and Nina emerge, together smiling. By which I conclude the United States and Montenegro are not at war.

The elite members of the delegation and senior State Department types are escorted into a posh dining room. The rest of us are left to search for vending machines or use the State Department cafeteria on the ground floor.

I know Nina is safe here but I'm uncomfortable being far away from her while she's not in her embassy.

After I've had a leisurely lunch consisting of coffee in a paper cup and Mars Bars, Nina and the Secretary of State emerge from the dining room looking happy and well fed. The press is unleashed and more photos are taken of Nina and the Secretary shaking hands and smiling broadly.

Janet collects us and we return to our cars. Nina gestures for me to join her and Janet in her limousine. The ambassador and Savich have gone off somewhere on their own.

"How did it go?" I ask, to be polite.

Nina slumps in the back seat and briefly shuts her eyes. Finally, rousing herself: "It went well. We both got what we wanted. There were some compromises on both sides. I hate compromise." She looks at me hard. "Tell me about the girl who was murdered last night."

"I wish I could tell you more. The Maryland police are investigating. The DC police are helping where we can."

"Who could do such a thing?" Nina asks. "Why would someone want to hurt that poor girl?"

I have no answer.

When the cars pull into the embassy garage, I say: "I have some police business. I believe your schedule calls for you to remain in the embassy the rest of the afternoon. With your permission I will go to police headquarters to deal with another matter."

"Of course. I'll be safe in the embassy. Janet and Viktor will look after me."

*   *   *

When I return to police headquarters, Cynthia Fletcher, Victoria West's theatrical agent, is waiting for me. Arms folded across her breast, she regards me warily. "Somebody murdered Vickie West," she announces to me, without preamble.

Cynthia Fletcher is easy to identify by the white streak running through her dark hair: as if she were hit by lightning. Very dramatic, I think. Very New York. Today in bright light she looks about forty. She's tall and slender and she wears a long, gray skirt that reaches her ankles. Her eyes are gray and suspicious.

"Am I allowed to smoke here?" she asks, holding a crumpled pack of cigarettes in one hand, a light in the other.

"I'm afraid not. This is a no smoking area."

"Damn! How do you get any work done?"

"If this is about the death of Victoria West, you should speak with my partner, Lucy Tanaka. She's in charge of the investigation now."

"I'm speaking to you on a personal basis: this is a private matter." She stuffs her cigarette package and lighter angrily into her large purse. "You need to know that Vickie did not commit suicide."

There's no point in telling Fletcher I already know that Victoria West was murdered. I need to know why this woman is so certain.

"How are you so sure?"

"Because I've known Vickie for years. She could not have killed herself. That means she was murdered. I thought you should know that."

We sit in the police department's waiting room, an area we sometimes use to meet with visitors who aren't serial killers. Its inoffensive decorations are meant to convey the message that the police department is more than prison cells and torture chambers. The nice upholstery and pretty pictures of our national parks probably fool no one.

"Was Victoria West right-handed or left-handed?" I ask.

Cynthia Fletcher looks at me with some annoyance as if I made a bad joke, then closes her eyes as people do when I ask that question, trying to reconstruct a remembered image. "Right-handed, I'm pretty sure," she says at last.

"Were you close to Vickie?" I ask.

"That's not any of your business."

"Were you close, Miss Fletcher?" I repeat. "And it is my business."

"I came here to talk with you. On my own volition. I didn't expect to be treated like a common criminal." She takes a deep breath. "We were close."

"Why were you at the theater the night Vickie died?" I ask. "You're not a member of the cast or crew."

"I was there to see to Vickie's flowers."

"Tell me about the flowers."

"On opening nights, I always bring a bouquet of two dozen, long-stemmed red roses. She loved roses."

I remember the bouquet of roses I planned to give her the last time I saw her. The bouquet I crushed under my foot.

"Vickie had to have roses on opening nights. Always two dozen. It was a kind of ritual for her."

"Where did you put the flowers during her performance?"

"I left them in Vickie's dressing room until it was time to pick them up and get them for her final bow."

"Did Vickie have a laptop computer?"

"Of course."

"We searched her dressing room. We found no laptop there."

"Maybe she left it in her hotel room."

"We've searched her hotel room. There was no laptop there, either. What do you think became of it?"

"I have no idea."

"Whose idea was this production of *Hedda Gabler*?"

"It was Vickie's idea; she very much wanted to do *Hedda Gabler*. She wanted to perform it once more before she was too old for the part. She even arranged to get financing for the show. She brought in Marty Close, the New York producer. Of course, Marty had conditions."

"Such as?"

"He insisted Arthur Cantwell be cast. Arthur performed with Vickie in the New York production of *Hedda Gabler* years ago. She and Arthur had a notorious love affair during the production. I think Marty thought it would be good publicity to bring the two lovers together again. He thought it would sell tickets."

"What do you think?"

"I think Marty Close's a creep. He also insisted that Garland Taylor direct the show. That created serious problems. Vickie was dead set against Taylor and at first it was a deal breaker. But Marty insisted Garland direct, and, in the end, Vickie had to agree: otherwise, no *Hedda*."

"Why was Vickie so opposed to Garland Taylor being the director?"

"They'd worked together and they didn't like each other. Besides, Garland has a reputation."

"For what?"

"For harassing actresses, particularly young, inexperienced actresses. Vickie didn't tolerate that kind of behavior."

"On opening night Miss West forgot her last line."

"She forgot one damn line."

"It was an important line. Isn't that strange?"

"Everything in the theater is strange."

"You left the flowers in Vickie's dressing room. That means you had access to that room."

"What of it?"

"Tell me about the original *Hedda Gabler* New York production."

"Vickie very much wanted to play Hedda. I was her agent; we were both just starting out in our careers. I didn't like the idea. I don't much care for Ibsen myself, but Vickie was insistent. She could be very strong-minded. As you know."

"Where does Arthur Cantwell come in?"

"He was cast in the original New York production. I have to admit he and Vickie made a fabulous pair on stage. I guess that's why they fell madly in love—or what passes for love in our make-believe world. The affair was open and scandalous, red meat for the New York tabloids. When the show closed, Vickie and Arthur flew off to a tropical isle and got married on some goddamn beach."

"I take it the marriage did not turn out well."

"The world is not a beach, Detective. Understand, Arthur is a world-class shit. After the divorce, they both remarried. Arthur married some supermodel. Vickie married her hairdresser, for God's sake."

I must have seen some of this in *Variety*, which I used to read in my New York days. It was painful enough back then. It still hurts when I hear about Vickie going off the tracks like that.

"I hate to say it, but *Hedda* was a sensation," Fletcher says. "It launched Vickie's career."

"Were you aware that Vickie and Arthur Cantwell were planning to marry when this show closed?" I ask.

Cynthia Fletcher's face pales. "Who told you that?"

"Cantwell told me."

She nods. "Vickie told me on opening night."

"Just before she was murdered."

Fletcher stares at me blankly.

"Were you in love with Victoria West?" I ask.

Cynthia Fletcher's face flushes with anger. "You should be ashamed to ask me that question."

"As a policeman I have no shame left."

"You're in a dishonorable profession then."

"I won't argue that."

"I wanted to be sure you understood. Vickie could not have committed suicide. You should know that—you of all people."

"Why do you think I should know that?"

"Because you were once in love with Vickie." There's a long, uncomfortable silence. "I knew she was seeing someone before she was cast in *Hedda Gabler* in New York. She never told me his name, but she talked about him. I'm pretty sure that man was you."

It doesn't matter now.

"Tell me what happened between you and Vickie the night she was murdered," I ask. "When she told you she was getting married again."

"I met with Vickie in her dressing room just before curtain, and she said there was something I needed to know. Arthur Cantwell was going to announce that he and Vickie were going to marry." Her voice trembles. She can no longer hide her fury. Or is it grief? "Am I now your prime suspect?"

"What makes you think you should be?"

"I'm the jilted lover. Isn't that one of the motives for murder in your sordid little world, Detective?"

"Some people think that makes *me* the prime suspect," I say. "Did you have an argument with Vickie?"

"We had a discussion."

"Did you also talk about someone named Valerie?" The name that Props heard Vickie yell at Fletcher the night of the murder.

Cynthia Fletcher's face freezes. "Valerie is none of your damned business." She rises to her feet and looks down at me, trembling. "I don't want to talk about Valerie. This discussion is over."

CHAPTER EIGHTEEN

"Are you here to arrest my boy, Detective Zorn?" The woman speaks to me through a screen door I know is secured by a single latch. She wears a faded housedress, a kitchen towel flung over her left shoulder. Her forehead and her arms are dusted with white flour. Helen Stephens is in her early forties, a bit worn, a bit frazzled, but still pretty.

"Not today, Helen. Maybe another time."

"In that case, come on in." She unlatches the hook, and I follow her into a warm and sunny kitchen. I smell something baking in the oven.

"Well, if you're not after Tommy, may I offer you a cup of coffee?"

She pours coffee into a large mug that informs me she's a supporter of Public Radio. Beneath us, the kitchen floor vibrates with the sound of bass guitar and heavy drums. In the many times I've visited this house, I've never seen or heard of a Mr. Stephens. Maybe Helen's a widow. Maybe the mysterious Mr. Stephens ran off with a cashier from the local Safeway. Maybe he's locked up in the attic. Maybe I'm better off not knowing.

"Tommy's in the basement. Is he in trouble?" she asks.

"He's probably in trouble. But I don't know about it."

"Thank God," she sighs.

"Someday he's going to step over the line," I say. "Someday the FBI's going to come down hard on him and his friends. And I may not be able to help next time. You better keep an eye on him."

"I try but I really don't know what it is they do down there."

"I want to speak with them."

"I'll let them know you're here so they can hide their stash or whatever it is they need to hide." She walks to the door to the basement and calls down the stairs. "Officer Zorn is here, boys. He'll be coming down in a moment."

Helen and I talk a while, speaking about the recent weather. When I've finished my coffee, I rinse out the mug in the sink and go to the door to the basement.

"Thanks, Marko," Helen says. "I appreciate what you've done. I'm sure Tommy does, too, although he'll never say so."

The basement is dim, lit by a dozen glowing computer screens. The walls and ceiling vibrate with the pounding sounds of some death metal band I don't recognize. A dozen or so faint figures lounge around the room. One man lies on a couch, his back to the room. A couple of young men sit at what was once a Ping-Pong table now scarred with years of coffee stains and cigarette burns. A fat kid is curled up in an old armchair, its stuffing leaking out, reading a comic book.

No woman is in evidence; there never is.

Every flat surface is heaped with computers and electrical equipment lashed together by cables and wires. On the walls are old movie posters and a sign that reads, "No Swearing No Spitting." The air is fragrant with the smell of French fries, pizza, and marijuana.

A couple of the figures raise their heads and glance at me without interest as I pass through. The group calls itself Kosmic Anomaly. I have no idea why.

I work my way through the crowded room and stop at the table. A kid no more than seventeen with bleached blond hair cut in a Mohawk is working at a computer keyboard. He looks up at me but makes no eye contact. He never does.

"Hello, Tommy," I say.

He shrugs and returns to his computer. I'm told Tommy is a genius at computers and hacking the internet. The FBI certainly thinks so. There's no point in my staying to talk with him. Our conversation is over. I've already lost Tommy to cyberspace.

"Welcome to our den of iniquity, Officer Zorn," the man lying on the couch mumbles without turning around to look at me. "To what do we owe the honor?"

I haul a wooden kitchen chair close to the couch, and the man slowly rolls over. His name is Paul Whitestone and he was once a high-level official in the National Security Agency. That was before he served time in a federal prison.

"Don't worry," I say. "You're not about to be busted." I have to shout to be heard over the music.

"Can I go back to sleep then?"

"No. I need your help."

Paul's around fifty and badly needs a shave. "You want our help? Isn't that probably illegal?" he asks.

"Do you really care?"

Paul sits up and takes a crumpled cigarette from a jacket pocket, lights it with a butane lighter, and studies the glow at the end of his cigarette. "What kind of help are you looking for?"

I take a copy of the paper the embassy code clerk gave me—a copy of one side only, not including the handwritten message about danger—and pass it to Paul. Paul puts on a pair of glasses and studies the paper.

"It's a code, obviously," he says. "Is this USG?"

"Nothing to do with the US Government."

"So what is it then?"

"I believe it's a message either going to or coming from the embassy of Montenegro."

"Does this embassy know you have it?"

"I certainly hope not."

"I won't ask how you got it." He returns the paper to me. "A lot of hard work. Not interested."

"I may have to insist," I say.

"Is that a threat?"

"If it was a threat, you'd know it. It's more like a promise. I'll keep the FBI off your back, at least for a while longer."

"Guys, kill the sound," Paul yells. "I need to hear what this policeman has to say." After several seconds, the music stops. "Why do you want to read this?"

"A young woman gave this to me—a woman who worked at the Montenegro embassy as a code clerk. Sometime last night she was brutally murdered. I think she was trying to ask me for help. A message may be hidden in this code."

"That's heavy." Paul twists the paper in his hand. "What language is the clear text in?"

"I suppose it's whatever language it is they speak in Montenegro."

"That makes it a south Slavic language. One of the Balkan ones. Yo, who here speaks Slavic?" Paul calls out to the room.

"Stevie speaks Romanian," a voice from the dark announces.

"That's not Slavic, idiot," Paul fires back. "Anyone else?"

"Peter speaks some Bulgarian. His dad came from there."

"Close enough. Where's Peter now?"

"He's at school—in detention," the fat kid with the comic book announces from across the room.

"Somebody go to the school," Paul orders. "Pick Peter up and bring him here. Tommy! Get over here. I have a project for you."

This Kosmic Anomaly is supposed to be a democratic collective and have no hierarchy and no leader, but like all organizations made up of lazy, undisciplined people, if anyone is prepared to think, he becomes the leader.

Tommy emerges from the dimness and Paul hands him the paper. "Break this," he says. "You know the drill."

Without a word, Tommy takes the paper and disappears.

"This is almost certainly a substitution code," Paul says to me. "That means, we can't solve it."

"You can't?" I try to hide my disappointment.

"We can't use a brute force attack. For one thing, the text is too short to do a letter-frequency analysis, and we don't have the computer power. Even if this is an off-the-shelf code, which it probably is, it would take us years. Maybe with a quantum computer, a bit less." Paul waves at the electronic equipment. "What we have here are bits and pieces of computers we got from Best Buy."

"How about your friends at the National Security Agency? I'll bet they have already broken the embassy's code."

"I don't have any friends left at the Agency."

"Are you saying it's hopeless?"

"I never said that. If you can't get in the front door, go in the back door. Can you think of any words that might appear in the message that could help us take a peek behind the curtain?"

"Nina Voychek," I say, writing the name on the back of the sheet of paper I give Paul. "She's the new prime minister. She's just arrived in Washington and there should be chatter about the trip."

"Any other names?"

"Lukshich. Vuk Lukshich. He's the ambassador at the embassy where I found this. And try Goran Drach." I write out the names. "How do these names help?" I ask.

"We will use side-channel analysis."

"Can you explain that?"

"Absolutely not. In the first place, you wouldn't understand. Second, if you did, it would spoil the magic we do here."

CHAPTER NINETEEN

I'D PARKED MY Honda Civic rental car across the street from a
small park two blocks from Helen Stephens's house. I don't want
anyone, friend or enemy, to connect me with what goes on in
Helen's basement. I didn't have time to exchange the rental car I'd
used yesterday for a different one this morning. I know I'm taking
a chance doing that. If somebody identified me driving the Civic
yesterday I could be a target. I decide to turn in the Civic at the car
rental service and pick up a different car at another agency later
this afternoon.

As I approach my car, I sense something is wrong—not big wrong,
something small wrong—but wrong enough to make my skin tingle.
I look up and down the street and see nothing out of place. There is
no suspicious figure stopping to light a cigarette, pretending not to
look at me. No slow-moving van cruising the street.

I turn my attention to the Honda and I see it immediately. On the
right rear fender there's a small black smudge.

I like the cars I drive to look smart. Even a rental car. Even a Honda.

The black smudge wasn't there when I parked here an hour ago.

The smudge seems to be tar, probably from the road surface, and
it looks like someone knelt on the ground next to the car and leaned
in close, pressing against the side of the car for balance: Why would
someone want to do that?

It doesn't take long to find out. Under the chassis, clamped to the rear differential housing, are two objects, each about seven inches long and maybe four inches wide. They've been smeared with tar or mud so they almost disappear into the dark undercarriage of the car. They're connected by two short, thick wires.

I make my call and within less than fifteen minutes, several police cruisers and a large truck arrive. The first one out of the truck is Ron Ensler, chief of the police bomb squad. We've known each other for several years, and almost everything I know about bombs I've learned from Ron.

"Are you the one who called in a bomb threat?" Ron asks.

I point to the Honda. "It's attached to the differential."

"I might have known." Ron looks at me funny, then calls out: "Code Red. Now!"

Half a dozen men and two women climb out of the truck, putting on HAZMAT and protective gear. They clear the area around the car, several going house to house to tell the occupants to evacuate their homes immediately. Ron and one of his assistants inspect the underside of the car using high-powered flashlights.

"It's a bomb," Ron tells me.

"I know it's a bomb," I say. "That's why I called you. What are you going to do about it?"

"It's too dangerous to move."

"So?"

"We'll blow it up."

"What about my car?"

"That, too."

It takes almost half an hour for Ron's team to clear the area. The bomb squad strings up yellow police tape at each end of the block blocking off all traffic, car and pedestrian. Several fire trucks arrive with firemen geared up ready to do their thing. The bomb squad crew drapes a heavy steel containment net over the car.

Then my Honda Civic explodes.

The firemen converge, putting out the fire, which takes almost thirty minutes, leaving a heap of twisted and charred steel and melted plastic on the street.

Ensler takes off his HAZMAT helmet; his face red and sweating, while his team removes the steel containment net from what's left of my car and others search the wreckage for bomb fragments.

"That was a real motherfucker," Ron tells me. "This your car?"

"Was."

A couple of Ensler's people come up to us and a woman holds a piece of burnt and twisted metal in her gloved hand. "Part of the detonator," she tells Ensler.

"What would make it go off?" I ask.

Ensler turns the piece of metal over in his hand. "That was no amateur job—highly professional. You don't see those much. I can't be sure, but I'd say it's one of those detonators that is triggered when the vehicle reaches a certain set speed, say twenty-five miles an hour for example. Very professional."

"What am I supposed to do with that mess you left on the street?" I ask.

"It's your car. Deal with it." Ron climbs into the bomb squad truck with his crew and cheerfully waves goodbye.

As I ride in one of the police cruisers to return to the embassy I try to remember whether I checked the box for insurance when I rented the Honda.

CHAPTER TWENTY

"Have any of you jokers seen the prime minister?" Janet is yelling as I walk into the waiting room outside Nina's private quarters. Janet turns to Viktor Savich. "That damned woman has disappeared. She just finished hours of press and TV interviews and retired to her private quarters to rest, she said. Now she's gone and vanished."

Janet and her team disappear into the labyrinth of rooms in the residential section of the embassy, searching for the prime minister.

"Where's Nina?" I ask Viktor, who seems quite calm.

"She's safe as long as she's inside the embassy."

I'm beginning to have second thoughts about that. At the back of my mind I have questions about His Excellency the Ambassador and I'm no longer sure Nina's completely safe here.

"I think I know where she went," says Savich. "Come with me."

I follow him into Nina's private quarters, which are empty, along a back corridor until we stop at a small door.

Savich opens the door and I follow him down a set of steep, narrow steps. At the foot of the steps, we're in what appears to be a series of storage and workrooms. One room is filled with locked file cabinets. Another has industrial-size washing machines and dryers. We pass quickly through what seems like a disused conference room.

Savich swings open a door and we step into a large, institutional kitchen with gas ranges, stainless steel sinks, slate-topped worktables, and a walk-in refrigerator: Nina Voychek stands at one of the worktables.

"Nina! You can't disappear like this," I say.

"I'm so sorry," Nina answers. "I didn't mean to make trouble. After I heard about the murder of our code clerk, I needed time by myself, I needed time to grieve for that girl."

"How did you manage to get out of your private suite without Janet or her people seeing you?" I ask.

"There's a back entrance to the basement. There always is. When I was an undergrad in New York, I worked summers as a house cleaner on the Upper East Side. I learned there's always a back entrance to the servants' quarters."

While Savich escorts Nina back to her private quarters, I return to the waiting room. After a half hour, during which I have a heated phone discussion with the rent-a-car company, one of Nina's assistants approaches. "The Prime Minister would like a word with you."

Nine Voychek sits on a small settee in her private suite.

"I apologize for the trouble I caused," Nina says softly. "That was stupid of me. I've already apologized to Janet." She takes a deep breath. "I was deeply affected by the death of Yulia Orlyk and needed some time by myself to deal with what happened—and to deal with personal memories."

Nina wraps her arms tightly around her body. She's nervous and tense—something I haven't seen in her. Her jaw is clenched.

"Tell me," she asks, "how was Yulia killed?"

This is not the first time someone has asked me specifically how Yulia Orlyk was murdered. Most people don't ask that. Most people don't want to know the details. I try to remember who it was that asked me that question before: it seems like it should be important.

"She was strangled," I tell her.

She studies my face closely. "Do you mean she was garroted? Is that right?"

"Yes, ma'am. How did you know that?"

"It's Nina, remember." She takes a deep breath. "Did they hit her in the face?" she asks.

"Yes."

"They like to do that to women."

"I can't imagine what it must have been like," I say.

Nina Voychek shudders, almost a spasm. Her face flushes. "I can imagine." She gasps. "I know how the garrote feels around my neck. I've died that way several times."

She pulls the scarf from her neck and reveals a dark wound around her throat: the same wound I saw around the neck of Yulia Orlyk. The same wound I saw around the neck of the dead guard at the theater.

"That's my gift from Goran Drach," she whispers and turns away. "I'm sorry." She hastily covers the wound, embarrassed. "I promised myself never to do that. It's selfish of me."

She takes a deep breath. "I need a drink; would you be so kind as to get me a scotch and one for yourself, if you're allowed to drink while you're on duty. I'm rather shaken," she says. "I'm not sure I trust myself to walk across the room just now."

I pour her a glass of scotch and water and fix one for myself.

"Marko, I ask that you be discreet about this." She touches the scarf wrapped around her throat. "I consider my scars to be a badge of honor; but they're a private honor."

"Were you the one who insisted I be assigned to your security detail?" I ask, handing her a glass of scotch.

"Did somebody request your involvement specifically?" She sips her drink thoughtfully. "That's curious. It wasn't me. Somebody on my staff, do you suppose? I'm certainly happy it worked out that way. I feel safer with you around."

"You have your own people. That should make you feel safe."

"It should, but it doesn't. I know my friends and supporters are here to protect and help me. But with you I feel truly safe."

"Why? We're strangers."

"It's because we *are* strangers that I trust you. The people who accompany me have been through the agony of my country, and they bring their own memories and emotional baggage. How could it be otherwise? Three times someone has tried to kill me. These attempts involved people I thought I knew and trusted. You're a stranger who brings no personal agenda. I can't tell you what a comfort that is for me."

"I'll do my best."

"You asked when we first met whether I'd lost anyone during the Revolution." She takes a deep drink. "His name was Sasha and he was a poet. We planned to marry, but it didn't work out. When I returned to my country from the States, I became engaged in opposition politics, and I had no time for love." Her face is frozen, lost in her own thoughts and memories. "I was a bit older than Sasha and more experienced; I'd had affairs in college. Nothing serious, but Sasha was an innocent.

"Then Mykhayl Drach issued the Special Emergency Decrees and opposition politics became very dangerous. Newspapers and radio and TV stations were shut down. Men and women were fired from their teaching positions and arrested. Ordinary people were recruited as spies for the Secret Police—Goran Drach's police—forced to inform on their friends, on members of their own families. Soon, no one trusted anyone." She stops and again stares into the middle distance. "And then the ethnic cleansing started."

"If it's too painful, you don't have to talk about it."

She shakes her head. "I have no one I can take into my confidence anymore; no one I can really trust." She lifts her now-empty glass. "Do you think you could fix me another?"

I pour us both fresh drinks.

"Then the day came when Drach's secret police came to our apartment and arrested Sasha and me and took us to the St. Nikolas Central Prison. I was held there for seven months: in solitary confinement. Twice I was brought before the high Tribunal and charged with treason against the state. Twice I was condemned to death. Twice I was taken to the execution chamber, the garrote tightened around my neck until I passed out. But I lived. I suppose I was more valuable to them alive than dead.

"Many of my followers were arrested and taken there. Many were executed, including members of my family. Drach's thugs tortured my poor brother, Filip. They demanded he sign a document denouncing me as a traitor. He is not strong but he held out as long as he could. Finally, he signed a statement saying I was a CIA agent. Then they let him go."

"And Sasha?"

She closes her eyes. Her face is hard with loss—or is it rage? "I was forced to watch his execution, which was by garrote, of course. The garrote is the preferred means of execution used by the former regime for special prisoners. It used to be called 'Drach's necktie'. They brought Sasha into the execution chamber where there were boxes of Sasha's books and poems. They forced Sasha to watch as they burned them. All his life reduced to a pile of ashes. Then they murdered him."

There's a gentle knock on the door.

"Come," Nina says.

Janet Cliff opens the door and looks suspiciously around the room. "Just checking. Is everything alright here?"

"Everything is fine," Nina answers. "Marko is looking after me."

Janet gives me a hard look. "I'll be right outside the door if you need me." Janet silently closes the door, leaving me and Nina alone again. Nina sips her drink, huddled on the settee. "This business with the code clerk has shattered me: I feel personally responsible—guilty."

"It wasn't your fault."

"Wasn't it? My presence has caused destruction to many people. My work caused Sasha a terrible death. By coming here to Washington, I'm responsible for the death of that young woman, I'm sure of it. How can I not feel guilty? Now it is you who's in danger."

"I must tell you," I say. "There was an attempt on *my* life today. Somebody planted a bomb in my car."

"Were you hurt?" She sits up straight, concerned.

"I found the bomb before I drove the car. It's been safely disposed of."

"That's awful. You must be very careful."

"The attempt may have nothing to do with you, Nina. A few days ago somebody shot at me. And more recently, I was attacked by some unknown person in the basement of a theater. These things happened before you arrived in the US. Maybe they have nothing to do with your presence here."

She looks skeptical. "Do you really believe that? And there is the murder of my embassy code clerk. I can't dismiss all this as coincidence. I couldn't stand to have you on my conscience as well."

"I'll make sure you won't have to."

CHAPTER TWENTY-ONE

LUCY IS STANDING at the edge of the stage when I arrive at the theater. "Natalie Esmond, the actress, is on her way," Lucy says. "She'll be here any minute. The props girl is backstage waiting for you."

"It won't take me long," I say.

"I've already questioned Props. She doesn't know anything useful. She just joined the production a few days ago. She was a last-minute replacement when the former props manager left unexpectedly. She has no prior connection with any member of the cast or crew. Absolutely none with Victoria West."

"Where does your investigation stand?"

"I wish I had better news. The whole team of homicide detectives and I have been over the scene again and again. We've interviewed every member of the cast and crew and everyone in the theater on the night of the murder. That includes four stagehands, an electrician, two concession-stand folks, and a coat-check girl. Everyone except those in the audience. The people in the audience were never near the stage."

"Did you find any ringer in the group you interviewed?"

"Roy Hunt concentrated on the women, but he didn't get anywhere. He swears they're all innocent. I've spoken personally with each one as well. Maybe they're not quite as innocent as Roy claims, but there are no killers among them as far as I can see. With maybe one exception. Cynthia Fletcher. She was Victoria West's agent."

"What's wrong with her story?"

"Her relationship with Miss West was more than professional."

"Meaning?"

"They were . . . very close."

"Don't be squeamish, Lucy. You mean they were lovers?"

"Maybe. And Victoria West was about to announce she was going to marry Arthur Cantwell. Maybe Fletcher killed Victoria West in a fit of jealousy. She seems high-strung and she was at the theater that night, but no one remembers seeing her all the time."

"Anything else?" I ask.

"Cynthia Fletcher made several withdrawals from her bank account, which is now close to zero balance. She claims her fees have dried up in recent weeks."

"How about members of the cast and crew?"

"I've pulled up police records on everyone. I found nothing suspicious. Interesting, maybe. One of the actors, Tim Collins, was once charged with assault, but the charges were dropped."

"Who's Tim Collins?"

"He's the actor you interviewed. The one on that TV series *The Phantom*."

"Who did he assault?"

"He tried to beat up some theater critic he met in a restaurant. He didn't do any serious damage. And Arthur Cantwell withdrew $100,000 from his investment account the day before the murder."

"Do we know why?" I ask.

"He claims it was to redecorate an apartment in New York for Vickie and him to live in. He also has a serious gambling problem."

"Does he owe money to anyone in the production?"

"Nothing I could find. Cantwell did buy two round-trip tickets for Aruba a few days ago. But they were open tickets with no fixed departure date.

"A sound designer, a man named Carl Soames, borrowed almost $81,000 from some New Jersey loan sharks. But he was in New York at the time of the murder and his alibi is solid. And there's one more thing. Michael Toland, the stage manager, admits to owning a Smith & Wesson revolver. He keeps it in his desk in the stage manager's office."

"The same gun that killed Vickie West?"

"The same make and model but a different gun. Hanna's checking it out."

"Has Toland's gun been fired?"

"Not recently. You should know that the gun is unregistered."

"Why didn't Toland register it?"

"He said he forgot. A couple of the stagehands had minor offenses and some drug possession charges, but nothing stuck and that was years ago. I'm afraid it's all pretty thin. I hate to admit it, but we're nowhere."

"We'll get there. Keep the faith," I urge.

"By now we should have some sense of motive. I can find no reason why anyone would want to harm Victoria West. She was well liked. She'd worked with members of the cast and crew for weeks in rehearsals and previews and there'd been no sign of any problems. Many had worked with her in previous productions and were her friends."

"Not everybody was her friend."

"Everyone involved had a stake in the production being a success. With her death, they're all out of a job. At first, I put my money on Arthur Cantwell," Lucy says. "He seems like someone who could commit murder."

"More likely as a victim than as a killer," I say. "Do you still think he's a suspect?"

"That doesn't make sense to me. He and Vickie were going to be married. Why would he kill the woman he supposedly loved?"

"It's true, married couples usually wait until after the wedding ceremony to kill one another. And they already had their opportunity when they were first married."

"It looks like we're nowhere."

"I'm going to talk to the props girl now," I say. "Call me when Natalie Esmond gets here."

The props girl, whose name I seem to remember is Lily, is waiting for me at her table backstage, sitting in semidarkness.

"Can I ask you a few more questions, Lily?"

"Sure," she whispers.

"You only recently joined the *Hedda Gabler* production as a replacement."

"That's right. The former props person left, and they needed someone to take her place."

"Who hired you?"

"Mr. Taylor."

"Had you worked for him before?"

"No, sir. Someone at the Guthrie told Mr. Taylor I was available. He was desperate and he called me."

"No interview?"

"Who interviews props?"

"Had you ever met Miss West before you joined the production?"

"I saw her in the movies."

"You didn't know her?"

"No, sir."

"Did you have any connections with her after you joined the production?"

"She introduced herself on my first day. That was it. She was very nice that way."

"How about the other members of the cast and crew? Did you know any of them?"

"I never knew or heard of any of them. Except maybe for Mr. Collins. I saw him on TV in that terrible spy series." She smiles a sweet smile.

"Where are you from? Not from around here, are you?"

"I'm born and raised in Cedar Rapids."

"Natalie Esmond's here," Lucy calls from the stage.

"Thank you, Lily. You've been very helpful. You can leave."

She cocks her head and smiles. "Thank you, Detective Zorn."

A pretty woman, about thirty, is waiting on stage.

"Please take a seat, Miss Esmond." Lucy gestures toward several chairs she's arranged on the set for the interview. "We have just a few questions."

Lucy dives in with her questions about what Natalie saw and heard in the minutes leading up to the murder of Victoria West.

While this goes on, I let my mind wander. I trust Lucy's meticulousness. She'll spot anything wrong or inconsistent in Natalie Esmond's statements. Not that I expect any.

"Miss Esmond," I say during a pause in Lucy's questioning. "Did you know that Victoria West forgot her final line in her performance?"

"Sure. We all heard about it."

"Why do you think she did that?"

"I don't know. It happens sometimes." Natalie Esmond shifts in her chair. Until now she's been watching either Lucy or me steadily, poised, not breaking eye contact. Now she's looking at the door to the drawing room, then at the floor.

"Did Vickie often forget her lines?"

"Never. I never heard her hesitate on a line or a cue. She was line perfect in our first table read-through. She was a true professional."

"Natalie," I say, "I want you to think very carefully about this. Did you talk to Miss West before her last performance?"

"Just a few words." She looks away. "I was upset."

"Why were you upset?"

"I'd just got some disturbing news. Vickie stopped by my dressing table, she saw I was upset, and she tried to comfort me. She was always very kind that way."

"What news did you receive?"

For a moment I think Natalie's going to close down on me; her face is rigid, even a little hostile.

"What was it?" I ask again. Gently.

"One of my New York friends sent me a text message."

"Saying?"

"She told me about a memorial service for a friend in New York. An actress."

"And this upset you?"

"For sure. This girl . . . she'd just died. It was a real shock."

"What was the name of this girl who died?"

Lucy is watching me, puzzled, trying to figure out where I'm going with this.

"Is that important?" Natalie asks.

"Humor me. You said something to Victoria West about the woman who died. Tell me her name."

"Valerie Crane."

"Did Vickie West know Valerie?"

"They knew one another."

"Was Victoria West upset?

"It was shocking news."

"Tell me."

"Valerie Crane was a beautiful, young actress with enormous talent. She'd been in some small parts in several prestigious productions and got good notices. We all figured she was on a roll to a successful career."

"And?"

"She committed suicide." Natalie stops until she can get hold of herself. "She had a day job as a barista somewhere. She put in her normal workday, went home, and hanged herself."

"Did she have an acting job at the time of her death?"

"She was between jobs. She was looking for work but wasn't having any luck getting cast."

Natalie chokes and for a few minutes I hold back my questions.

"Were you close to Valerie?" I ask.

"Not really. We met at parties and auditions. That kind of thing."

"But you were deeply affected?"

"Of course I was affected. How could I not be? Those of us in the profession ... it's a kind of sisterhood. Valerie was about my age. We competed with one another, trying out for the same parts. But we were always on good terms, sharing tips on upcoming auditions, gossip. You know.

"But when something like that happens... you can't help asking: How could she *do* that? What was going on in her life we didn't know about? Could her friends have seen this coming and done something for her? Did we somehow let her down? Could that have been me?" She takes a deep breath. "Such a waste." After a moment: "Is that all?"

I look at Lucy. She shakes her head; she has no more questions.

"What has Valerie's suicide got to do with Victoria West's murder?" Natalie asks as she gets to her feet. She holds her hands in tight fists. "I don't see it."

"I'm not sure what the connection might be," I say. "But my instinct tells me Valerie's suicide has everything to do with why Vickie forgot her last line. And why Vickie was murdered a few minutes later."

CHAPTER TWENTY-TWO

As I leave the theater after my interview with Natalie, a limousine pulls up, and Horst, one of Cyprian Voss's bodyguards, steps out and gestures for me to get in. He holds a machine pistol in his right hand, close to his body so it can't be easily seen by others on the street. He pats me down, using his left hand, his eyes flicking back and forth, searching for danger.

"The man wants to talk to you. Get in. We're in a hurry."

I look over Horst's shoulder, expecting to see Raoul, but the driver is a stranger to me.

The car is in motion as soon as I'm inside, moving fast. I squeeze myself into the back seat corner. Cyprian Voss takes up most of the space. He holds a large, soiled handkerchief in one hand. He sniffles and wipes his nose.

In this confined space he seems even larger than normal. He probably feels uncomfortable being so close to another human being. Not half as uncomfortable as I'm feeling.

I can't see where we're driving. Velvet curtains have been drawn over the car windows, shutting out the rest of the world.

Voss seems deflated, if a man his size can be said to deflate.

Voss never meets in public like this, so this meeting can't be good. Nothing about this unscheduled meeting can be good.

"There's been a change of plans." Voss's voice is hoarse.

"A little late for that, isn't it? I'm fully engaged in your assignment."

"Not anymore, you aren't. You must abandon your protection of Prime Minister Voychek. Immediately. There is to be no further contact between you and Voychek or her entourage."

"I can't agree to that."

"Of course, you can. It's just a job. And I'm paying you."

"It's not just a job. Others have instructed me to protect Nina Voychek while she's in the country."

"Who has given these instructions?"

"The United States Secretary of State, for one."

Voss makes a dismissive gesture with his free hand as if what I'd said was a trivial matter.

I have no intention of telling Voss that the head of the FBI Criminal Investigation Division also gave me the same instructions. That would probably upset him.

"You made a serious mistake during the Chicago business. I cannot allow something like that to happen again."

"You said you were happy that Mykhayl Drach was killed. You said something about having relatives in Montenegro."

"Did I say that? I have no relatives in that part of the world. I lied."

I'm not surprised he lied to me. It would make no difference to Voss if he did have relatives who'd suffered at the hands of Mykhayl Drach and his brother. Normal human relations are alien to Voss. He'd told me he had a personal stake in Drach's death just to obfuscate his real motive: money.

"I'm not backing out of my responsibility to protect Nina Voychek," I say.

"Why on earth not?"

"I have a strong personal commitment to seeing that Nina Voychek comes to no harm."

I sense Voss's mass recoiling as if I might be infected. "That's very unprofessional of you." He blows his nose into his handkerchief. "That would be so unwise. In our business the first rule is never to allow an assignment to become personal."

"I'm afraid it's too late for that. I've come to admire Nina Voychek. Even to like her. And I admire what she's doing for her country."

"Your sentimental drivel bores me."

"I'm not going to abandon her."

"You disappoint me. Stop your protection of Nina Voychek. That's an order."

"No."

"What?"

"I said no."

"This is not a request. This is a direct order."

"I don't take orders from you."

Voss blows his nose loudly.

"What's this all about?" I ask. "Why are you terminating the protection job? Is someone paying you off to betray Nina Voychek? Has Vladimir Putin gotten to your organization?"

"There's no need to be rude, my boy."

"So now you're going to run away?" I ask. "You're going to get on your private plane and leave Nina Voychek to the tender mercies of Vladimir Putin and his Russian thugs? Doesn't that bother you at all?"

I think I hear Voss laugh softly behind his dirty handkerchief.

"I won't be a party to betraying her," I say. "Have you no moral scruples?"

"I don't know where you got the idea I had moral scruples," Voss says. "I thought you a better judge of character than that."

I understand now; Voss has decided my activities are putting him in danger.

"What are you afraid of?" I ask.

Voss makes a pretense of laughing. "Afraid? Why should I be afraid?"

"I know you're afraid. I can smell it."

"There is reason I should be afraid. And you, too. Raoul was murdered last night."

This I didn't expect. From the look on Voss's face, neither did he.

"What's this all about?" I ask.

"It's a message. To me. And to you, Detective. Raoul was garroted. We both should know what that means. Back off."

"Horst must be upset," I say.

"He's in shock."

Raoul was a trained bodyguard. Probably a trained killer. Not an easy man to take down. Next to impossible to murder. Somebody very special must have done that job. And the use of a garrote? That's getting close to home.

"I might be next," Voss sighs. "Or you."

I reach into my pocket and grasp my cell phone. I know when the moment comes, I'll have to move fast. Voss is probably not armed but Horst is and the driver as well. And after what's happened to Raoul, they will be ruthless defending themselves and their boss.

"I don't suppose I'm going to get paid," I say, trying to make our conversation sound normal, almost friendly, as if I hadn't figured out he was going to have me killed.

"Paid? Of course not. You didn't carry out your side of the bargain."

Bargain? I'm puzzled by what he says. "What do you mean, 'my side of the bargain'? There was never a bargain. Just a straightforward assignment: protect Nina Voychek."

"Don't be naïve."

I should have known. At that first meeting with Voss at the Thai restaurant, I knew Voss was not telling me everything, but I didn't figure out what it was he was hiding. My job was never just to protect Nina Voychek. My job, unspoken, was to find her assassin and kill him. By being assigned to Nina Voychek's security team, I'd be close to the assassin who would expose himself and I could eliminate him. That was Voss's plan.

The assassin is still very much alive and is now a direct threat to Voss and his organization. Raoul's murder was a hint of things to come.

"Pull over and stop the car," Voss bellows. I feel the driver jam the breaks and the car swings over toward the curb. "Horst, you know what to do."

I pull my cell phone from my pocket. My fingers find the photo and flash button, and I point the phone at Voss's face. He sees me and recoils, turning his face away. The flash lights up the interior, just as the limousine comes to a stop. I can see Horst leap out, machine pistol in hand, and reach for the car door handle.

"Tell Horst to stand down." I add the words "Cyprian Voss" to the photo and transmit to Lucy. It's not a full-frontal picture; more of a profile. But more than enough to identify him through FBI and police facial recognition files.

Horst pulls open the door and aims his machine pistol at me. He can't fire. Voss and I are in close quarters, and in the darkness he might hit his boss. He'll wait until I'm out on the street to make his move.

"Forget it, Voss. Your man's too late."

"Did you just take a picture of me?" Voss demands. "Did you just take a picture of me?"

"I'm afraid I did. It's already been sent to the police. If anything should happen to me, the police, the FBI, and who knows who else, will know you're responsible. Give up, Voss. You've lost this round."

Voss shrinks back into his corner and blows his nose.

I need something more from Voss, but this isn't the time to make demands. I can't test Voss's patience too far. I need Voss and his gunmen to be far away before I make my next move.

"I'm leaving," I say. "Tell Horst to stand back. If he so much as looks at me funny, it's the end for you."

I get out of the car, keeping a close eye on Horst, who makes no threatening move with his machine pistol. Voss nods from the back seat and Horst climbs back into the car and it moves off, fast.

I wait until it's a block away, then call Voss's cell number.

"What is it now, Zorn? Our business is done."

"The game's not over just yet, Cyprian." He hates it when I call him by his first name. "There are two more things you need to do before I let you get onto your plane parked on some private strip somewhere."

I can hear Voss breathing heavily.

"There are a few details we didn't take care of while we were in your car. A couple of points I didn't want Horst or your driver to overhear."

"What do you want?"

"First: I want to be paid."

"You didn't dispose of the assassin."

"I'll dispose of the assassin in due course. In the meantime, transfer $250,000 to my private Luxembourg account."

Voss grunts.

"Second: I want the name of the assassin."

Silence on the other end of the phone. I think I hear a sigh.

"If you refuse," I tell Voss, "I'll have the FBI informed you're in the country. I expect the FBI has a thick file on you and would love to ask you some questions. And if you're thinking of escaping to some foreign country with no extradition treaty with the US, I'll inform the FAA and maybe NORAD as well. You won't be allowed to take off. And if you do get into the air, you'll be shot down. I guarantee. Now: What's the name of the assassin?"

"I don't know his real name. I only know him by his code name.

"What's his code name?"

"Domino."

I haven't heard that name in a long time although Domino's kind of a legend. I don't know his real name, of course, or what he looks like. I don't know where he comes from or his nationality. I just know he's the best there is in his special field. He has the reputation for being a crack shot with a handgun. They say he never misses. And he always favors a head shot.

"How do I find Domino?" I ask.

"Nobody finds Domino. He finds you."

"You never had direct contact with Domino?"

"Certainly not. I never want to. Nobody has. Anybody who's seen his face doesn't live. All contacts with Domino go through intermediaries and are done by phone or text message. People who need his services use a middle man."

"No one has ever seen Domino's face?"

"There's only one man who did see Domino's face. And lived. A man I think you once knew. Someone you had dealings with when you were a NYPD cop, according to my files."

"What's the name of this man I was supposed to know in New York?"

I'm pretty sure I can guess who it is, but I want to hear Voss say the name. I need to be certain there isn't a second man out there I don't know about.

Giving me information for free hurts him. In Voss's world, information is money. Telling me what I want to know is like burning money.

"The name of the man who saw Domino face-to-face is Asa Forest," Voss murmers.

I remember Asa well. He was the New York mob's accountant and bookkeeper. Turns out he was also skimming from the mob. When they found out they sent two hoods after him. Asa Forest managed to kill them both. So much for being a mild-mannered accountant. Then the mob sent for Domino to do the job properly. That's when Asa saw Domino's face. The next day, Asa turned himself into the NY police and pleaded guilty to a double homicide and to racketeering charges. Asa knew the game was up for him. No one ever escapes from Domino.

"This Asa Forest seems to have disappeared," Voss goes on. "Four or five years ago. My guess is Domino got to him. The $250,000 payment is on its way to your account now. If you are able to kill Domino, you will receive a generous bonus. Final advice: Find Domino and kill him."

"If I don't?"

"Domino will find you and kill you. You can count on that."

CHAPTER TWENTY-THREE

I'M IN AN unfamiliar part of town. I'm not even sure whether I'm still in Washington. I could be somewhere in the Maryland suburbs. Across the street there's a small strip mall. I go into a store and I call Officer Bonifacio. The store owner tells me where I am and Bonifacio says he'll pick me up in fifteen minutes. When Bonifacio arrives, I can see his patience with me is wearing thin.

"How did you get way out here, Detective?" I notice he doesn't call me Marko. "I was supposed to pick you up at the theater."

"I was hijacked."

He looks at me with genuine concern.

"It won't happen again."

"I hope not."

"Me, too. Now take me to National Airport."

"Sir?"

"I'm going to leave town for twenty-four hours. I'll be back tomorrow afternoon. I'll call you as soon as I know when my return flight arrives and you can pick me up at the airport."

"Are you going to be safe where you're going? I promised Captain Townsend I'd keep a watch on you."

"I'm going to the safest place on the planet."

* * *

My plane lands and we're informed by a member of the cabin crew that the local time is six forty a.m. That's about the time I usually go to sleep. We've arrived at our destination: a town in Colorado called Pueblo. The passengers on my plane struggle to get their luggage from the overhead bins. I'm traveling light with no luggage and I join the other passengers as they shuffle up the aisle. Eventually, we enter the airport waiting room. The flight had been smooth; I was actually able to get a couple of hours of sleep, which I badly needed.

I had a contentious talk with Janet yesterday evening when I called her from the airport and told her I had to be out of town for the better part of the next day. She protested, reminding me of the responsibility the Secretary of State had given me. She seemed to forget she'd thought I was mostly in the way. She finally relented and added additional agents to Nina's security detail and said I could go.

I pick up a container of coffee and a bun drenched in sugar at a concession stand before I find the driver I'd reserved before I left Washington. He's leaning against a late-model Chrysler parked in the airport pickup zone. The car looks comfortable enough for a long drive.

The driver holds a handwritten sign reading "Cooper." I use the name Cooper when I travel and don't want my identity advertised. It's a common name and one easy to remember. There's nothing more embarrassing than inventing a secret cover name and then forgetting it.

"Good flight?" the driver asks. It's a greeting, not a question, and I climb in without answering.

"The dispatcher said a long drive. There and back. Where we headed?"

"ADX Florence."

The driver turns and studies me. He wants to know who he's got in his back seat. He must conclude I don't look like a terrorist or a mass murderer. Then again, terrorists and mass murderers don't look much like terrorists or mass murderers.

Satisfied I'm not going to kill him, he starts the engine, turns on the AC to full blast, and pulls out of the airport pick-up zone.

"You a lawyer?" the driver asks.

"A friend."

"I didn't know the guys in there had friends."

"One does."

When we reach the outskirts of the town of Florence, I ask, "Do you get a lot of passengers coming here?"

"Sure. All one-way, of course." He laughs at what must be his standby joke for passengers headed to Florence. He's probably told it a hundred times.

"There it is." The driver points to a group of low, brick buildings ahead of us. Nothing particularly unusual except for the watchtowers manned with machine guns and double, twelve-foot razor-wire fences that surround the complex.

It really does not look like much from the outside. Not like some fortress prisons you see in the movies: black and storm-battered. But this is the US's Super Max prison, the most secure prison in the country. Maybe the world. The home to the worst, most dangerous, men in America.

The outside is not especially intimidating. Not much worse than your average Holiday Inn.

Inside, it's hell.

Behind a thick, bulletproof plastic barrier are two uniformed guards, heavily armed: one, a beefy man, and the other a slightly less beefy woman. Above me is a narrow slot through which I make out two more guards inspecting me carefully.

I'm in a kind of lobby area except there are no chairs or couches to sit on. The walls are painted a soothing color of mud brown and there are some photographs of Colorado mountains. The floor is covered with a nice floral-pattern linoleum.

I slip my DC driver's permit and police ID through a narrow slot in the plastic barrier. One of the guards takes my ID's and immediately makes copies and, I assume, transmits facsimiles to the US Bureau of Prisons in Washington.

"My name is Marko Zorn. I'm here to see Warden Cousins."

One of the guards studies his clipboard. "You're not on the visitors' list, sir."

"This is a kind of last-minute thing. I didn't have time to go through your bureaucratic chicken-shit routine."

"No visitors are allowed without prior authorization from the Bureau of Prisons," the guard announces officiously.

"Could you manage to inform Warden Cousins that Detective Zorn wishes to see him?"

"That's not allowed."

"That's not allowed?" I exclaim in feigned outrage. "Are you not permitted to speak with your own warden?"

The guards are losing patience with me. It's time I bring out my secret weapon.

"Norm Cousins and I are old friends. He will want to see me. Otherwise..."

"Otherwise what?"

"Otherwise I will be obliged to deploy the nuclear option."

The two guards step back from the barrier, hands on their weapons.

"What do you mean, *nuclear option*?" the male guard asks, his voice a bit shaky.

"I'm going to piss all over your pretty floor."

"What did you just say?" the female officer demands, swallowing hard. Her companion is speechless.

"I said, unless I receive satisfaction to my request to see my old friend Norm Cousins, I will be obliged to piss on your lobby floor. It will be an awesome sight, I guarantee."

The lady guard's immediately on the phone. There's a lot of urgent back-and-forth behind the plastic barrier.

"Stay where you are," the male guard shouts at me. "If you make any move, any move at all, you will be arrested."

"For what?"

"For showing disrespect for the Bureau of Prisons."

I stand reasonably motionless for what seems like an endless wait. Finally, the inner security door behind the reception desk opens and another guard appears with lots of fancy stuff on his visor. He's accompanied by two more armed guards.

I step through the security door that closes with an ominous clang behind me. The officer with the fancy hat leads me along a brightly lit corridor. We pass rafts of cameras and motion detectors.

"I like your cap," I say, to be friendly. "Are you a general or something?"

"You're on thin ice, sir. Very thin ice. Don't push your luck."

We stop at a large door above which is a sign reading "Warden," Another smaller sign reads: "Mr. Norman Cousins." My escort knocks and we step into an office with large windows overlooking a parking lot. The windows are covered with heavy steel mesh.

The office is furnished with a standard government-issue metal desk, several steel filing cabinets, a couple of uncomfortable-looking metal chairs in front of the desk. A large color photograph of a middle-aged woman wearing an evening gown hangs on the wall behind the desk. A series of smaller headshots of what I assume are senior officials of the Bureau of Prisons adorn the walls.

Sitting at the desk is a small, nervous man: Norman Cousins.

"Did you just threaten to urinate on my lobby floor?" he demands.

"I was provoked."

I decide to take one of the uncomfortable chairs facing the desk even though Norm didn't invite me to.

"Welcome to the Florence Federal Correctional Complex," Norm says. "What the fuck do you want?"

I met Norm Cousins years ago when I was a young detective newly assigned to the NYPD narcotics unit. There'd been an infestation of drugs at Rikers Island and I was part—a very small part—of a task force assembled to "take care" of the problem. Norm was the warden there at the time, and we got to know one another. Not friends. Just law enforcement officers assigned to do an impossible job.

It soon became clear to me that Norm was part of the problem. He wasn't selling drugs or anything. Just turning a blind eye to what was going on in return for some cash bonuses. When the DEA and the NYPD broke up the organization supplying drugs, Norm kind of slipped through the cracks. And maybe I had something to do with that. I think I may have misplaced his file. Norm owes me big-time.

"What do you want?" Norm repeats. "Why are you here in my prison? It can't be for anything good."

"I'm here to see Asa Forest."

Norm stares at me for a long moment. Then announces: "No."

"I've got to speak to Asa."

"Our rules are very clear on that. No visitors. Except attorneys and medical personnel. When absolutely essential. You're not in the least essential."

"How long has Asa been here?"

"Five years, I think. Go away."

I wonder what it must feel like to achieve the highest station in his chosen profession. In a dreary office with a view of a parking lot

surrounded by the most dangerous men in the world. I can't help
thinking of Satan in Milton's *Paradise Lost*: "Better to reign in Hell,
than to serve in Heaven."

Was it worth it, Norm?

"Why is Asa here?" I ask. "Why is he in a maximum-security
prison? I thought your SuperMax was designed for men who'd
committed the most horrendous crimes: terrorists and mass murderers, people who would be a threat to our national security and the
general population if they escaped. That doesn't fit Asa Forest. He's
a mild-mannered bookkeeper."

"Did you ever hear the inside story of his sentencing?" Norm
answers. "After you guys arrested Asa he told the DA he'd plead
guilty and agreed to turn state's evidence and testify against the Mafia
families. His testimony sent a lot of guys to Attica. But Asa made
one condition—that he be sentenced to a SuperMax federal prison.
Weird, don't you think? Most people go to great efforts not to be
sent here. But here he is."

"I want to talk to Asa."

"Request denied," Norm announces. "You may leave now."

"Do you ever hear from the old crew?" I ask. "Is Darren keeping in
touch? I lost track of him when he left prison. And how about Foley?
He was due for release last March."

Mention of these names from the past, all members of the gang
distributing drugs at Rikers, all of whom served serious prison
time, all of whom worked with Norm at Rikers—fails to cheer
Norm up.

"Go to hell."

"Contact Asa and tell him I'm here. Tell him I need to talk to him.
Then I'll leave quietly. If I run into Darren or Foley, I'll give them
your best wishes."

Norm sighs and picks up his desk phone.

The room is small; the walls are gray concrete; here there are no windows. The room is lit by fluorescent bulbs secured into the concrete ceiling and covered by thick plastic.

There's a single table in the center of the room, on two sides of which are facing seats. The table and the seats are concrete and are bolted to the floor.

I sit for almost ten minutes alone in the room, waiting. It's eerie. There's no sound at all; not from the corridor outside or anywhere else in the prison complex. I could be on the surface of the moon although I expect the moon surface would be more inviting.

There's a click at the door lock, and two guards usher in a man, handcuffed and shackled, wearing a blue jumper. The man is old and frail, stooped, his once luxuriant hair now mostly gone.

The guards guide the prisoner to the table, where he sits on the concrete seat. They release his handcuffs but leave the shackles on his feet. They secure the foot shackles to an iron ring in the floor. They then step away and stand near the door, but close enough to hear what the old man and I say to each other.

Asa Forest and I study one another for a long, silent moment. I think of asking him how he's doing but decide that's a pretty stupid thing to ask under the circumstances. Finally, it's Asa who breaks the silence.

"How is Laura?" A simple question, asked without emotion.

"Laura is fine."

"She must be out of high school by now."

"She's in college. At Oberlin. She's studying music."

"Is she happy?" Asa asks.

"I haven't spoken to her in three years. I thought it best to keep my distance. She knows how to get in touch with me if she's ever in trouble: if she ever needs anything."

"Will you see her?"

"When she graduates from college, I may go for the graduation ceremony."

"Does she ever ask about me?"

"She does. There's not much I can tell her."

"Does she know where I am?"

"She knows you're somewhere."

By mutual agreement with Asa, I stay away from his daughter. I was able to get her a new identity, but her life is still at some risk. Laura saw Domino's face once and that's normally a death sentence. As long as Domino's alive, she's in danger. I've never told her about the danger, except in general terms. She understands she must never tell anybody who her father is or anything about her early life or what she saw that evening. Her foster parents know nothing about her past or her father.

I've never talked to Laura about what happened although she must remember the night she and Domino stood face-to-face. Maybe when she's older I'll tell her more. For the moment, she's safe. No one can find her. Not even Domino can find her.

Asa never asks about money. There's a fund for her in a bank in Rochester in a numbered account; Asa knows I'll see his daughter is taken care of. He knows he can trust me to do what's right for Laura.

"Are they treating you okay?" I ask.

"The mattress is too thin. It gets too hot in summer. The food's all right. I have terrible neighbors. Ted Kaczynski, the Unabomber, is in the cell on my left. Zacarias Moussaoui, one of the guys who planned the 9/11 bombing, is on my right. Some neighborhood!"

Asa and I met when I was still with the NYPD. We got to know each other in the course of one of my investigations and we both took a liking to one another, although he was a thief and I was a cop. I keep telling myself, there *is* a difference. I was pretty sure Asa was working for the Genovese family and I was pretty sure he was ripping off the mob. Asa was playing a dangerous game. One he eventually lost.

When someone ratted on Asa to the mob, he was as good as dead. The Genovese family sent two hit men after him and they nearly got him, but he managed to get them first and escaped. That's when Asa came to me. He knew his time was up and the family would send someone else. For reasons I still can't explain to myself, I agreed to help him, and I found him a place where he and his daughter could stay.

Then Domino appeared.

At that time, I'd never heard of an international assassin named Domino. It turned out the Genovese mob used him for special jobs. As did some of the other families. Not to mention others around the world. The Genovese family was by then in a panic mode. They knew if Asa turned on them, they were screwed, so they brought in Domino to fix things up.

"Tell me what happened that evening you saw Domino," I ask.

"It was a long time ago. What does it matter now? It's ancient history."

"It's not history to me. I need to know exactly what you saw."

"I was living in the apartment you'd found for me and Laura up in Spanish Harlem. It was about six thirty in the evening; I was in the kitchen cooking spaghetti and tomato sauce for dinner. Laura was in her bedroom doing her homework.

"Suddenly, I became aware I was not alone. I turned and a man was in the kitchen. A man I didn't recognize but I knew absolutely he was there to kill me."

"Describe him for me."

"He was ordinary-looking. A slight build, maybe about five feet seven. I didn't pay much attention to his appearance. I was preoccupied by the gun he was pointing at me."

"How old was he?"

"In his thirties. I only saw him for a second, you know."

"Describe his face."

"Nothing special. Except . . ."

"Except what?"

"He smiled. A sort of sweet smile. And his eyes—I'll never forget his eyes. He had large brown eyes."

"What happened when you saw him?"

"I was holding the pot of boiling tomato sauce and instinctively threw the pot at his head. At his smirking smile. I hit him hard. '*Scheisse!*' he screamed, and he grabbed at his face."

"You're sure that's the word he used?"

"That's what he screamed. 'Scheisse.' He stumbled out of the kitchen, trying to wipe the boiling sauce from his eyes. There was blood on his face. I think I must have cut his head badly with the pot."

"What happened next?"

"I heard him stumbling down the stairs. Then I turned and saw Laura."

"Are you sure she saw the gunman?"

"She saw him. Why else do you think I've chosen to live out my life in a SuperMax penitentiary? It was either here or suicide and I knew I'd never have the courage to kill myself. But I also knew if that man ever found me, he'd force me to tell him where Laura was, and I could never allow that to happen. Never."

It's obvious now why Asa insisted on being sent here. The Super-Max is so secure no one can ever escape from it. By the same token, it's so secure no one can ever get in. Asa has placed himself in the safest place to hide on earth. The one place even Domino can't get at him.

"The man who you saw in your kitchen that night," I say, "The man sent to kill you—his name was Domino."

Asa nods. "I always suspected that was who it was."

After the attack, Asa called me and asked for my help. When I arrived, Asa was shaking with terror. I saw blood on the steps. Domino must have received a serious wound in the head.

Asa and his daughter packed their few belongings and I moved them out. The next day, Asa turned himself into the NYPD. He knew there was no place to hide from Domino. I found a safe place for his daughter to live.

"Did you know Domino?" Asa asks.

"I knew the name."

"When you did the books for the Genovese family," I ask, "were you the one who made the payments to Domino?"

"That was me. Of course, I never used Domino's name. I never even heard the name. He was just a numbered account at the Bank of Trinidad and Tobago."

I know nothing about the Bank of Trinidad and Tobago, but I know what kind of bank it must be. A bank located in a country that has passed laws to protect depositors with secret bank accounts; a bank that has accounts that can be accessed only with special account numbers. A bank used by people who want to keep their financial dealings secret. Clients trying to avoid paying taxes. Clients involved with money laundering, espionage, drug trafficking.

The IRS and FBI are always trying to break in. The banks always try to keep them out.

Asa pauses and smiles wistfully. "I realized only later that the account transfer I'd made the day before was for my own murder. Ironic, don't you think?"

"I don't believe in irony. Can you remember any specific payments you made to Domino's numbered account? Like the dates and maybe who the contracts were for?"

"I was never told what these contracts were for. Sometimes I could make a guess. I'd read in the papers about some killing and make a connection with the payments I'd made. There was a Jeweler named Roth with a shop on Fifty-second Street. And a soldier from the Bonanno family. I don't remember the others."

"Who was your contact with the mob when they wanted payments made to Domino?"

"A man named Guido Profaci. He was a longtime member of the Gambino outfit."

"When the mob wanted to hire a hit man for a special job, do you know how they contacted him?"

"I was never involved with that side of things. I do know they always used a middle man, a sort of fixer. Even the capo had no direct contact with Domino. It was always through an intermediary."

"Do you know the name of the fixer?"

"Not a name. But I know who the payments were sent to. I know the capo always referred to the middleman as the Greek. No name, just 'the Greek.'"

"'The Greek' is good enough for me. Can you remember the access and account numbers for the Trinidad bank you used to pay Domino?"

"The access number is easy. It was 'Suite 319.' That was part of my office address in Manhattan."

"And the account number?"

Asa hunches over nervously. "After all these years?"

"After all these years."

He closes his eyes for a moment, then nods. "I'll never forget that number. I think, on my dying day, I'll whisper that number into some priest's forgiving ear."

He takes a breath and recites a series of nine numbers and letters, speaking in a steady voice, slowly, not raising his voice, but not whispering, so as not to draw the attention of the guards.

"8LM539620," Asa says. Just once.

I have to remember the sequence perfectly from hearing it one time. One time only.

We sit across from one another in absolute silence while I chew on the numbers and letters Asa has given me. I repeat the series over and over in my head.

Then I nod to Asa to let him know I've got the code.

"Time's up," one of the guards announces. "Fifteen minutes is over." They unlock Asa's shackles from the floor, lift Asa to his feet, and reattach his manacles.

"Why did you want the codes for the numbered account?" Asa asks me.

"I'm going to put Domino out of business. And I'm going to find a way to put Domino's money to some good use. All that money he's been paid to kill people will go to benefit others. When he hears what I've done—and I'll see to it that he does hear—that will make Domino go crazy."

CHAPTER TWENTY-FOUR

MY FIRST TASK on the morning of my arrival back in DC is to screw Domino.

As arranged, Lieutenant Bonifacio is waiting for me in the arrivals section at National Airport.

"Any problems?" he asks.

"Everything went according to plan."

"Where to now?"

"Do you know any computer cafés? Somewhere I can use a computer to transact some business. Some place that's out of the way."

"You can use a computer at police headquarters."

"Not for my kind of business."

The computer café Bonifacio takes me to is in a rundown section of southeast Washington. I find an empty table. Bonifacio sits some distance away to give me some privacy. The presence of an armed, uniformed police officer has a depressing effect on the clientele and the café is soon empty.

I log on to one of the computers, using a fake ID, and download the Onion Router operating system. Immediately I'm in the dark Web where no one can find me or my IP address. It's a world I feel right at home in.

From here I create a new account at the Chase Manhattan Bank in the name of F. N. U. Domino. It takes a little longer to create a charitable trust in Domino's name and then direct that the trust be converted to a pledge. I used the name "Calvin Coolidge" for the account originator. He won't mind. This is not a secret account. Just a normal bank account that can be traced. But because of the Onion operating system, my transaction can't be traced back to me or my IP or to this computer as the depositor. I then complete some pointless forms regarding the pledge that no one reads. I've done this before and I know the drill.

I then make a series of calls, mostly to South Bend, Indiana, and after a lot of transfers and "on holds," I reach the man I need: The Reverend Timothy Sullivan. After a few awkward moments, the Reverend Timothy Sullivan and I are friends for life. I explain what I need and, with the help of Lieutenant Bonifacio, get the fax number of the café I'm in.

End of Act 1.

A few customers come into the shop, take one look at Lieutenant Bonifacio, and decide to have their coffees elsewhere.

Now for Act 2.

I log on to the Bank of Trinidad and Tobago site and enter Domino's password and secret account number: 8LM539620.

A voice comes on—a mellifluous baritone with a light Caribbean accent—obviously prerecorded—asking whether I wish to make a deposit to the account—press 1—or withdraw from the account—press 2. Or speak with a bank manager—press 0.

I press two and the recorded voice asks the amount I wish to withdraw.

I punched in the amount of $3,420,000 US dollars, the entirety of Domino's secret account.

One of the few good things about dealing with computers in bank transactions is the computer never indicates surprise or shock. Or even curiosity. I expect if there had been a real person at the other end, they would have registered some reaction, at least a gulp. The computer couldn't care less how much money's in the account or what I do with it. All the computer does is ask me to confirm the amount.

"I say 'three million four hundred and twenty thousand dollars,'"

"Thank you," the nice voice says. "Transaction complete. Have a nice day."

No real human being is ever on the other end of the line at banks with secret numbered accounts. These banks worry about the IRS or the FBI snooping and using voice-recognition software. The bank managers don't want to know who's depositing funds or for what purposes. They want to keep their hands clean. And their customers happy.

The recorded voice asks me whether I wish to take delivery in person or have the funds transferred to another account. I punch in the account number at the Chase Bank in New York I'd established for this purpose.

I feel a sense of profound satisfaction as I log out. I'm all done. And Domino is all done, financially speaking.

"Thanks for waiting," I say to Lieutenant Bonifacio as I close down my computer. "A fax message should be waiting for me in the manager's office. See if it has come in."

It's there as I had arranged with Reverend Sullivan. It's short, one page, and gives me what I need to shoot down Domino.

"Do you know the Northumberland Hotel in downtown Washington?" I ask Bonifacio as we leave the café.

"Of course."

I tuck the fax into my jacket pocket. "Then let's get out of here. I have a date with a lady."

* * *

Cynthia Fletcher stands at the entrance to her hotel room. She holds the door only slightly ajar, a sign she does not want me to come in.

"I have questions," I say.

"Is this really necessary? I'm packing. Getting ready to go back to New York."

"It's really necessary. I won't take long."

Grudgingly, she opens the door wider, and I step into her room—a small, modest, typical hotel room. Lying on the bed is a suitcase, half packed, and next to it lies a pile of neatly folded blouses, skirts, and a jacket.

"When we spoke last time," I say, "you told me Vickie owned a laptop computer."

"That's right."

"That laptop has disappeared."

She shrugs.

"You had access to Vickie's dressing room where she kept her laptop when she was at the theater. You said you put her flowers there."

"Okay. Many people had access."

"You could come and go in her dressing room without anyone noticing."

"So?"

"Did you take Vickie's laptop?"

She looks away. "Are you saying I'm a thief?"

"I'm not accusing you of being a thief. I don't care if you picked up Vickie's computer without permission. I just need to examine it."

"What's so important about that damn computer? What's your obsession with looking at it?"

"It might include information about Vickie's murderer."

She looks obstinate. I figure I'm going to have to use threats. "If you refuse to give it to me, that would be obstructing a murder investigation, which is a crime."

"Why are you so sure it was me who took it?" She holds out her arms in a pretense of being handcuffed. "Are you going to arrest me? Drag me to jail in shackles?"

"Not unless I have to."

"Anyone could have taken that computer. Vickie never locked her dressing room. She usually left her laptop on her dressing table. I warned her about that many times, but she never listened."

"I know you took that laptop. Please give it to me."

"What's on that laptop is private. That's not for prying eyes. Not even yours."

"I'm pretty sure someone has already looked at what's on that laptop. I promise I'll return it to you when I'm done."

"There are private communications on that computer. Communications Vickie never intended for people other than me to see."

"I'll be very discreet. Your private relationship with Vickie won't be made part of the official murder investigation record. But if I find something that reveals the killer, I will have to use it."

"There are email exchanges between Vickie and me I would not want to see made public. We were often very frank, maybe too frank, in expressing our thoughts and feelings."

"I'm not easily shocked."

"I'm not trying to protect myself. This is for Vickie. I don't want her name smeared in the press. Is that too much to ask?"

"When did you take the laptop?"

Her shoulders sag. She's giving up the game.

"After Vickie was found dead; while you and your officers were doing your search, I slipped upstairs and found the laptop on her dresser."

"Why did you take it?"

"My first instinct was just to take something that belonged to Vickie. As a kind of memento. So much of our two lives were bound up in those email exchanges. I dreaded the thought that some stranger would read her messages."

"Have you opened the laptop and read them yet?"

"I couldn't. It's too painful. Maybe later."

"Give me Vickie's laptop."

She stands rigid. "Why should I trust you?"

"I'm afraid you're going to have to."

Without a word, Cynthia goes to the bed and rummages deep into her suitcase and pulls out a black laptop.

"Is there a password?"

"It's 'orison.'"

"Did you use your real names in your exchanges with Vickie?"

"Never. As you can see, Vickie was careless with her computer. While she was on stage, she had to leave it in her dressing room. She thought it would be safe there. Everybody else would be on stage or occupied with the production."

"What names did you use for one another?"

Cynthia Fletcher almost looks embarrassed. "In our private correspondence, she called me Miranda."

"What name did you use for Vickie?"

"I called her Ariel."

She places the computer in my hands. "Please take good care of this. It's all I have left of Vickie. All I have left of our lives."

* * *

On returning to my house, I arm all security systems and place the laptop on my desk in what I laughingly refer to as my "study." This is one of the few rooms in the house with no windows. Here I have privacy as well as security.

I sit at my desk, a Regency antique I bought in London a few years ago in an antique store on Jermyn Street. I'm pretty sure the owner cheated me but I'm quite fond of it. On the walls is my very private art collection. A large late-Renaissance painting of Sebastian, his body pierced with arrows, covers my wall safe—an ancient Mosler bank safe. It's where I keep my records away from prying eyes. And stacks of cash, in various currencies, including dollars and euros, even a small stack of Chinese yuan. Here I keep my passports and identification papers of various nationalities and in various names, all with my picture. I also store here a small arsenal of weapons. The painting that hangs over the safe is so disturbing that it should discourage all but the most dedicated burglar from trying to break in.

Each piece of art represents a successful job, some of them for Cyprian Voss.

I plug in Victoria West's computer and fire it up. The start-up screen shows an image of the three witches from *Macbeth*. The legend on the screen warns "STAY OUT."

I poke around the keyboard. Someday, I tell myself, I must really learn how to use these things. For a while I get nothing except Microsoft gibberish. Then something instructs me to sign in and I type in "orison."

Almost immediately I'm in—and I go to the email files. There I find Vickie's extensive email correspondence. Hundreds of messages. Vickie was one of those souls who can't bear to delete anything.

The messages begin with today's date dozens, maybe hundreds, of incoming bewildered, condolence emails, the senders obviously having just heard of her death, unsure about what happened, what was true. What not.

I skip back through the recent emails to the date of Vickie's death. The bulk of the messages are about theater business: schedules, contracts, publicity. Nothing to explain anything about her murder.

I realize I'm not going to find anything useful among these files. I have a sudden revelation as I remember that Cynthia Fletcher told me that Vickie often used a secret name when exchanging emails on very private matters. "Arial." The name I always associate with her from the first night I saw her on stage. That name must have meant something very special to Vickie as well.

I search for the name "Ariel" and suddenly there are scores of messages to and from Ariel. All of them connected to "Miranda," who I know is Cynthia Fletcher.

Before me stretch page after page of expressions of affection interspersed with gossip. I feel uncomfortable reading these intimacies between two women—one a woman I once loved. I feel like I'm violating them in some way and I skim over these quickly, not reading carefully . . . looking for what I'm not sure.

Cynthia Fletcher told me that only she and Vickie used these names and no one else knew about them. But that isn't true. At least one other person knew the name "Ariel" and knew who it was. Garland Taylor in my interrogation of him on the night of the murder said he and Vickie were close, and he used the name "Ariel." I know now that was a lie. Only Vickie and Cynthia Fletcher knew these names. The only way Taylor could have learned the name "Ariel" is if he'd read Vickie's correspondence on this laptop.

Two days before the opening of *Hedda Gabler*, the email exchanges between Ariel and Miranda stop. I wonder why.

On a hunch, I search for emails between Vickie and Valerie Crane and find an email from Valerie saying she's been blackballed from any New York theater production.

In her urgent reply, Vickie encourages Valerie to be strong and to keep looking for work. She asks who it was who blackballed her.

Valerie doesn't answer that question. Instead, she tells Vickie she's too depressed to go to auditions anymore. In her response, Vickie promises to help Valerie straighten this out as soon as she gets to New York. She'll talk to people.

Several days seem to pass without any further exchanges. Then Vickie sends another email to Valerie asking how she's doing and asking again who's blackballing her.

Valerie's message is short. "It's hopeless, Vickie. I'm too ashamed to go to casting calls. But I need to tell somebody about something terrible that has happened to me. Please don't repeat this to anyone. If you do, I'll be in more trouble than I'm in already. Three weeks ago, in the middle of the run of the play, Garland Taylor invited me to his apartment to go over notes on my performance. We were half-way through the production by that time, and it was a little late to be making changes. I was uncomfortable in going, but he suggested that other members of the cast would be there, too. When I arrived at Taylor's apartment, he was drunk. And we were alone. After a very short time, he began pawing me. To put it bluntly, Garland Taylor raped me. He said if I told anyone about this, I'd never work in theater again. I never told a soul about what happened, but Taylor thinks I did, and he's seen to it I'm not cast in any more plays. Please keep all this to yourself."

It looks like Vickie must have replied almost immediately.

"Valerie, please don't do anything rash. I know this is horrible for you. I will take care of this situation. And I'll take care of Garland. I plan to do something that will make theatrical history. Something so outrageous, that Garland will be ruined for life if he's not charged with a capital crime. I plan to announce to the whole world what Garland did without mentioning your name, and I'm going to pick

the most dramatic moment I can and I'm going to inform the most
powerful people in Washington what kind of man Garland Taylor
really is. During my curtain call speech, I will denounce him. Please
keep my plans to yourself. This must come as a complete surprise and
shock to Garland until the very last minute. If he suspects what I'm
planning to do, he will try to stop me. He may even use force. He's
quite capable of it, I'm sure. Maybe I might give the bastard a sneak
preview of what's in store for him. Let him sweat a little. Maybe I will
improvise some dialogue at the end of the play he'd understand as
a warning, but nobody else would, and it would be too late for him
to stop me. Please give no one a hint of what I'm planning. Vickie."

There is no response from Valerie. But on the opening day, the day
of Vickie's murder, Miranda sends an email addressed to Ariel.

"I've just received horrible news. Valerie is dead. Her body was
found in her apartment this morning. She'd hanged herself. I hate to
give you this news on opening night, but I felt you needed to know."

Vickie's reply was almost immediate. "Justice will be done. Ariel."

I close the laptop. That simple message to Miranda, I suspect, was
Vickie's death warrant.

*   *   *

Lieutenant Bonifacio drives me to my next appointment, also in
a downtown hotel. Not a real appointment. I'm going to show up
unannounced and very much unwelcome.

CHAPTER TWENTY-FIVE

THE OLD MAN wears a satin dressing gown and points a gun at my face. "Get out or I kill you," he spits at me.

"That's not exactly the warm welcome from an old friend I was expecting," I say.

The last time I saw the Greek was in Venice when he was living in a *palazzo* on one of the less fashionable canals, surrounded by several armed guards, two mean-looking hounds, and several beautiful, slender women who lounged around an empty pool drinking Asti Spumante. I knew him then as Nikos.

He's frail now, slightly stooped, and he wears round, rimless glasses, the lenses a dark opaque green. His hair is gray and thin and he needs a haircut and a shave and he's wearing blue velvet slippers. The years have not been kind to Nikos.

His gun hand shakes. From old age or fear? Palsy? I can't tell.

"Go away, Marko," he croaks. "I don't want to talk to you!" He tries to slam the door in my face but he partially loses his balance and his concentration, and I quickly relieve him of his gun, an old Luger that looks like a souvenir from World War II.

I slip the Luger into my pocket and step into his hotel suite. Nikos moves away, staying well out of my reach. As far as I can tell, he's not carrying any other weapon but you never know. Nikos was once extraordinarily skilled with knives.

I step over the threshold and we're in a sitting room of a large hotel suite furnished with a couch and several armchairs. To one side is a desk on which lies a violin with a bow and some sheet music.

"I wonder what the FBI would find if they looked into your presence here in the US," I say. "What do you suppose they'd find?"

"I was in New York shopping."

"Fashion week isn't until next spring. And this isn't New York. What were you shopping for?" I ask.

He gives me a disgusted look. "For a violin, if you must know. All I did was buy one violin. Go away."

"Is that the instrument you bought?" I point to the desk where the violin lies.

Nikos sits in the armchair, silent. Next to the chair is a small side table. He's angry and frightened.

"That violin looks expensive," I say. "You must have paid a lot for it."

I can't see his eyes but sense they flick to the violin. "That's not an ordinary instrument," he says. "It's an Amati."

"Why did you buy it?"

"It once belonged to Constantine Buchholz. I heard him play it many times and I fell in love with its sound. I tried to buy it from him, but he refused to sell. Constantine died last year—of natural causes, I assure you. A month ago his instrument came on the market at a New York auction sale. I knew I had to have it."

I remember when I saw him in Venice, he'd sometimes slip away to what he called his studio and play his violin for hours. Then I dismissed it as a harmless eccentricity. Now I know it's his obsession.

"You're no musician," I say. "You're a thief and a facilitator for murder. What's your interest in expensive violins?"

"When I was a child, I wanted to become a professional musician. It turned out I had no talent, but I could never stop playing." He rises and crosses to the desk, lifts the violin and caresses it gently. It's dark wood has a beautiful veneer. "This gives my life meaning and purpose. Listen to its voice."

He tucks the instrument under his chin, picks up the bow, closes his eyes, and plays a short passage from a Paganini's 24 Capricci. The playing is barely adequate but the instrument's sound is rapturous.

Nikos stops and stands silently, eyes closed, then carefully replaces the instrument on the desk and sits back in his armchair, his hand resting casually on the side table next to him. "Can you understand why I had to have it? Do you have soul great enough to understand?"

I sit in a chair next to the desk, the violin within easy reach.

"Why are you here?" he asks.

"Somebody's been trying to kill me. I thought you might know who."

"How would I know that? I'm retired."

"Of course you are. Being a middleman for murder is a young man's game. But I think you've come out of retirement. Probably for the biggest pay out you've ever gotten."

"Why would I get involved in the business again? It's dangerous and tiring."

"You got back into the game because one day you read in the paper that an Amati violin you've been craving for years was going to be sold at auction in New York. I remember hearing of an Amati selling for six hundred thousand dollars recently. Where do you get that kind of money?"

"Who knows?"

"What resources does an old man like you have?"

He shrugs, but I sense his eyes darting to the small table next to him.

"I think you have one invaluable resource. You know the right people. So you let it be known in certain circles that you're back in the game."

Nikos is suddenly holding a Browning automatic pistol he's snatched from the side table and pointed at me. "This conversation is over." His voice croaks, but his hand seems steady.

"How many guns do you have?"

"As many as I need."

"Put that thing down. Somebody might get hurt." I reach across the desk and snatch the Amati violin and hold it in front of me.

"Don't!" Nikos screams, jumping to his feet; his hands shaking in panic, his face white.

"Don't hurt my violin," he pleads. "Please."

"This is awkward," I say. "You, pointing a gun at me. Me, holding your precious violin. We could go on like this all day, I suppose, but that would be silly. Sit down and put that damned gun away and I'll put your Amati down and we can talk sensibly."

Cautiously, he sits again and puts the Browning automatic back on the side table but still within easy reach: I hold the Amati violin in my lap.

"I think you have a contract for a major assassination."

Nikos shrugs. He's not going to tell me what I need to know without additional encouragement. This is not what I want to do. Nikos is old and fragile. He can't stand up to me, even if he has a Browning automatic next to his hand. I must be careful.

"The commission for the person who recruits an assassin must be substantial," I say softly. "But not substantial enough to buy this violin. I think you did more than just recruit a hit man for a job."

Nikos glares silently at me through his dark green glasses.

"Please. Don't make any sudden moves," I say. "I've been under a lot of stress lately and I might accidentally drop your Amati violin. That would be a shame."

The old man shudders but stays quiet.

"Why are you still here in the States?" I ask. "Why aren't you back home, playing your precious violin?"

He glares at me. At least I think he does. It's hard to tell through his dark glasses.

"Because your job's not yet done," I say. "I expect you're here as an on-site advance man, is that right?"

Nikos crosses his arms defiantly but says nothing.

"My guess is you're here to handle special arrangements. Maybe to record the target's movements, identify locations, recruit backup personnel, and plan escape routes. Is that right?"

Silence from Nikos.

"Is the local talent from the Brooklyn branch of the Russian Mafia?"

He twists in his seat. Body language like that usually indicates somebody is ready to talk. I go for it.

"Did you hire someone named Oleg Kamrof to do site surveys for you?"

"I won't tell you anything." He stares at me sullenly.

I grasp the violin by the neck. "Don't make me do something we'd both regret. All these guns around here make me nervous and when I'm nervous I tend to drop things. I asked you, why are you still in Washington?"

The man winces. "There have been complications with the contract."

Here we go. Most people find it almost impossible not to talk after a while. I guess it's a human instinct.

"Meaning?"

"My contact who represents the principal demanded some last-minute changes to the work order and that's created serious difficulties for me."

"Who is your contact?"

Nikos looks longingly at his Browning. *Can I get at it?* he's thinking. No, he realizes he's too old, too feeble. Too slow. He must surrender.

"You once recruited for the mob in New York and Chicago."

"If you say so."

"I say so. Which of the Five Families in New York did you recruit for?"

"All of them. I wasn't particular."

"Who is your contact when you need to reach a hit man?"

Nikos sighs and shifts in his chair. "A man named Anton Briand."

"Who is this Anton Briand?"

"A man I used to work with in the old days. He contacted me a few weeks ago and we met in Brussels. He had a big job for me."

"Who was this Briand working for?"

"He never said. He probably didn't know. There are always at least two cutouts between me and the principal, the one paying the bills."

"So even if you're caught, you could never reveal who's behind this operation."

"That's right. That includes you."

"Where's this Anton Briand now?" I ask.

"The French police pulled his body from the Seine. One bullet in the head."

"Who'd Briand want killed?"

"Briand and I initially agreed on the contract on Nina Voychek, the prime minister of Montenegro. It was originally to be carried out in Montenegro during some village festival. That's when I first contacted the man to do the job.

"Two weeks later, Briand contacted me again. Urgently. He said his principal needed to amend our contract. We negotiated a substantial supplemental payment."

"What was the amendment he wanted?"

"The original contract was for the assassination of the prime minister only. Very simple given that the man I recruited to do the job is the best in the business. Now Briand insisted on adding two additional names."

"Two new names?"

"For this he was prepared to pay top dollar. And there were other requirements."

"What requirements?"

"The hit had to be to done in Washington, not in Montenegro. And it had to be done while the prime minister was in Washington on a state visit."

"And the two additional names?"

"I have no idea who they were. Briand said he'd arrange that directly with the man I recruited to do the job. Which was fine with me. But Briand indicated that one hit had to take place in a theater in Washington and had to be done on opening night. That tied it down to a specific date."

I feel my heart beat fast.

"Briand also insisted the same hit man do all three jobs. He did not want to involve additional personnel. Less risky that way."

"You had to arrange a murder in a theater on opening night? That must have been a problem."

"I've managed worse. I asked around among my former contacts and found an ideal solution. Somebody—somebody with no connection to Montenegro or the prime minister, but with a connection to some Washington theater—was in the market for a professional hit man to kill the same actress."

Oh, oh! I think I just went down a rabbit hole here.

"Are you saying you found someone else who was in the market for a hit man?"

"It happens more often than you'd think."

"A hit man who was supposed to do a contract on the same person?"

"That is a bit unusual. I agree."

"How did you manage that?"

"You're asking for trade secrets."

"I'm a cop and you're an accessory to murder. You have no trade secrets from me."

He looks longingly at the Browning. "About a month ago I was contacted by one of my old associates. Somebody wanted a contract on an actress. This was long before I knew anything about the Nina Voychek hit. The principal looking for this contract was an amateur."

"What do you mean by 'amateur'?"

"Not someone involved in organized crime. It was a civilian. You know. Some wife who wants to off her husband so she can marry the pool boy. A businessman wants to get rid of a partner over some business dispute. It was the bread and butter in my business when I was still active."

"So you discovered some 'amateur' out to remove a professional actress."

"I almost recruited some local thug to do the job when Briand contacted me about the Voychek job. For that I needed a true professional and figured: Why not combine the two contracts? Save a lot of trouble and money. Briand agreed."

I'm having a little trouble here. This seems to be altogether too neat to be believable. Am I being drawn into a minefield of lies? Maybe, but I don't see what Nikos has to gain by lying about that.

"How much was the principal paying for the two additional hits?" I ask.

"One million, three hundred thousand, plus expenses for the total package."

"Who's bankrolling this?"

"I don't know. It would cost me my life if I ever heard the name."

"Do you want to guess?"

"Considering that large amount of money involved, I'd say it would have to be some state actor."

No surprise there. But now we come to the jackpot.

"What is the name of the assassin you hired?"

"I don't know his name."

"Is your hit man known as Domino?"

The old man jerks in a spasm of shock and takes a moment to answer. "The young ones can't be relied on. They're sloppy and they're careless. It's not like the old days."

"Is he Domino?"

Nikos nods. "That's one of the names he uses. For a job like Voychek I needed a top gun, like Domino. I used to employ him from time to time in the past. He's very expensive but he's totally reliable: I needed someone very special. You know, no loose ends. Domino never leaves loose ends."

"What is Domino's real name?"

Nikos laughs. "I have no idea what his real name is. Or what he looks like. Or where he comes from. I've never had direct contact with him. All arrangements are through intermediaries."

"How can I find Domino?"

"Not to worry. He'll find you."

I cross the room and take the Browning from the side table and remove the clip. He looks anxious as I toss the rounds to the other end of the room, but he doesn't try to stop me.

"What's Domino got against you?" he asks as I walk to the door.

"I assume somebody's paid him to do the job."

"Want a word of advice? If you can't get rid of Domino, let him know you're on to his game. Get the word to him he's now the prey. That'll make him extra cautious and he'll hide in the shadows where he lives. That won't stop Domino, but it'll slow him down."

"I'll leave your violin by the door," I say.

"Can I have my Luger back?"

Using my handkerchief, I wipe the Browning and clip clean of my prints and toss them across the room. "I don't think that's going to help much," I say. "Be careful who you open the door to."

CHAPTER TWENTY-SIX

IT'S TEN FORTY-TWO at night and I'm listening to Dave Brubeck's *Take Five* when the phone rings

"Somebody's trying to kill me." A male voice on the phone is hoarse with terror.

"Who *is* this?"

"It's me, Aubrey Sands. I'm at the theater," the voice on the phone whispers. "Help me."

It comes back to me: the mystery-book writer.

"I told you to stay away from the theater."

"I know who killed Victoria West. He's going to find me."

"Get out of there," I tell him.

"I know how it was done."

"Are you listening to me? Get out. You're trespassing. You're breaking the law."

"You were right. It was never a locked room mystery at all. It was always misdirection."

"Leave now!"

"I can't. I can hear him moving around backstage. He's looking for me. He's going to kill me."

"Where are you?"

"I'm on the stage set. I think he's heard me. He's coming now."

"I'll send help."

"I hear footsteps." Aubrey's voice trembles.

"I'll be there right away."

The phone goes silent.

I call police dispatch and send a police team to the theater, then call Lucy. "I just talked to a man who's at the Capitol Theater. He's that mystery book writer and he's terrified. He's in the theater now and claims there's someone in the theater with him who's threatening to kill him. I've sent a police patrol."

"I'll go now," she says. "I'll send a police cruiser to pick you up, and we can meet at the theater."

My heart sinks when I reach the Capitol Theater: half a dozen police cruisers are stopped in front, their light bridges flashing red and blue. It's the middle of the night and it's raining hard, but a few curious people clutching umbrellas are watching the scene, kept at a distance by uniformed police officers. I rush through the front doors of the theater, hurry through the lobby, and into the auditorium.

Lucy Tanaka stands on the stage set speaking urgently to a police officer. I run down the aisle and up the steps to the stage.

Aubrey Sands lies on his back on the floor in the middle of the stage. He wears a pale pink shirt and his eyes are wide open in terror. A golden cord has been wound around his neck, cutting deep into the flesh, leaving a livid wound.

Lucy stands above him. "This is where I found him. Is he the writer who wanted to help solve the murder case?"

"That's the man."

"I've called Hanna and the medical examiner personnel," Lucy says, "And I deployed officers at all entrances. The building is in lockdown in case the killer's still in the building. I'll do a search."

"I can do that," I say.

"It's my case. My responsibility. I'll take the search."

"Be careful," I say. "The man who did this may be armed and is certainly dangerous and desperate."

Lucy opens her jacket and takes her Glock service weapon from her shoulder holster. "I'm ready."

Hanna and the medical team arrive and go directly to the body. "Dead," Hanna announces. "Looks like the victim was strangled. At . . ."

"At around two thirty-two or soon after," I say. "I spoke with the victim on the phone at two thirty-two."

"It looks like he was strangled with this fancy gold cord," Hanna says.

"It was a part of a prop," I say. "The cord was attached to the hilt of the saber hanging above the fireplace."

I step into the empty drawing room. It's as I remember it from the night of Victoria West's murder except now there are traces of fingerprint powder on the doors and around the walls, and the outline of a body in white tape is on the floor marking the place where Vickie died.

I try to concentrate and visualize the room as Aubrey must have seen it. I shut out the voices of the medical team and the crime scene technicians and immerse myself in the room, breathe its air.

What did Aubrey see that I'm not seeing? I wonder.

Lucy joins me. "I've checked the backstage area and the dressing rooms. So far, we've found no one. I'm starting on the rest of the building."

"Be sure to take a uniformed cop with you."

"Will do."

Lucy's nervous and wound up—that's not her. It's late and we're all tired. But it's more than that. Something has gotten to Lucy. I can tell.

It takes us more than an hour to complete a preliminary investigation and to secure the crime scene.

"There's nobody in the building," Lucy says when she joins me on the set. "We've gone from the attic to the basement, including the shop."

"I expect the killer's long gone," I say.

"Did Sands tell you anything about his attacker?"

"Nothing. But he did say it wasn't a 'locked room' murder. He told me it was all misdirection."

"What did he mean by that?"

"Have you ever seen a professional magician show? They do all these elaborate tricks using complicated sets and capes and top hats and wands and attractive women and bunny rabbits. That's all meant to distract the audience. Most of the tricks are done by sleight of hand. Done in plain sight but in a way the audience doesn't see it happen. It's all misdirection."

Lucy and I leave the theater together and we sit in her car, Lucy in the driver's seat. I sense she needs to talk.

The windshield is smeared with rain and we stare through the glass at the blurred red and blue flashing psychedelic lights of the emergency vehicles parked in front of the theater. We watch in silence as the medical team rolls a gurney with the ruined body of Aubrey Sands covered in a heavy cloth and places him into an ambulance.

"Have you ever killed anybody?" Lucy asks, out of the blue.

"Are you all right?" I ask. I'm worried about her.

"I'm wondering whether I might have made a mistake," Lucy says at last. She doesn't start the engine but sits, gripping the steering wheel, her knuckles white, not looking at me. "Getting into police work, I mean. Maybe I'm not cut out for this job."

"I hope you're not thinking of quitting on me. You're a good cop."

"Police work is what I've always wanted to do. Now I'm having doubts."

"Seeing the man killed like that ... that was a shock. It would be a shock for anybody. Nothing wrong with feeling upset."

"Some people thought," Lucy says, "at least in my family—they thought it wasn't natural for a girl to be a cop. My parents' dream was for me to become a dentist or something. At least a dental hygienist. But I chose law enforcement. I believe there are people who want to destroy the foundations of our civilization, people who steal and cheat and kill. And they'll keep doing it unless somebody stands up to them. Someone has to be willing to defy the barbarians—to stand at the gate—or civilization will collapse." Lucy looks at me, an embarrassed smile on her lips. "Does that sound as pretentious to you as it sounds to me?"

"Do you think the barbarians are getting through the gate?" I ask. "There are days when I think so."

She sits for a long moment in silence, struggling for words, then looks directly at me. "Tonight—suppose the killer had been hiding in the theater somewhere? Suppose I'd walked in on him? Suppose the killer had a gun? Waiting for me?"

"It's okay to be scared. We're all scared in situations like that. It's only natural."

"That's not it. Being scared—I can deal with that." She pauses. "Do you know I've never had to use my weapon except in training exercises. Not once. Not in a real situation. Suppose I'd faced the killer tonight?"

"You've been trained for that."

"I'm not sure how I'd act. Tonight, searching backstage—it suddenly came to me—suppose I came face-to-face with the killer? I'm not sure I could shoot a man. Not even to save a life. Not even to save my own life."

CHAPTER TWENTY-SEVEN

IT'S ALMOST FIVE in the morning when my phone rings. Right when I'm finally falling asleep, of course. I'd just gotten in after I'd seen that Lucy was safe at home. She's anxious and I know I'm going to have to do something for her.

"I have something you must see," a voice on the phone says.

It takes me a few seconds to recognize Paul Whitestone's voice. He never identifies himself on the phone—for obvious reasons—although I'm sure the FBI and the National Security Agency have voice-recognition software that will identify him. I'm not pleased to be wakened at this hour, but I suppose I should be grateful that Paul and his hacker collective are still working this late at night on the decoding project I gave them.

"You've broken the code?" I ask.

"In part."

"Can it wait till tomorrow?"

"It *is* tomorrow. Your life depends upon you seeing this. Trust me."

He gives me the address of a Starbucks on Wisconsin Avenue. "Take an outside table; away from other people. Seven sharp. I won't wait."

The phone connection goes dead.

It's much too early in the morning to call Lieutenant Bonifacio. I figure he deserves a good night's sleep, so I collect my new rental car that

I'd parked in my garage—a beat-up old Kia—and arrive at the rendez-vous ten minutes early and survey the area to ensure no unwanted guests are hanging around. I buy the largest coffee Starbucks has to offer and sit at an empty outside table, above which stands a large green umbrella that gives me some protection from the light drizzle. There are a few other customers at the other table, who look like nurses and technicians headed for early shifts at nearby doctors' offices.

Today's Metro section contains several articles about Victoria West, most of them complaining about the incompetence of the hapless Metropolitan Police. I see nothing about the murder of Aubrey Sands. Of course, the print edition would have gone to press too early for that story, but on my iPad his murder is spread all over the *Post's* website: "Distinguished Writer Murdered!" "Mystery at Scene of Murder of Famous Actress." "Mystery Author Found Dead in Theater."

Paul Whitestone takes a seat opposite me, his face strained. "What the fuck have you gotten yourself into this time, Marko?"

"I beg your pardon."

"Last night—about two in the morning—we made a partial break-through. Enough to read part of the message you gave me. Enough to know I don't want to read the rest."

"Does that mean you're not going to tell me what it says?"

"It means we're done. I've ordered every note the team made—every query—destroyed, erased from our hard drives. If we're ever raided, there'll be no evidence. I told the boys to go home. I'm dissolving Kosmic Anomaly. It's time the kids got a life."

Paul takes a sheet of crumpled paper, slightly coffee-stained, from his pocket and places it on the table between us. I can see it's a copy of the encrypted message I gave him, now covered with handwritten notations in various colors.

"The text you gave us appears to be the end of a much longer message. Tommy first hacked the embassy's clear-text communications, the stuff they send back and forth dealing with administrative matters. These messages can give us clues about what's in coded messages—certain repeated phrases such as greetings and titles and common references."

"I get it." I'm impatient and wish Paul would get to the point. "What did the message say?"

"'Eyes only.' 'For the ambassador.' Then stuff we couldn't read but which seemed to do with an important trip. We recognized some of the names you gave us. 'Nina Voychek' and 'Goran Drach.'"

"Go on."

"And a word that made no sense at first but which seemed to be a name: Domino. Then Tommy had one of his epiphanies. Tommy worked out the date-time signatures. From there he was able to work out several passages. Of course, they were in some Slavic language so we had to translate what we had, which was a complication as our translation staff is a fourteen-year-old kid who wanted to play *Mortal Combat* instead. Tommy finally worked out one full sentence."

"What did the damn thing say?"

"When Tommy showed me the translation, I closed down the project and sent everyone home. That's when I knew it was time to terminate Kosmic Anomaly."

"You've lost me."

"See for yourself." He pushes the page across the table to me.

I put on my glasses and read quickly through the message. In between what seem to be random numbers are mysterious hand-written notations. When I look up, Paul has gone; I don't expect to see him again.

"Oh, shit," I hear myself saying aloud as I come to the last sentence of the message. Several people look over at me, startled.

The text reads: *Domino advised. Further failures unacceptable. Prime minister and Zorn must die before PMs departure from US.*

CHAPTER TWENTY-EIGHT

LUCY LOOKS STRESSED this morning and I know I have to do something or she'll be of no use to me.

"There's something I need you to do for me," I tell her. "I want you to shoot some targets at the firing range."

She looks up at me and shakes her head impatiently. "I'm fully qualified on small arms."

"I know that but I need to show you something."

The range is "cold" this morning—no one is shooting or preparing to shoot.

Nelson Towne, the chief arms instructor and, this morning, the range master, waves cheerfully from his desk. He is a tall, thin African American dressed, as always, in a business suit, with a vest and jacket and bow tie with polka dots.

"You here to learn how to shoot, Marko?" he asks. "It's about time." Nelson disapproves of the fact I rarely use a weapon—he's convinced I'm afraid of guns—and he's also convinced that most police officers on the DC police force are unqualified in the use of firearms. "There'd be a lot fewer deaths if the police learned how to shoot better" has been his mantra for as long as I've known him, which has been a long time. Unfortunately, no one pays much attention to him.

"No shooting for me today, Nelson. But I'd like you to give my partner here, Officer Tanaka, a refresher course in handguns."

Nelson looks surprised. "Officer Tanaka's not on the firing schedule today."

"Can you see if you can fit her in? Lucy and I are involved in a murder investigation and last night one of our witnesses was killed. So we know we're dealing with a dangerous criminal. I'd feel better if Lucy was completely comfortable with shooting her weapon."

"Is this really necessary?" Lucy demands. "I know how to shoot. I've been through the system. I'm totally comfortable with firing a gun."

"I know that. This is different."

"Happy to take care of you, Officer Tanaka," Nelson says.

Nelson leads Lucy to one of the firing booths and supervises the unloading and inspection of her Glock. They put on ear protectors, and Nelson watches as Lucy prepares her weapon and takes a shooter's stance. I retreat to the waiting room outside where it's quiet.

After fifteen minutes, Lucy emerges from the range, holding a paper target, folded neatly into squares.

"How'd you do?" I ask.

"Take a look for yourself." She unfolds the target showing the silhouette of a man holding something in his right hand, maybe a knife, maybe a gun. Three shots entered the target's upper abdomen; two more struck the chest.

"Good shooting," I say.

She looks at me intently. "But you don't really think it was good shooting, do you? You think I could have done better."

"Look at the silhouette," I say. "It's supposed to be a man, maybe six feet tall."

"Around that."

"Maybe two hundred pounds. Maybe more."

"I hit him right in the chest."

"This is not a TV show like *The Phantom,* where the hero takes one shot and his opponent goes down. That's not the way it works."

"How is this different?"

"Your aim was great—perfect even—but you failed. You didn't achieve what you had to in a gunfight."

"What didn't I achieve? I shot the bastard." Lucy's getting defensive, even angry at me.

"Your primary objective in a gunfight is to stay alive. To do that, you've got to take your opponent out in the first exchange. Your opponent might have been wearing body armor. Even if he wasn't wearing a Kevlar bulletproof vest, you could have lost the fight. You hit your opponent in the chest—a big, heavy man like that—he'd probably still be standing. Especially with you using a small-caliber weapon. He could still stay on his feet long enough to get off a shot at you. He might be fatally wounded, but he's still extremely dangerous. If he's big enough and mad enough, he could even charge you, firing his weapon. Remember the mantra for close-quarters shooting—'one shot one kill'. In a firefight you must be able to immediately disable your opponent."

"What would you have done?"

"Me? I would have gone for a head shot—"

"Sergeant Towne said I should always shoot for the center mass. That was what I was taught in small-arms training when I entered the police academy. I was told never to shoot for an arm or leg or the head."

"That's what they teach all police recruits. As far as that goes, that's fine. You shoot for the center mass because that's an easy target. If you have backup, that will work. But if you're alone—facing a determined, armed opponent who's a trained killer—you will fail. I would have shot for the T-Box."

"What's a T-Box?"

"It's a target point where the nose meets the forehead. Military and police security shooters aim for the T-Box, especially in hostage situations where there is no time for a second shot."

"I thought you didn't believe in guns."

"I don't, but there are times when they are necessary."

"The space between the eyes and over the nose is an awfully small target."

"Very small. Easy to miss. And if you miss, you're dead.

"But you think I should go for a head shot."

"You're a good shot, Lucy. Your target proves that. But I don't think you're ready yet. You would have to perfect your hand-eye coordination."

"You mean practice."

"It takes more than practice. Your weapon must become part of your body and your mind and you must have total psychic concentration. When that moment comes—when you face a killer, your mind and body are one, totally focused on one thing—destroy your opponent. You must not think. It's almost a spiritual thing. It takes years of learning to achieve that degree of concentration. It's hard to describe."

"I don't think I could do that—shoot somebody in the head. I've never shot anybody. Never had to face that. I don't think I could."

"You're thinking. Thinking is fatal. The most important thing in a confrontation with an armed killer where someone's pointing a gun at you: never allow yourself to think, never hesitate. Hesitation is death."

"I can't."

"You don't know what you can do or can't do until you're in the real situation."

Lucy is more anxious than I've ever seen her. I pretty well know what she's going through. She's thinking about what I just told her, running the scene through her mind—imagining herself facing an armed opponent.

I've made my point. I now need to get her to think about something else.

"Let's look at the surveillance footage I got from the embassy," I tell Lucy. "And get the tapes we got from the Chicago police showing the two killers entering the chess club in Chicago."

When we meet in the projection room, Hanna has already cued the embassy security tapes to start about ten p.m. on the evening Yulia Orlyk, the embassy code clerk, was murdered. We watch the scene in silence, and for a long time, we see no one enter or leave the embassy. We make out the lights of passing cars. Traffic's light at this time of night and there are no pedestrians.

"There it is," Lucy says softly, urgently. She leans forward and points to a black, or dark-colored, SUV pulling into the driveway in front of the embassy.

"Can you make out the plate numbers?" Lucy asks.

"No way," Hanna answers. "The picture quality's crap."

A moment later the door to the embassy opens and a figure at the bottom of the screen steps out onto the front stoop and stops. Although the image is dark and grainy and the figure has her back to the camera, I know it's Yulia Orlyk. She's wearing a raincoat and clutches a purse and an umbrella in her hands.

"Time?" I ask.

"Eleven fifteen," Lucy says.

"Why is she just standing there?" Hanna asks. "Why doesn't she get into the car?"

"That's because she's confused," I say. "She called for a taxi, but this is no taxi. She's not sure what to do."

Nothing happens for several seconds. The woman stands motionless under the glass canopy above the embassy door and there's no movement inside the car. Then both front doors of the SUV open and two men emerge.

The driver walks around the front of the SUV and talks to Yulia. He's short and slight and wears a dark raincoat. He gestures angrily and it looks like he's yelling at her.

The man who'd been in the passenger seat is big. As a car passes, for a second, the man's bald head and face are caught in its headlights.

The bald man steps forward, grabs Yulia by her left arm. Yulia tries to pull away and reaches for the embassy doorbell. The two men pull her away violently, and there's a momentary struggle as she tries to free herself. Then she's pulled into the back seat of the SUV, where she's seated next to the bald man. The small man jumps into the front seat and the SUV moves quickly out of the picture frame.

We sit in silence for a minute, hardly breathing, then run through the film again, and again a third time.

"Can you identify the car?" I ask.

"Probably a Ford Bronco," Lucy answers. "Probably black. There are maybe a thousand like that in the metropolitan area."

"Let's look at the Chicago surveillance tapes," I say.

Hanna pops in the tapes and we're looking at a busy street scene in any large city. It's a bright, sunny day and the sidewalk is crowded. Mostly men and women looking at their cell phones. Normal people walking along a normal street. Two men appear and stop. Unlike the embassy tapes taken at night in subdued lighting, the images here are clear and sharp. I don't recognize one of the men. Just an average young guy in a hoodie. The other man I know immediately. He's older, maybe thirty, tall and bulky, and he's bald. The same guy who abducted the embassy code clerk we just saw in the embassy CCTV tape.

The two men disappear from the scene.

"The two men are about to enter a chess club in Chicago," I say. "They're about to commit murder."

At that moment, the door to the projection room bursts open and the bright room lights switched on.

"Everybody, stay where you are," Roy Hunt shouts. "Keep your hands where we can see them."

I'm surrounded by two uniformed police officers, one of whom puts a meaty hand on my shoulder.

"Detective Zorn, I'm arresting you for the murder of Nikos Mazarakis," Roy announces. Roy is now in full junior-detective mode, a moment I'm sure he's dreamed of ever since he joined homicide.

"Roy, get out of here," Lucy shouts. "We're in the middle of reviewing surveillance tapes in connection with two murders."

I get to my feet, brushing the cop's hand from my shoulder.

"You have the right to remain silent," Roy drones.

"Who is Nikos Mazarakis?" Lucy demands. She's boiling mad.

"Calm down, Roy," I say.

"Anything you say can and will be used against you in a court of law."

"Shut up, Roy," Lucy snaps.

I give a hard look at the two cops Roy brought with him as backup, and they step back, a bit abashed.

"You have the right to an attorney," Roy persists.

"Roy," I say, "You're making a fool of yourself."

"If you cannot afford—"

"Stop it," Hanna shouts. Hanna is normally soft-spoken.

"What's going on here?" I demand.

"You heard me. I'm arresting you on suspicion of murder."

"Tell me again who it is I'm supposed to have murdered."

"I'm booking you. You can get the charges through your attorney."

"Roy," Lucy says loudly, "you're acting crazy. This is Marko you're talking to. Have you lost your mind?"

"There's been a murder and Marko's our prime suspect," Roy protests, touching his mustache.

"Who is Nikos Mazarakis and what's he got to do with Marko?" Lucy demands.

The thrill of arresting me is beginning to wear off, and Roy, facing Lucy's fury and Hanna's scorn, is beginning to have doubts about this whole arrest business. But he tries to put on a brave face for the benefit of the two cops backing him up.

"A man named Nikos Mazarakis was found murdered in his room at the Franklin Hotel about an hour ago."

"What's that got to do with me?" I ask.

"You were with him."

"I think I'd better go to the crime scene and take a look around," I say.

"You? *You* want to inspect the crime scene?" Roy explodes. "You can't do that. You're the suspect. I just arrested you."

"Roy, you're an idiot. And I respect that. Just let me do my job. I'm going to the Franklin Hotel now. Lucy, Hanna, come with me. You too, Roy, if you want."

CHAPTER TWENTY-NINE

THE HOTEL SUITE looks about the same as when I left Nikos. Except now it's full of police detectives and Hanna's crime scene inspectors. The other difference is the presence of a corpse spread on the floor. Surrounding the corpse are the splintered remnants of an Amati violin.

"You know this man?" Roy demands, pointing to what remains of Nikos. "He some friend of yours?"

"He's an acquaintance," I say.

Lucy is watching me anxiously.

"The deceased registered in the hotel under the name of Miles Acton," Roy announces in a tone that makes him sound like he's testifying in court. "According to one of his passports, his name was also Nikos Mazarakis, Nikos Howard Thornbridge, and Olaf Stein. The front-desk receptionist said a man fitting your description, Marko, entered the hotel yesterday and left about thirty minutes later. He identified himself as Marko Zorn and showed her his police ID."

"Marko," Lucy intervenes, "you should have a union rep with you before you answer any more of Roy's questions."

"You stay out of this, Detective Tanaka."

"It's okay," I say. "I'm happy to answer Roy's questions. I came here to pay my respects to the late Nikos Mazarakis. Except he wasn't 'the late' at the time."

"Why were you here?"

"I heard Nikos was in town and I came to say hello."

"What was your business with him?"

"No business. Just a couple of old acquaintances talking about old times. We had a mutual interest in musical instruments."

"There are bits of wood all over the room," Roy announces. "They look like they come from a fiddle of some kind. What do you want to bet your prints are all over this fiddle?"

"Could be. I told you I was here in this room talking with Nikos Mazarakis. I may have picked up the violin while talking to him."

"What I think happened," Roy says, "was you and your 'old acquaintance' got into an argument and you hit him on the head with the fiddle. Then you strangled him."

"Why would I do that?"

"I don't know. I don't know why you do any of the things you do. You're already a suspect in the murder of Victoria West and in the murder of that book-writer fellow. Now you're connected directly with this victim—whatever his real name is—who was clearly an international criminal."

"Roy," Lucy says with unsuppressed satisfaction, "when did this murder take place?"

"Approximately two hours ago."

"Marko couldn't have been involved," Lucy says. "He's been with me for the last few hours."

Roy looks seriously deflated. Lucy's exaggerated the time we spent at the shooting range and viewing the CCTV tapes, but I'm not going to point that out.

"Satisfied?" Lucy demands angrily.

"I'm not finished with you, Zorn," Roy sputters. "I have a lot more questions. Did you know your friend carried a gun?"

"He was not my friend, just an acquaintance."

"He had a Browning automatic with him," Roy announces. "Loaded but not fired. And a Luger, a real antique. Also loaded. And a sawed-off shotgun next to his bed. A real music lover, wouldn't you say?"

I can only shrug

"Take a close look at the body," Roy says, trying to get his edge back. "Maybe it'll jog your memory."

Nikos is spread on the floor, half enclosed in a body bag.

"Cause of death?" I ask Hanna.

"Almost certainly strangulation. Subject to confirmation at the lab."

"Same as the guard at the theater?" I ask.

"The MO looks identical," Hanna says. "I've found an interesting item,"

Hanna holds up a transparent evidence bag. "A single strand of hair," she says. "Quite long. Blond. Certainly not the victim's."

"Can you get a DNA sample from the root?" I ask.

"There is no root. This is not real human hair. It's almost certainly a wig."

Nikos said Domino never left loose ends. It looks as though Nikos was a loose end.

I lean close to what's left of Nikos. A thin wire is wrapped tightly around his neck.

"What's that around his neck?" Roy asks, looking over my shoulder

"I'd say it's a violin E string."

CHAPTER THIRTY

MEL GIFFORD STRIDES past the "Train Arrivals and Departures" sign in Washington's Union train station. Lieutenant Bonifacio has dropped me there, and I've told him to stand down until I call him. He reluctantly agreed. I need him out of the way: his presence would have compromised my exchange with Mel.

Mel's eyes flick back and forth impatiently, looking for me in the crowd. He can't be missed. He stands six foot three and cuts an imposing figure and has heavy, expressive eyebrows. I've seen Mel in court looking almost magisterial, pacing in front of a jury box, defending his clients charged with racketeering, fraud, arson, and, occasionally, murder. His eyebrows rise and fall in shock when an opposing attorney dares to object to something. He's fun to watch in action.

It took major cajolery and threats on my part, including calling in some favors, to get Mel Gifford to come to Washington rather than meet me in New York. I'd already taken a day away to visit Asa in the SuperMax prison, and I don't want to be away from Nina any more than I have to. At the moment she's in an interview with CNN inside the embassy, then she'll be getting ready to go to the reception at the Lincoln Memorial, where I'll be present to add protection. For the moment she's surrounded by security in the embassy and is safe.

This meeting with Mel is essential. To do what I have to do—to scare Mel speechless—I need to be face-to-face with him so I can reel him in.

Mel is accompanied by a young woman: lithe, with curly blond hair and a figure that stops traffic. She wears a tight-fitting, tartan miniskirt with matching vest and stiletto-heeled shoes.

"This better be good, pal," Mel says as he wades toward me through the crowd of passengers arriving from New York. He does not look happy. As a matter of principle, he does not like to talk to cops and he does not like to leave New York. And he especially doesn't like talking to me in some foreign city like Washington. We've crossed paths from time to time, so he's learned I'm not someone he wants to antagonize. But he has an overwhelming need to know why a DC cop wants to warn a New York attorney urgently about an immediate threat to the five New York Mafia families.

I hold out my hand to the pretty blond lady. "I'm Marko Zorn."

We shake hands. She has a firm grip.

"Nice to meet you, Mr. Zorn. I'm Gloria Felt. I've heard so much about you." She smiles sweetly, but her eyes are hard and intelligent. I decide I better not mess with her.

"Gloria's my right-hand man," Mel announces, laughing at his little joke.

Gloria looks sour.

"Let's get outta here," he says. "This place is worse than Penn Station. Is there anywhere around here we can get a decent drink? We were on the Acela and the levee was dry."

"Why didn't you take a flight out of La Guardia?" I ask as I lead them to the main station doors.

"Mel's afraid of flying," Gloria whispers to me under her breath.

Gloria's new to me. I can't quite figure the relationship between these two. She speaks with a pronounced Long Island accent and looks smart. For now, that's all I've got to go on.

"There's a place nearby," I say. "The coffee's okay. I'd steer clear of the food."

I take Mel and Gloria to a bar across the street. They're both visibly shocked at the ambiance and wince at the loud, pulsing music on the loudspeakers. The place is almost empty except for one guy at the bar, nursing a beer. We take a seat at a table in the corner far from the bar.

Gloria wrinkles her nose. "What's that smell?"

"Don't ask," I say.

"Can we get the management to turn down the sound?" she asks.

"The noise is a good thing, honey." Mel says. "If Zorn's wired, whoever's on the other end won't be able to hear a damn word we say."

A middle-aged woman with big hair shows up at our table to take our orders. Mel asks for a Manhattan. Gloria and I pass.

Gloria looks around at the bar with distaste. "What a dump," she says. "You come here often?"

"It suits me," I reply.

"What's this about?" Mel asks loudly over the music. "You said you had to tell me something about a threat to one of my clients. Why couldn't you just come see in my office in New York to tell me? It's a lot nicer than this hole."

"I'm busy."

"Ever heard of the telephone?"

"Not good for what I have to say."

Mel heaves himself forward. "Understand, I don't normally travel farther than 100th Street. Four hours on a goddamn train. Who rides on a train anymore? This had better be good."

"You won't be disappointed. There's something your clients need to know," I tell him. "Something that might involve the United States Attorney for the Southern District of New York."

Mel winces at the words "the United States Attorney" as if I'd uttered an obscenity. Gloria, who's been slumped in her chair looking bored, sits up and studies me closely. She tugs modestly at her mini-skirt that only draws attention to her shapely legs. I make an effort to keep my eyes politely averted.

"Could you be more specific?" Mel says. "What is it my clients need to know?"

"Some of them may soon be in serious trouble."

The woman with big hair serves Mel's Manhattan. "You want peanuts?" she asks but doesn't wait for an answer and leaves.

The glass doesn't look clean. This is not a Manhattan kind of place.

"What is it you want to tell us, Detective?" Gloria is losing patience. "We've come a long way to accommodate your schedule. Mel had to clear his calendar for the day. Not good."

"I thought Guido Profaci might have a special interest in what I have to say."

"I've never heard of anybody by the name of Guido Profaci," Mel says.

"The law firm of Gifford and Sullivan is listed as counsel for Guido Profaci in seven criminal cases a few years ago. Did I get that wrong?"

"What business is it of yours who our clients are, Detective?" Gloria asks. "That kind of information is confidential. Attorney-client privilege, you know."

"I doubt that your client list is privileged, Ms. Felt. But, just as a hypothetical, let's say you had some association with Mr. Profaci. Perhaps you'd like to pass along some information to him about what one of his contract employees is up to."

"That might not be practical," Mel observes. "Profaci's not available these days. He was last seen at the bottom of the East River. I could arrange a personal appointment with him if you want."

"I believe, in the past, Mr. Profaci, on behalf of the people he repre-sented, made use of the services of a certain individual."

"Understand," Gloria says firmly, "we do not acknowledge that Mr. Profaci was ever a client of the Gifford and Sullivan law firm or that we have ever had any dealings with that individual. Or that he ever existed. And, in addition, Mr. Profaci was a beloved member of the community and a respected businessman, involved in construction, and he has an unblemished record. Check the Better Business Bureau. You'll see."

"This Profaci character was known as a consigliore to the Commission." I say.

Gloria actually smiles at that. Gloria is easily amused. "The Commission?" she asks. "What Commission?"

"I understand the Commission is a group of men who coordinate the activities of the Five Mafia Families in New York and in Chicago."

"Then you understand wrong," she fires back. "There is no such thing as the Commission. There is no such thing as the Five Families. There is no such thing as the Mafia. It's all a myth concocted by the *New York Post*."

"I have reason to believe your client Guido Profaci, over the years, transferred large sums of money to a numbered account at the Bank of Trinidad and Tobago."

"Who is the account holder?" Mel asks. He's getting worried now.

Mel knows me well enough by now to drop the charade that he's never heard of Profaci. He knows that will only irritate me. Gloria, on the other hand, is new to the game, and she hasn't yet learned not to screw around with me.

"I don't know the real name of the account holder. But I believe he's known to some as Domino."

Mel's hand jerks and he spills half his Manhattan. He snatches a paper napkin from the table and dabs at his wrist and jacket cuff.

Gloria's reaction is one of sudden anxiety. She studies me through squinted eyes.

"I thought dominoes was a game people played with little tiles with dots on them." Gloria smiles sweetly at me. "We don't play games."

"I don't play games either," I say.

"Why should we or our clients care about this man, Domino?" Mel asks.

Mel wants me to say more. Gloria, I think, wants me to shut up and stop talking. One of them knows more than the other. One of them may even know who Domino is. One has at least heard of him. Which is which? And who's in charge of this conversation?

I decide I'll be the one in charge. "I thought you and your clients should know that this man, known to some as Domino, may be going through some kind of a midlife crisis."

They both look puzzled.

"What's a midlife crisis?" Gloria asks.

"And why should we care?" Mel asks, still dabbing at his jacket cuff.

"Because one or more of your clients has, over the years, paid Domino large sums of money through Mr. Profaci, for services rendered. For highly irregular services."

"We don't know what you're talking about," Gloria says, without much conviction. "What has this got to do with us or our clients?"

"Within the last few days," I say, "Domino's secret numbered account at the Bank of Trinidad and Tobago has been emptied out. The entire amount, $3,420,000, is gone."

"What happened to the money?" Mel asks.

I've got his full attention now. No more games.

"The entire amount has been deposited to an account in the Chase Manhattan Bank in New York."

For the first time since we sat down, Gloria looks worried. "Why should we be concerned?" Her voice is shaky.

"I think you and your clients should be concerned because it sounds to me like Domino might be going through some kind of crisis of conscience."

I might as well be speaking Urdu. Maybe they're unfamiliar with the "conscience" concept.

"Maybe he's got religion," I say. "Maybe he's gone a little gaga. That can happen to people in his profession. People in his line of work are often unstable. As you know."

"We don't know anything of the sort," Gloria murmurs.

I have them both hooked. Time to draw them in.

"Maybe he's turned over a new leaf," I say. "Maybe he deeply regrets his life of crime and the things he's done for your clients. Maybe he wants to make amends for his past evil deeds. Who knows?"

"Why should I believe you?" Mel asks, hitching his chair even closer to the table and leaning into me so our faces are inches apart.

"Why would I lie?"

"You're a cop. Cops lie. That's what cops do."

"How do we know you're not just making all this up?" Gloria asks. "Maybe there was never an account in this Trinidad bank."

Gloria doesn't know me or she wouldn't ask me that question.

"You or your clients can easily check out what I'm saying. Somebody in the organization has Domino's secret account number so he can make deposits. Somebody who's taken over Mr. Profaci's responsibilities. He can call the bank and ask."

Mel sits back in his chair and looks at his now empty Manhattan. His eyebrows droop.

"All he has to do is make a phone call to the bank," I say encouragingly. "He can confirm in a couple of minutes what I've been saying —that Domino's account has been emptied."

"Where did he put the funds he withdrew?" Mel asks.

"That's the interesting part," I say. "A real surprise."

"Go ahead, surprise me."

"Domino has made a very generous gift to charity."

"Are you kidding me?" Mel asks. He's abandoned the pretense he's never heard of Domino. "Get to the point. Who gets the money?" Mel's fidgety as the enormity of the problem begins to sink in.

"Domino has created a scholarship fund for the University of Notre Dame."

"Jesus," Mel blurts. "No way."

"Is Domino even Catholic?" Gloria asks.

"Let me show you something." I remove a folded sheet of paper from my jacket pocket. It's the FAX I received this morning at the café. I spread it out on the table in front of Mel and Gloria.

Mel puts on a pair of bifocal glasses and leans over the table to study the paper. "What's this?"

"It's a press release from somebody called the Reverend Timothy Sullivan on behalf of the Board of Fellows of the University of Notre Dame. It's announcing the pledge of a gift to the University of $3,000,000 to establish a scholarship endowment for ex-felons and people with problems with the law in their youth. It's to be called the Domino Scholarship."

Mel is sweating visibly now.

"The Reverend Sullivan says the donor wishes to remain anonymous," I explain. "He then bangs on about forgiveness, mercy, and redemption. It's very inspirational."

Mel and Gloria look at me open-mouthed. The fish is caught. Time to pull it in and gut it.

"Is Notre Dame's going along with this?" Mel asks at last. "Seeing as how Domino is what he is?"

"The University knows nothing about Domino. As far as they're concerned, Domino is just a name. All they know is that some generous donor who wants to remain anonymous has made a substantial pledge to the University. From what I hear, the University is delighted with the gift and with the program. They may even name a chapel in Domino's honor."

"Oh, my God." Gloria buries her head in her hands.

"Why would Domino do such a crazy thing?" Mel asks.

"I can't answer that. I've never met this Domino and I know nothing about him. But it sounds to me like Domino may have become a new man. Admirable, don't you think?"

"You think maybe Domino's gone crazy?" Gloria asks.

"I can't say what his mental condition is. And I certainly have no idea what else he's going to do. Maybe he still observes *omertà,* the code of silence, in which case your clients have nothing to worry about. But personally, I wouldn't count on that."

It's time for the gutting knife.

"What if Domino decides," I ask, "to talk to the US Attorney? Or the Manhattan DA's office about contracts he's carried out for one or more of the Five Families. To clear his conscience. That would be a major headache for some people."

"Gotta make a phone call," Mel says suddenly, then, to Gloria: "Book us on the next flight to New York." He looks a bit frantic. "Send copies of that press release thing to everyone on the Commission. Tell them to set up a meeting for tonight."

Mel rushes out of the bar and onto the sidewalk. Gloria gets on her phone and makes flight arrangements. I watch Mel through the dirty front window as he talks into his cell phone, reading from the press release. His face is red.

Gloria puts away her cell phone. "Who the fuck are you?" she asks.

"I'm an officer with the Metropolitan DC Police Department."

"Let me rephrase that question: Why are you giving us this information? Why is a police officer offering us a warning, and through us, to our clients? That raises all kinds of red flags for me."

"Maybe I'm just being a good citizen."

"In our business, there's no such thing as a good citizen. Do you know Domino? Did he tell you about giving his money to charity?"

"I've never spoken with Domino and never met him . . . not that I know of. I don't even know what he looks like.

"The truth is, I sense that Domino has been close to me. I feel certain he's been watching me. We may even have met. Maybe even have talked. He could be that lone man sitting at the bar drinking a Coors. How would I know?"

"What's in this for you?" Gloria asks. "I don't believe there's such a thing as a free lunch. What's your angle?"

"Domino has become something of a personal problem for me. I'd like to see him closed down. Or, at least, forced to take cover for a few days."

"If what you told Mel about Domino turns out to be true,'" Gloria says, "some of Mel's clients will be happy to close Domino down. Disloyalty is frowned upon in their world."

I get to my feet. "Understand, I never asked you or your clients to do anything about Domino. I hope that's clear."

"Of course you didn't."

As I leave the bar, I wave at Mel, who's still on his phone. He's preoccupied and doesn't wave back. I'm pretty sure that within minutes somebody in his organization will be on the phone to the Bank of Trinidad and Tobago to confirm what I told him. And probably about the Notre Dame scholarship, as well. That will be a dead end, of course. They will never find out who anonymously pledged the funds to create the Domino scholarship.

The next step will be an emergency meeting of the Commission to decide what to do about Domino. Finding Domino will not be easy. The mob has never had direct contact with the man, probably has no description of him and doesn't know where he's hiding. But at least the word will be out on the street that the mob is after him. Domino will know he's a hunted man. Even if he avoids the mob's clutches in the short term, he's going to have to hunker down and stay out of sight. At least for a time. That should cramp his style.

I hope.

And give me the time. I now know the only way to guarantee Nina's safety is to eliminate Domino. Even if I get Nina out of the country, Domino, and his masters, will be waiting for her when she returns to Montenegro where they will certainly try to kill her.

Domino must be stopped here in Washington before she gets on that plane.

For the moment she's safe in the embassy with Janet and her security team, but I know her safety won't last long.

CHAPTER THIRTY-ONE

THE LINCOLN MEMORIAL is getting ready to party.

The last thing I did before leaving home for the reception was to go to my office and open the Mosler safe. From there I selected a weapon appropriate for a diplomatic reception—a black oxide Ruger SR40c 9 mm automatic. It's small and light and won't ruin the drape of my Brioni tuxedo jacket but it carries a big punch. I only hope I won't need to use it. I don't normally carry a gun and I went through some soul-searching before deciding to arm myself this evening. A gunfight in a crowded reception like this would be a disaster. But the risk of an attack against Nina tonight is great. Not to mention me. After what I learned from the decoded message, I knew I had to be armed.

Lieutenant Bonifacio picks me up promptly at my home to take me to the reception at the Lincoln Memorial. I don't mention to him that this evening I'm armed and his presence is not strictly required. I figure an additional police officer may prove an advantage.

The State Department security teams are in place when I arrive: some have bomb-sniffing dogs, and several men and one woman, using high-powered flashlights, are crawling around and under the tables set up to hold food and drinks, looking for explosives. There are several security teams weaving through the area inspecting everything. People from the National Park Service are stationed around the periphery of the Memorial.

The scene is cheerful. Tables have been set out with bunting in the colors of the United States and the Republic of Montenegro. Waiters in tuxedos arrive and lay out plates and flatware and crystal glasses along with buckets of ice and bottles of wine wrapped in colored cloths. A music stage has been set up.

Lincoln and his memorial have never looked so festive.

It's twilight when the caterers appear with their Styrofoam containers and lay out food. There seems to be a lot of grilled meat on skewers, which I assume is some specialty from Montenegro and smells delicious. Chafing dishes are fired up and large platters are heaped with stuffed grape leaves and shrimp dishes.

Waiters prepare to circulate with trays filled with food and drink.

There will be armed security men and women who will move discreetly among the guests. Fat lot of good that will do, I think. This is the worst possible place for security. Janet is deploying her troops as best she can. She does not look happy. It's beginning to get dark and lights are turning on, bathing the reception area in a warm glow. The caterers are followed soon after by a group of men and women carrying musical instruments.

Lucy and several of the more presentable members of the DC homicide squad arrive to serve as backups to Janet's main security team.

"Are you armed?" I ask Lucy. She opens her blue linen jacket, revealing her Glock 26 9 mm. Her appearance is smart and professional and she looks calm, but I'm not fooled. She's tense and uneasy. I hadn't intended to ask her to join the protection detail this evening, but she insisted on taking part. Of course, from her perspective, tonight is a test. She needs to prove to me and to her fellow detectives she's up to the job. Most of all, she needs to prove this to herself.

Janet was at first not pleased with my idea of using police officers to provide extra security. She's convinced the police are cowboys who will shoot anything that moves, particularly anything that looks different or funny. I expect she has nightmares of my guys arresting the ambassador of Nigeria or shooting the foreign minister of Nepal. After once again surveying the reception site, she has reluctantly agreed to a police presence—at a distance.

I did not include Hanna in our police contingent. She's not qualified in small arms, and her Orioles cap would not have fit in with the high-fashion couture favored by the rich and famous invited here this evening. But Bonifacio is a real addition.

The Ruger is comfortably tucked in a holster under my left arm.

I confer with Janet and we agree my people will help control the periphery, taking their positions at the bottom of the grand steps leading up to the Memorial and at the VIP entrances. Janet has had wooden barriers set up at the foot of the steps so no wayward tourist will wander in.

I stand near the bandstand and listen to musicians tuning up. Some are dressed in conventional musician getups for events such as this—black suits and white shirts and black bow ties for the men, the women in long, ankle-length, black gowns. They'll be the ones to perform familiar show tunes and dance standards. A separate group of musicians are dressed in what look to be some eastern European or Balkan outfits, with shiny, knee-length boots and puffy-sleeve blouses.

I stand next to one of the musicians, who's smoking a joint held in his curled fist, to keep it invisible.

"Did they fly you in from Montenegro for this event?" I ask.

The man shakes his head. "We all come from around here. I'm from Baltimore."

"There's a Montenegrin community there?"

"Big enough to support a small music group like ours. We play mostly at weddings. You know, the old folks eat food from the old country, dance some of the old dances, embarrass the teenage kids by making them dress in traditional costumes. The old folks love it." He drags on his invisible joint.

"You're from Montenegro?"

"My mom and dad were. They came to this country to escape the Drach regime."

A tall, young man carrying an accordion case on his shoulder stops beside us. He's costumed in the ethnic getup: black jodhpur-like pants, a white shirt, and maroon vest. "Are you the guy who's supposed to get the music parts?" he asks, holding up a fistful of music sheets.

"Where's Georgi?" the man with the joint asks.

"Couldn't make it," the accordion guy says. "Took a bar mitzvah gig. Asked me to sub tonight. Where do I go?"

"Join the others on the stand. I'll take one sheet. Give the rest to the others; I'll join you in a minute."

The man nods and hurries away to join the other musicians on the bandstand.

"We're supposed to play the national anthem of Montenegro tonight. None of us know it; it changes every few years. The embassy supplied us with copies of the new scores."

He shows me the music sheet he's holding. The lyrics are in a language I can't read and the score looks like a bouncy quick-march.

"Shouldn't you practice this?" I ask.

"We'll fake it as we go along," he says. "We do this all the time. Nobody knows the difference."

Somebody from the bandstand calls out, and the man drops his partially smoked joint and crushes it under his boot into the ground. "We're about to start." He smiles and climbs up into the bandstand. "Enjoy the show," he says.

A moment later, the musicians in formal getups begin to play a medley of show tunes.

The first guests are arriving. All are well-dressed; some look vaguely familiar. I recognize a few senators and congresspeople. The men wear tuxes or are in formal dress uniforms, the women are in long dresses. A famous TV actor is surrounded by admiring fans who ought to know better. There's a tall African American who looks familiar. A woman standing near me says, in an awed voice, that he's a famous rock star.

The place is quickly filling up, with clusters concentrated around the open bars. There's a lot of chatter and careless laughter.

As the band plays a chirpy foxtrot, I mix with the crowd, looking for faces that don't belong. The weather is warm and pleasant and the atmosphere is cheerful and I see no danger.

Abruptly the band stops playing the foxtrot and the guys with the accordions strike up some lively ethnic dance piece. Maybe it's the Montenegro national anthem. Who knows? This must be the signal that Nina Voychek and her entourage have arrived. She's dressed in a floral embroidered evening gown with a white silk scarf around her neck. An excited stirring spreads among the guests, and I move toward the VIP entrance.

Nina enters. To her side is her ambassador, leaning down and whispering into her ear. Behind her follow Janet and Viktor Savich and the guy with the steel-frame eyeglasses, the deputy chief of mission.

A man—I'm guessing from the State Department—rushes up to Nina Voychek and there's a lot of happy banter. The ambassador and the State Department guy lead Nina into the thick of the crowd, where there's discreet applause and burbling from the distinguished guests. Everyone looks happy—except Janet and Savich, who don't like the scene at all. Nina and her group move through the crowd, pausing long enough for a few polite exchanges with the distinguished guests.

Carla Lowry, the chief of the FBI's Criminal Investigative Division, is speaking with some dignitary in a tuxedo who wears a raft of medals on his chest. To my surprise, Carla leaves her conversation companion and works her way through the crowd toward me.

Her eyes dart, briefly, at the small bulge under my left arm. She knows I'm armed but says nothing.

"The reception seems to be going well," Carla says.

"It's still early."

"My people in Chicago have picked up your man, Jovanovich, and he's tucked in, safe and sound."

"I appreciate that."

"What can you tell me about a man called Nikos Mazarakis?" Carla asks.

"He's dead."

"I know that. I also know that you visited him in his hotel room before he passed away. The MO is close to that of the murdered code clerk from the Montenegro embassy. What were you doing with the victim?"

"Visiting an old friend."

"Nikos Mazarakis is, or was, nobody's friend."

"Acquaintance, then."

"He was a dangerous man involved in a nasty business over many years. What was he doing here in the US?"

"He was acting as an advance man for whoever is planning the assassination of Prime Minister Voychek. I met with Nikos to ask him who was paying the bills."

"Did he tell you?"

"He didn't know or was too frightened to tell me."

"It looks like he had good reason to be frightened."

"He did confirm that the assassin is a man known as Domino."

Carla catches her breath. "That's new."

"Do you know anything about this Domino?" I ask.

"I've heard of him, of course. Over the years his name has cropped up. Not in a good way."

"Nikos told me Domino has been contracted to carry out the three killings."

"Three?" Carla asks. "I thought there was just Nina Voychek."

Carla glances over her shoulder, looking at the crowd. Nina is nowhere in sight. "Who are the other targets?"

"I'll get back to you on that," I say.

"Watch your back." Carla disappears into the shadows and into the happy throng.

I stop by one of the three open bars and study the servers. They look like all the other servers in every reception I've ever been to: mostly college kids making a few extra bucks. The waiters carry trays of food and napkins and toothpicks in little glass bowls. I see nothing wrong.

I also feel sure I'm missing something.

Janet Cliff passes by and gives me a tight smile. I catch a glimpse of Nina in a huddle with Secretary of State Cross and her ambassador. They're standing at the base of the Lincoln statue and seem to be having an intense conversation. I decide not to interrupt them.

I stand at the top of the grand stairs and inspect the police barrier at the bottom: more a psychological barrier than a real one, I think. Nothing a determined killer couldn't get through.

A young couple stops near me and the man takes pictures of the crowd using a Canon SLR with a large telephoto lens. I move away. I don't like my picture taken. By anyone, for any reason.

"Say, buddy," the young man calls to me. "Can you take our picture? Midge and me?" He hands me his camera without waiting for my answer and instructs me on how to take a picture even though all these cameras function more or less the same.

"We've set it for telephoto, you know, us in front." The young couple line up for their photograph. She must be about twenty, pretty, with curly, brown hair. She wears a nice frock she probably bought for this special occasion. The man looks like a mid-level bureaucrat who managed to wrangle an invitation to the reception to prove to his girlfriend how important he is.

"Can you try to get us with some famous people in the background?" the young man asks. "Maybe the rock star?"

The couple smiles broadly, leaning into one another so they can be centered in the picture frame. They have beautiful teeth.

I peer through the viewfinder. "I'll count to three."

I pan over the crowd, foreshortened through the telephoto lens, and see Nina and her entourage in the distance. Carla Lowry is engaged in an intense interchange with some senator.

Then I see something I shouldn't be seeing. Standing in the shadow of one of the massive columns that fronts the Lincoln Memorial is a tall, sinewy man with a narrow face and close-set eyes talking to a second man. As suddenly as I see them, the two men move into the shadows. But before they disappear, I recognize the tall man and I toss the camera to the couple and sprint into the crowd, drawing my Ruger.

"You never said 'three,'" the pretty woman calls out indignantly. "I wasn't ready."

I dive through the tangle of guests.

"That was rude," the young man yells after me.

The tall man I saw through the camera is thirty feet away now and is emerging from behind a table laden with champagne bottles. The second man I saw with him stands just to one side. The tall man sees me, turns, and disappears. The second man raises his right hand—wrapped in a thick, white towel—and points at me.

At that moment, a waiter steps in front of me. "Curried shrimp, sir?" he asks before crumpling to the ground and dying, his silver tray and shrimp dropping to the stone floor with a clatter. A large red stain seeps through the front of the waiter's starched white shirt.

It's horrible but there's nothing I can do for him. He's gone.

I sprint after the shooter, who's ducked behind a large tent and, for a moment, I lose him. The crowd's thicker here, knotted around one of the bars. The people in the crowd surging forward are trying to catch a glimpse of the famous Nina Voychek, and for a moment, they give Nina and her entourage physical protection. Nina's almost invisible in the scrum of people surrounding her, making her an impossible target.

I see Janet Cliff and gesture to her to follow me to where I think the shooter is headed.

"Shooter," I yell. "Male. Five nine. Shot one of the waiters. The shooter's somewhere behind that tent."

Janet's on her radio calling for reinforcements, giving directions. She runs ahead of me, her weapon drawn, streaking through the crowd that still does not yet sense something's gone wrong.

The shooter is using a weapon with a sound suppresser and no one heard the shot.

We swing around the corner of the musicians' stand and we're almost on top of the tall man. He stands at the far end of a table laden with wineglasses and buckets of crushed ice and he fires at us, but it's a wild shot and misses. Janet takes aim at the shooter, but she can't return fire safely. Too many people are crowded behind him.

The shooter grabs the edge of the table and heaves it over, upending it onto us, and we're for a moment stopped, showered with wine-glasses and ice.

We catch up to him at the top of the steps that lead down to the Mall. Lucy is approaching us from our left, Glock in hand. My heart stops. I think he's going to turn and fire at her.

From behind me there's a laugh and the pretty brunette girl I'd seen before, oblivious to what's happening around her, brushes past me to assume a pose at the top of the steps, with the Reflecting Pool, the Washington Monument and the US Capitol in the distance. Ahead of us is the Mall, black in evening shadows. Surrounding it is a necklace of light of the city of Washington.

The shooter is now halfway down the grand staircase, intending to make a break for it at the bottom of the steps. I remember him now—the man who so graciously offered to share his cab in the rain when I was headed for the Montenegrin embassy. Standing at the bottom of the grand staircase is Lieutenant Bonifacio. He has drawn his service weapon and is waiting, feet apart, in a shooter's stance. He's too far away to get a good shot; impossible with all the people standing at the top behind us. But nobody is going to get past the lieutenant.

The tall man stops and spins around and fires. Janet crumples, dropping her gun to the ground, as she falls to one knee, grasping her abdomen, spurting red blood through her clenched fingers.

Lucy's ten feet away with an unobstructed shot at the shooter.

"Lucy!" I yell. "Shoot! Shoot now."

She freezes.

The pretty girl with the curly brown hair who wanted me to take her picture a few minutes ago must have heard me call out and she moves away, instinctively.

I aim the Ruger.

The shooter's head explodes and he drops, rolling down the stone steps, leaving a long streak of red behind him.

Lieutenant Bonifacio is bounding up the steps toward me. He must be afraid I've been hurt. I gesture for him to stop. There is no need for him to come further.

The pretty young woman, standing a few feet away from me, stares at me, openmouthed, speechless. There are specks of blood on her nice new frock—Janet's blood.

CHAPTER THIRTY-TWO

RICK TALBOT, JANET'S number two, eases Janet to the ground, pressing a compress into her abdomen wound. "The shooter?" he demands.

I nod at the corpse splayed far down the steps. "Dead. Head shot."

Lucy crouches at my side. "Are you okay, Boss?"

Her face is ashen. I don't have time to answer.

"Any other shooters?" Talbot yells to me. He's already on his phone calling for backup and ambulances.

"At least one other. Big man, bald. Take care of Janet," I shout. "I'll get the prime minister out of here."

I holster my Ruger and grab Lucy by the arm and we push our way through the crowd. A woman somewhere screams and I hear voices yelling behind me. It's beginning to dawn on the guests that something terrible has happened.

"Out!" I yell when I reach Nina and her entourage. "Into the car."

Viktor Savich grabs Nina's arm. Nina starts to protest, but she goes with us as we run through the VIP exit, surrounded by Janet's security men, who provide an impenetrable barrier as we push through the crowd. Somewhere in the distance, I hear a waltz.

Savich pulls open the door to the limousine and pushes Nina inside.

"Take one of the cruisers," I call to Lucy. "Go back to headquarters."

"Marko, I blew it."

"Later," I tell her. "We'll talk later."

I'm in the limousine and it's already moving, the two flags on the fenders making us an obvious target. No time to remove them now. We're preceded by police cruisers, their sirens screaming. The lights inside the limousine are turned off, and we sit in total darkness. I know the limousine has bulletproof glass, but that's no comfort. A round like the 338 Magnum cartridge I found across from my house can penetrate bulletproof glass. Out the back window I see VIPs and their security teams tumble through the exits, trying to find their cars and drivers.

"What happened?" Nina whispers.

"The assassin," I say. "He shot Janet."

"Is she going to be all right?"

"She was wounded. I don't know how bad. Her people are taking care of her."

Nina covers her mouth with her hands.

"What happened to the shooter?" Savich asks.

"Dead," I say. "It looks like the killer had an accomplice."

In the dark, Nina takes my hand in hers. Her hand trembles as she whispers, "Am I to have another death on my conscience? God, please keep her safe."

"She was doing her duty," I say. "She knew the risks."

Nina squeezes my hand and we drive in the dark for a few minutes.

"Did the shooter say anything before he died?" Savich demands.

"He was dead before he hit the ground," I say. "It was a head shot."

"Janet saved my life," Nina Voychek murmurs from the dark of the limousine beside me. "If Janet hadn't shot that man, he would have killed me."

"That's right," Savich answers.

"She was doing her job," I say to her. "That's what she signed up for."

"Was Yulia doing her job when they tortured and strangled her?" Nina asks.

Ten minutes later, we pull into the embassy garage and Nina, closely surrounded by her security guards, is rushed upstairs to her suite. The rest of us follow, and Nina retreats into her private quarters, followed by Savich and Ambassador Lukshich.

After half an hour, the ambassador and Savich emerge. "The arrangements for tomorrow will proceed without change," the ambassador announces to the waiting security detail. "The prime minister will depart for Dulles airport tomorrow afternoon as scheduled. Exactly at 4:10 p.m. The schedule is very tight and we must leave on time. Detective Zorn and Mr. Talbot of the State Department Diplomatic Security Service will accompany the minister to the airport."

The ambassador smiles a thin smile. "I must report tonight's incident to my government. Please forgive me." He hurries off.

"How is Nina?" I ask Savich.

"Shaken, of course. But she's a strong woman and will manage. She's very concerned about Janet Cliff and may demand to be taken to the hospital tonight. I know this woman. Remember when she disappeared and we found her in the embassy kitchen? She's independent-minded and she does what she pleases. Now I must join the ambassador. He will have last-minute instructions for me."

Savich leaves me with seven members of the State Department security detail in the waiting room, all armed. They all expect there will be another attempt. Tonight or tomorrow. A man named Ludlow stands in front of the doors leading to Nina's private suite, holding a shotgun.

The security detail has taken over the room outside of Nina's private suite as a command post where members of different shifts will stand guard. Some of the security team stand at the top of the stairs. Two men are stationed at the embassy entrance to see that no unauthorized person gets into the building.

The door to the waiting room opens and a member of the embassy staff—a very tall, thin man in his sixties, wearing a tuxedo of all things—wheels in a trolley with what looks like a full dinner and heads to the door to Nina's private suit.

I tell the man to stop while I inspect the trolley.

"This is for Madam Voychek," the man in the tuxedo protests. "The Ambassador instructed the kitchen to prepare a dinner for the prime minister."

"I'll take it into the prime minister," I say.

The tall man looks annoyed. "We must not let it get cold."

"I'll take full responsibility," I say.

He nods but does not look happy.

The dinner consists of a thick sirloin steak with roasted potatoes and asparagus. To one side is a silver bowl with béchamel sauce. A silver wine cooler holds a bottle of Dom Pérignon champagne, frosted with condensation. Next to it stand four champagne flutes. To one side is a stack of heavy linen napkins embroidered with the seal of Montenegro and cutlery.

I examine the trolley carefully. I pick up the tray. There's nothing suspicious underneath. I examine the underside of the trolley and find no bomb or deadly scorpion lurking there. The sirloin steak looks harmless if a bit overdone. I sniff the asparagus and detect nothing amiss. The seal on the champagne bottle is unbroken. I sample a small portion of the béchamel sauce with a silver spoon and hesitate. There's something off. I can't be sure what it is, but I'm not sending the béchamel into Nina.

I give the béchamel sauce to Rick Talbot and ask him to have it delivered to the police lab as soon as possible for testing. It's probably harmless, but I'm in no mood to take chances.

I tell the man in the tuxedo to bring another full dinner exactly the same as that prepared for the prime minister, minus the béchamel sauce. Immediately.

The server looks anxious. "I can't do that. Only the ambassador can order a dinner like this. I would have to consult His Excellency."

"Then you'd better get a move on and consult His Excellency. If another identical meal is not here within twenty minutes, I will be obliged to consult His Excellency in person. And that will annoy us both."

The man in the tuxedo makes a small bow and leaves the room. I tell the members of the security detail to help themselves to the dinner on the trolley, minus the champagne.

I call the hospital and am told Janet's in surgery and the doctors believe she will survive.

Twenty minutes later the man in the tuxedo appears again with an identical trolley with the same dinner items. He looks terribly put-upon. "Will that be all, sir?" he asks with the tone of arrogant obsequiousness all professional waiters master.

"That will be all. I'll see to it that the prime minister gets her dinner."

After inspecting the second trolley and its contents, I knock gently on the door to Nina's suite and hear her say "Come," I open the door and push the trolley into her sitting room.

She's on a couch in the same clothes she wore at the reception. Her face is pale and drawn, her hair loose and disheveled. One strawberry-blond curl falls across her forehead.

"What's that?" she asks, almost smiling when she sees me.

"I think it's your dinner, Nina."

"I never ordered dinner."

"Compliments of His Excellency, the ambassador."

She stands up and studies the trolley and its contents, scowling slightly. She lifts the cover from the steak and potatoes. "What was he thinking? I can't eat anything. Not after what happened tonight at the reception. Would you please take this away? I don't want it in my room." She slams the cover down.

I start to wheel the trolley out the door.

"Please keep the champagne. And a glass. Two glasses, please. I wouldn't want to see the champagne go to waste."

I push the trolley out into the waiting area and return to Nina's suite.

"Please join me," she says.

I shut the door. "How is Janet?"

"She's in surgery. The doctors are optimistic."

"Thank God." Nina sits back onto the couch and presses her hands to her face. "I've been so worried about her."

Nina seems to crumple. "Viktor Savich told me the assassin was killed."

I'm not sure how much Savich has told her or how much she knows about what happened at the reception this evening. She's obviously deeply shaken. Her hands are trembling. I don't want to see her go to pieces. I doubt Nina Voychek has ever gone to pieces.

"I think I could use a drink," she says. "Would you be so kind as to open the champagne? Two glasses."

I peel off the foil wrapper from the Dom Pérignon, twist out the cork until it makes a satisfying pop.

"Stay with me for a while," she says. "I need someone to talk to."

I fill two flutes with champagne. Nina and I toast one another.

"*Nazdravlje,*" she says.

"To life," I reply as we touch glasses. "Would you like some music? I find it sometimes helps settle my nerves."

Nina looks around the room, almost helplessly. "There's a TV here. And some speakers. I haven't figured out how they work."

I take my phone from my pocket, switch on the Apple Music, and turn on Bluetooth to connect my phone to the room speaker.

"What's your pleasure? Rock and Roll? Jazz? Big Band? How about some Wagner?"

"I've had quite enough Wagnerian *Sturm und Drang* this evening. Can you get dance music on that telephone of yours?"

"I can get any kind you want."

"When I was growing up in Montenegro, I lived in a small village in the mountains, our only entertainment then was our local village festivals. Of course, we didn't call it entertainment. Four or five times a year, the village would organize a festival. Honoring some saint, celebrating spring or harvest time. There would be music and traditional food. And dancing. We would dance round dances. We call it *kolo* dance. I don't suppose you can get one of those dances on your phone."

"I don't think my music app is that broad minded."

"When I was at Columbia, I used to go out dancing in the evenings with the kids in my class."

"What kind of dances did you like?"

She takes a sip of champagne. "I took dance lessons. Can you believe? Actually, I loved it. Twice a week I'd go to a dance studio on upper Broadway and get swung around the dance floor by some would-be Latin lothario. It was a different world then. Can you find a tango on your gadget?"

I hunt through the menu and find not one but several tangos. I switch it on, and we are transported to Argentina, or at least some aural facsimile of Argentina. There is the sound of an accordion, a violin, and some bass string instrument.

Nina smiles happily.

I stand, bow, and hold out my arms in what is supposed to be a Latin American gesture of romantic courtesy. Probably something I once saw in an old Hollywood movie. I'm only missing the ruffles on my shirt and brilliantine in my hair to complete the image. This is as close as I can come to being a Latin lothario.

Nina rises with a broad smile, and our bodies entwine, my left hand lightly touching her waist, my right hand holding her hand. She dances with suppleness and grace, her body comfortable in my arms. As we get into the rhythm of the dance, Nina begins to improvise—a swing, a deep dip. I know how to dance the tango, but she's way ahead of me. She has the dance in her blood.

We move around the floor of her suite, trying to avoid bumping into the furniture. We almost collide with the couch, but Nina skillfully swings around just in time without losing the beat.

A phone somewhere in the room rings and she stops.

"Excuse me." Nina stops and looks at the caller ID on the phone.

"Sorry. I've got to take this call. It's the President of the United States."

I turn off the music as she picks up the phone. "Yes, Mr. President . . . I'm just fine, thank you." She looks across the room at me and covers the speaker with one hand. "I need to talk to him. Will you excuse me?"

The evening is over. There'll be no more champagne; no more dancing. I feel a pang of regret. I want to hold her for a little while longer, to feel her lithe body sliding under my hands. I wish Nina would ask me to stay.

I know that's hopeless.

"Good night, Nina. Your security detail is right outside your door. There's no need for you to worry. You're safe tonight."

"Until tomorrow," she whispers, and smiles uncertainly. Then speaks into the phone.

I go to the door and step into the waiting room, glancing one last time at Nina Voychek as she stands, the phone clutched in her hand, speaking urgently. I shut the door silently.

Four members of the State Department security detail are sitting at a small table finishing up what's left of the two meals the man in the tuxedo delivered. A new man named Fergusson stands at the door to Nina's private suite holding the shotgun.

Savich stands by the door, waiting for me. "How is Nina holding up?" he asks.

"She's on the phone with the President. She may be a while."

"There's no need for you to stay here any longer, Detective. I know you've had a taxing day. The security here is tight." He gestures at the squad of armed guards in the room. "I suggest you go home and get some rest. We want you at your best tomorrow when you accompany the prime minister to the airport."

Savich may be right about security inside the embassy. It does seem in good shape. But . . . after this evening's attack at the Lincoln Memorial, I feel unsure.

"You're right, Viktor. I should get some rest."

Savich gives me a warm smile. Then he leaves.

I follow him out the door and head down the marble steps to the reception desk, where the same pimply-faced man I met the first day stands behind the desk, talking to the two security men Rick Talbot stationed at the front door.

Savich unlocks the outer doors, and I walk onto the street. I sense Savich and the others watching me as I leave. I walk two blocks north of the embassy, stopping to be sure no one is following me, then reversing my course and head back, using a different route so no one in the embassy can see me approach.

I stop at the entrance to the embassy garage, where a DC police cruiser is parked, blocking the driveway to prevent any unwanted intruders. I speak for a couple of minutes to the two bored cops, then go to the garage door. To one side a cyber lock has been installed in the concrete wall. I punch in the cyber code 821914 that Savich gave me. There's a clinking sound and the doors rise slowly.

As soon as there's just enough room, I slip under the rising door, stop the door mechanism, and press the Close button.

The garage is dark and I have to use the light from my phone to see my way to the far end. I'm alone. Just the two limousines and me. I move quietly past them and find the door to the embassy. It's unlocked and I step through into a corridor that leads to the elevators and the stairs to the chancery and the residential area.

I skip the elevator. It would make too much noise. Somebody would hear the elevator mechanism and want to find out who's prowling around the embassy this late at night. I take the stairs to the second floor and immediately step back into the waiting room of Nina's suite. The room is as it was when I left it twenty minutes earlier. The security detail has consumed the last vestiges of the second serving of the steak and potatoes.

"Anything happen while I was away?" I ask.

There are a couple of negative grunts.

"Any word from the prime minister?"

"Not a thing," Fergusson, the guard with the shotgun, answers.

I'm tempted to open the door to Nina's private suite and see if she's still on the phone but decide against it. She deserves her privacy. Instead, I collect a blanket from the security detail's room and find an empty couch not far from the entrance to Nina's suite.

"I'm going to try and get some sleep," I tell the security team. "If anything happens, wake me right away." I roll over and shut my eyes. For a while I think about Nina and how she moved when she tangoed.

It's almost six when I wake up. I'm annoyed I slept so late. The members of the security team are now once again at full complement, all heavily armed. They assure me nothing happened overnight.

I wash up in an adjoining bathroom as best I can, run my fingers through my hair, try to get rid of the creases in my clothes, and leave the waiting room.

I once again take the stairs to the street level. I see no one as I go into the garage. I step into the empty garage, cross to the garage doors, punch in the cyber code from the inside, wait for the door to rise, slip under the door, close the door, and walk away briskly onto the street.

There's very little traffic at this early hour: only some delivery vans and a garbage truck. I see a taxi and hail it and I give the driver the address of the embassy of Montenegro. He looks at me funny. "That's two blocks from here. You want me to drive you?"

"If you please."

He shrugs and in a couple of minutes we're there. The embassy receptionist sees me through the glass door.

"Good morning," he says to me. "Did you have a good night?"

"Perfect," I reply.

CHAPTER THIRTY-THREE

"I FUCKED UP." Lucy looks up at me from her coffee, as I take a seat across from her at a table in the police department coffee shop. Her face is drawn and pale. The morning's *Washington Post* is spread out. "Terrorist Attack in Nation's Capital," "Massacre at Lincoln Memorial," the headlines read.

After checking with the security detail posted outside Nina's private suite at the embassy, I decided to return to police headquarters. I was reluctant to leave Nina, but she's well protected by Janet's security team.

"I totally fucked up," Lucy says again.

Several men and women, sitting at nearby tables, eating what passes for breakfast, look up at her in surprise.

Lucy is close to tears. "I just stood there. I had a clear shot at the son-of-a-bitch and I did nothing. Janet was almost killed."

"She's going to be okay."

"You could've been killed. Right there in front of me. I'm turning in my badge today."

"Don't do that. Give yourself some time."

"I lost it last night: I froze. You told me the difference between life and death is hesitation. In a moment of a life-or-death decision, your instinct must kick in—instantly. If you think, you said, you're dead.

Last night on those steps I thought—thought about killing a man. I thought about shooting a man in the head. I couldn't do it. I couldn't pull the trigger. That makes me useless as a cop. You know that."

She looks at me intently. "Marko, I have a question I must ask you."

"Okay."

"It's a question I wanted to ask you on the day I became your partner. Why don't you carry a weapon?"

"Sometimes I do. When it's really necessary. I was armed last night at the reception." I pat the Ruger in its holster under my left arm. "I still am."

"But usually you're unarmed. I'm your partner. I need to know."

"It's complicated."

"I'm sure it is. But the day may come when your partner, whoever that might be, is in danger, and your partner's life may depend on you taking action. I have a right to know what your hang-up with guns is."

I think carefully before I answer. I don't want to reveal more than I have to. I know that would complicate my relationship with Lucy, who's already stressed out about her own failure. At the same time, I know Lucy will not let me get away with some bullshit answer.

"The truth is, I'm not sure I can really trust myself with a gun."

"You're a cop. You've been trained."

"There've been times when I've been in a situation … where I came close to killing someone even though it was unnecessary. There have been situations where I wasn't sure I was in full control of myself."

"But you're the coolest, most controlled person I've ever met. I've seen you in desperate, dangerous situations and I've never seen you lose self-control."

"Control comes with practice and experience."

"What about instinct? Isn't that what you told me I had to trust? My instinct?"

"Instinct has to be trained and controlled—like any other skill."

* * *

My mind goes back to a summer in Maine. I was a few years out of high school when my life changed. I'd spent the day tracking my quarry: the boot prints along a trail led deep into the pine forest. This was a place I knew well. The man I was hunting was a city person; he knew traffic and sidewalks and grocery stores. This was my world, not his.

I'd been hunting in those forests since I was a kid and I knew every thicket and hill and ravine, every place where a hunted man might hide. I never doubted I'd find the man who'd raped and murdered my sister, Rose. I was good at tracking—born to it my dad used to say.

It was late afternoon when I found the man beneath a tree, half hidden in deep afternoon shadows. He was holding a Colt Python pistol. "This ain't no game, son," he said.

"You killed my sister."

He laughs softly. "What are you gonna do about it, boy? Call the sheriff?"

"I'm gonna kill you," I said, and shot the man in the head.

No need to tell Lucy about that afternoon. I've never told anyone what happened that day. That will always be my private memory.

"You've trained yourself to control your instincts?" Lucy asks. "Like some kind of Zen technique? Is that how it works?"

"It takes time and patience and discipline. I'm not sure I'm there yet. That's why I prefer not to carry a gun."

"I don't have the character for that kind of self-discipline," Lucy says. "Which is why I have no future in the police."

"Don't give up," I urge her. "Give it a few more days, at least until we close the Victoria West case. It's your case. See it through to the end."

She makes a helpless gesture. "We're nowhere on the West case. Or on the murder of Aubrey Sands, for that matter. Or the theater guard. And now we have the murder of that man in the hotel room."

"That's Roy's case."

"I've spent hours going through the records of everyone even remotely connected to these killings," Lucy says. "I'm nowhere. We may never close these investigations."

"The murders are all connected. When we close one, we close them all."

"How can you be so certain? I don't see the connection."

"Natalie Esmond told us what one of the connections was when we interviewed her at the theater."

"I don't see it."

"You will. You'll understand when we meet at the theater at one p.m. this afternoon as we planned.

"I've contacted all the major witnesses: the stage manager and Arthur Cantwell. And the director, Garland Taylor, along with the actors Natalie Esmond and Tim Collins. Including that props girl. They've all said they will be there."

"Where will you be until then?"

"I have to interview the people who catered last night's reception and talk to Janet as soon as the doctors will let me see her. I'll join you at the theater at one."

Lucy stands to leave. "The Medical Examiner's office sent photographs of the assassin who was shot last night. They'll be on your phone."

"Don't do anything rash," I say. "Don't quit on me."

CHAPTER THIRTY-FOUR

Tip Top Caterers is located in a small strip mall. Four large white vans are parked out front, each painted with the name "Tip Top" along with an email address and images of balloons and happy bubbles. Inside the small dingy office there is an absence of balloons or happy bubbles. A young black man stands at a long table near the entrance, packing glasses into a cardboard box.

"Are you in charge here?" I ask.

"Do I look like I'm in charge? You want Mrs. Sweet. She's the lady who runs this place."

"And how do I find your Mrs. Sweet?" I ask.

"Melanie," he calls out loudly. "There's a cop here wants to see you."

A door at the back of the room opens and an African American woman emerges, large-bosomed and smiling a broad, friendly smile. She holds two fabric samples in her hands—one pearl white, one a pale pink. "Which do you like, hon?" she asks. "It's for a wedding breakfast. They'll be monogramed of course."

"Is the breakfast inside or outside?" I ask.

"Outside."

"Tented or non-tented?"

"Tented."

"Go for the pearl," I say. "My name is Zorn. Marko Zorn. I'm from Metropolitan Police Homicide."

"You're right, I'll go for the pearl. You're here about that awful business last night at the Lincoln Memorial? What's the world coming to, I ask you." She drops the fabric samples onto a workbench. "A real shame. I lost one of my best servers last night: Manny was his name; I'm just heartbroken about Manny."

"I have some questions about the shooting."

"Then come with me into my boudoir." She leads me through a door into a small cluttered office.

Catalogs are stacked on the desk and floor. The walls are covered with photos of table-settings and flower arrangements. The woman holds out her hand and we shake.

"Melanie Sweet." She sits in a desk chair that squeaks loudly.

"Were you at the reception last night?" I ask.

"Some of my people were there. I had three events last night: a wedding reception, a bar mitzvah, and that business at the Lincoln Memorial. My job is to deal with catastrophes."

"Do you own Tip Top Caterers?"

"Some nice folks at the bank own it, dear. You want to know about the man we hired who shot somebody, I expect."

"What can you tell me about him?"

"Zilch. I've already explained all this several times to your people."

"You've been interviewed by investigators? Were they properly dressed and polite?"

"They were."

"Then they were probably FBI. I'm DC police: a different outfit."

"I told the others. I have no information on who that man was."

"Any paperwork? Any forms he filled out?"

"The other cops took everything. All my records, even my computer and goddamned cell phone! Everything. When do you think I'll get my stuff back?"

"Never. Maybe not even that soon. Tell me what you can remember."

"In addition to our normal catering requirements, we arrange for music groups. Not a problem for a small group with a keyboard. We do that all the time. But the embassy of Montenegro needed a group who could play some of their national music. No big deal. In this case, I started by contacting the musicians' union and the accordion community."

"There's an accordion community?" I ask.

"You better believe there is, dear. I put together the group over the weekend. Then one of the accordion players crapped out on me. He got a better-paying job at a bar-mitzvah. Then, next day this guy shows up saying he's looking for a gig and tells me he plays balalaika and accordion. Bingo! I'm in heaven. He told me he was a student at Penn. Looked okay to me. He had ID's. A Pennsylvania driver's license, too."

"Did he play the accordion for you?"

"You mean like an audition? I never ask for that. I figure who's going to admit to playing an accordion if they don't?"

My cell phone rings. It's Rick Talbot.

"How's Janet?" I ask, motioning for Melanie to wait a sec.

"She's in recovery and is doing well. She insists on talking to you. She wouldn't say what about. Just that she had to see you immediately. Can you come to the hospital? She's in the surgical ICU on the fifth floor. She said it's urgent."

"I've got to leave to go to the hospital," I tell Melanie. "Before I go I want you to look at something." I show her the photo of the assassin on my cell phone taken at the morgue this morning.

"Is this the man you hired?"

"I've never seen this man before in my life," she says.

"This man's name was probably Oleg Kamrof," I say. "I don't think he was a student at Penn."

"What happened to the guy I hired to play the accordion?"

"I'd say he's probably in a landfill somewhere."

CHAPTER THIRTY-FIVE

Lieutenant Bonifacio drops me off at the hospital and I tell him to wait until I call. The reception area is crowded with people carrying flowers and boxes of candy. Some clutch helium balloons saying "Get Well Soon," another balloon announces "It's a Boy." It must be visiting hours and the elevators are packed. I stand for a moment behind a young couple, the woman grasping an enormous teddy bear. I can see right away there's not enough room for the couple, the bear, and me so I take the stairs.

At first glance, the stairwell seems empty and the only sound I hear is my tread on the concrete steps. I'm almost to the third floor when I realize I have company. A large man emerges on the fourth-floor landing and stands motionless, looking down at me, his feet apart, bracing himself. He must be six three. He's heavyset and his bald head gleams in the fluorescent glare of the stairwell lights. He holds a small-caliber pistol in his right hand.

I look over my shoulder. A second man is running up the stairs toward me, two steps at a time. I recognize them as the two men I'd seen in the embassy CCTV film who kidnapped the young code clerk and left her body in a culvert in the rain. I hope it's them. I've been looking forward to meeting them in person.

When the man coming up the stairs sees me, he glances past me at the man on the upper landing, waiting for some signal. His hesitation is fatal.

There's not enough time for me to draw my Ruger. But I don't need to.

For just a second, I have the advantage, and a second is all I need. I spin around and charge down the steps at the man below me.

He looks surprised and braces himself, as he tries to aim his gun, but he's too slow, and I have the advantage of speed and momentum as I lunge into him. My motion lifts him off his feet, and I hold him in a bear hug, his arms pinned to his side. He can't get at his gun, which he drops to the concrete step. I hold him as a shield between me and the big man on the landing above, who's aiming his gun at me.

Then I lift him and twist him over the steel stairway railing, and for a moment he's balanced on top. His face contorts with terror as he realizes what's going to happen when I give him a violent shove and push him into the void. He tries to grab my arm but can't hold on and he falls over the railing with a scream, arms thrashing in terror, headfirst. I don't wait to see him hit the concrete floor three stories below.

I swing around. The big man is running down the stairs toward me. He hesitates as his buddy disappears over the rail. I draw my Ruger from its holster and fire once. At his head. The bald man pitches forward and slides down the steps, stopping a few feet from me, his gun resting on the step below him.

I wonder, does he think about the young woman he murdered on the side of the road? Does he regret what he did? Probably not thinking about much of anything at the moment.

I look up and down the stairs and see no one. No resident is out to grab a quick smoke; no nurse is on her way home after finishing her rounds. I have the stairwell to myself.

I push open the door to the fifth floor and step into a corridor painted pale green. The hall in front of Janet's hospital room is crowded with friends and colleagues from the State Department and the Diplomatic Security Service.

An intern, a powerfully built, black man, stands by the door. "Are you Detective Zorn?" he asks. "Mrs. Cliff said to let you see her as soon as you arrive."

Her intensive-care room is quiet and the lights are dim. Janet lies motionless in her hospital bed, hooked up to tubes and monitors. There's a faint, regular beeping and gurgling sound that I guess is a good sign. Her eyes are closed, and I think she must be asleep. A nurse sentinel stands next to Janet's bed, not allowing anybody near.

The others in the room are a young man who looks like an orderly and a man named Stark I recognize as a member of Janet's security team. He's there to protect Janet. An elderly African American couple sit in one corner, holding hands, and a girl, eight or nine stands next to them.

"My name is Zorn," I say to the nurse. "I'm told Janet wants to speak with me."

"The surgery was successful," the nurse tells me. "The doctors are hopeful, but the patient needs rest. She's asleep now. I'll call you as soon as she's able to talk."

I go to the elderly couple and introduce myself.

"I'm Vincent Cliff," the man says. "This is my wife, Sharon. We're Janet's parents. We just arrived from North Carolina."

"I'm pleased to meet you," I say. "I'm sorry it's under these terrible circumstances. I understand the doctors are optimistic."

Mr. Cliff nods. "They think she'll be fine. Do you know our daughter, Janet?"

"A little," I say. "We worked together over the last few days." I turn to the young girl. "And you are?"

"This is Rachel. Janet's daughter," Mr. Cliff tells me.

I never thought of Janet having a child. I guess I never thought to ask her about her family.

"Your mother is a very brave woman," I say to the girl. "A real hero. She probably saved the lives of many people. She certainly saved my life."

The girl looks at me with scorn that only a child can show for clueless adults.

Janet stirs in her bed and opens her eyes. Maybe she's heard my voice. She says something so softly I can't hear it. The nurse leans down to listen, then stands up and speaks to me. "The patient says she must talk to you. Please, a few words only. She needs rest."

Janet's eyes follow me as I approach her bedside.

"I need to talk to this man alone," Janet whispers. "Everyone else, stay away."

The nurse looks like she's about to argue.

"Everyone!" Janet's almost-shout is intimidating.

The nurse and the others in the room move quickly away, and I lean over the bed and speak softly to Janet.

"How are you feeling?"

"Like crap." She takes a deep, broken breath.

"You told me you always wanted combat experience," I say. "You finally got your chance."

"Fuck off, Detective. You're not funny." She gasps for air. "They say I shot the assailant last night. That's not how it happened, is it?" She takes another deep breath. "The shooter got me before I could get off a single round. You're the one who killed that son of a bitch. I saw you fire your weapon—it was you."

"You're going to be okay and the prime minister is safe."

From the distance comes the sound of multiple police sirens arriving at the hospital. I'm guessing somebody has stumbled across the two guys I left dead in the stairwell and has called 911.

Janet takes another ragged breath. "He was coming toward us. You were behind me, Detective. It wasn't the prime minister he was after, was he? Somebody wants *you* dead."

CHAPTER THIRTY-SIX

Two men, both wearing brown suits and white shirts and what seem to be identical green ties, grab me by my arms from both sides as I step out of the intensive-care unit. I can tell they're FBI. What have I done now?

"Detective Zorn, you're under arrest," one of them announces loudly. The second man pats me down efficiently and removes my Ruger.

"What am I being arrested for?"

"For the murders of Victoria West, Nikos Mazarakis, and the attempted murder of Nina Voychek."

"You are also carrying a concealed weapon, which is illegal in the District of Columbia."

"I'm a police officer."

The second man sniffs at the Ruger. "It's been fired recently."

"Come with us," the first man says.

"Come where?" I demand.

"To where we're taking you to."

"Who *are* you guys?"

"You have the right to remain silent," the first man says as they push me toward the bank of elevators. "Anything you say can and may be used against you in a court of law."

The irony here doesn't escape me. Except I don't believe in irony. These clowns want to arrest me for three murders I had nothing to do with. And just beyond the door to the stairs lie two dead men in the stairwell whose demise I had a great deal to do with.

The sooner I get out of here, the better.

"Come quietly or we'll have to hurt you."

The two men hustle me into an empty elevator, waving away others trying to get in, and we descend to the lobby. Lieutenant Bonifacio sees us and starts to cross the lobby to intervene. I wave him off. No need for him to get involved in my problems. I wouldn't want his record, which, I assume until now has been spotless, to be ruined by associating with me.

My escorts and I leave the hospital and climb into a waiting black SUV with tinted windows, parked directly in front of the entrance in a "No Parking" area. I'm shoved into the back seat between two burly guys one of whom is wearing way too much Old Spice.

We drive for maybe fifteen minutes through downtown DC and finally stop on a quiet side street with mostly small, two-story buildings. I'm hauled out of the SUV and taken into a brick building that looks like it could house a dentist's office. There's no sign on the door—not even a street number. I'm familiar with most of the FBI's safe houses in the city, but this one is new to me.

For a couple of minutes, we stand in an uneasy group in what, in a normal building, would be a lobby. My escorts talk among themselves in hushed whispers and then they gesture for me to move and we march down some stairs and along a corridor painted a faded green. They usher me into a room furnished with a wooden desk and four gray-metal chairs. If you've seen one interrogation room, you've seen them all.

My escorts take seats opposite me. One has a neatly trimmed, gray beard—I didn't know the FBI allowed beards—the other, somewhat younger, is clean-shaven. They both take identical notebooks from their jacket pockets—must be Bureau-issue, I figure—flip them open, and place them on the table in front of them.

"What's this all about?" I ask.

"We ask the questions here, Detective Zorn," the one with the beard answers.

"Questions? You have questions?"

The one with the beard stares at me. "You some kind of comedian? You hear the man, Gene? He's a comedian. You should be on *Saturday Night Live*. We've heard of you, Detective. You got a reputation as a major troublemaker and all 'round jerk. How is it you're able, all by yourself, to irritate most of the law enforcement agencies in this city?"

"It's a gift."

There's a long moment of sullen silence. "Were you at the reception last night at the Lincoln Memorial?" the one with the beard asks.

"You know I was. Along with several hundred other people."

"Why were you there?"

"I was working with the security group protecting the prime minister of Montenegro."

"You're not a security guard. How come you were providing security?"

"Beats me."

"That's not an adequate answer."

"I know, but that's the best I've got."

"You trying to be funny, Mr. Funny Man?"

I figure this is a rhetorical question and I don't bother to answer.

"Did someone hire you to attend the reception?"

"The United States Secretary of State."

"Why did he do that?"

"Ask him."

"We're asking you, comedian. He's busy."

"I'm busy."

I consider giving the two agents some additional lip but decide against it. As enjoyable as that would be, I don't have time for entertainment. I have an appointment in a very short time at the Capitol Theater with a killer.

"Tell us exactly what happened when Agent Cliff was shot."

"I was standing a few feet behind Agent Cliff," I tell them. "A man was coming at us, holding a gun. The man shot her."

"What happened to this man with the gun?"

"He dropped to the ground. It looked like he was shot in the head."

"Who shot him?"

"Hard to tell. There was a lot of confusion. I ran to Agent Cliff to see what happened to her and determined she'd been wounded."

"Then what did you do?"

"Several Diplomatic Security Service agents came, and I went looking for the prime minister."

"Why did you do that?"

"That was my job."

"What job?"

"I was part of the security detail there to protect the prime minister. Really, guys, are you not paying attention?"

"What did you do then?"

"I located the prime minister, got her into her car, and we left the scene. We drove to the official residence of the Embassy of Montenegro, where I left her."

"Detective Zorn," the man with the beard says, "you were seen snooping around the reception."

"Snooping is my profession."

"Before the reception began you were seen standing by the musicians' bandstand. Who were you meeting?"

"I wasn't meeting anybody. I was there because it was a good vantage point to observe what was going on."

"Were you looking for someone in particular?"

"No one in particular."

"What were you looking for?"

"Anybody who didn't belong there."

"Did you see anybody who didn't belong?"

"No."

"Except the man you claim shot Agent Cliff."

"Except him. That was later. Can I use your restroom?"

"You can use the restroom when I say you can."

I turn to the second man. "Do you ever have anything to say, Gene?" I ask. "Are you allowed to talk? Or is talking above your pay grade?"

"I'm asking the questions here," the first man announces.

"I'm getting bored talking to just one guy," I say. "I thought it might help improve the quality of our exchange if Gene jumped in now and then."

"You'll talk to whoever I tell you to, which is me," the beard declares.

"Have it your way, but I'd sure like to get some input from Gene. I'll bet he has some helpful ideas."

"Detective, you're failing to appreciate the seriousness of your situation. You seem to treat our investigation as some kind of joke."

"How *am* I supposed to treat it?" I ask.

"Three capital crimes have been committed. Maybe more."

"It looks like an assassin threatening the prime minister's life was killed," I say. "That's a good thing, isn't it?"

"There was an attempt on the life of a visiting head of state. One man, a man employed as a waiter, was shot and killed, and an employee of the US government was seriously wounded. Involvement in any of these incidents could be an act of treason."

"If you say so."

"Are you clear about how serious that is?"

"I want to use the bathroom."

"Two men were killed in one of the stairwells at the hospital you were visiting. One man was shot. The second seems to have fallen down three flights of stairs and broken his neck."

"You're telling me this because?"

"You were at the hospital when this happened."

"If you say so."

"We say so. Do you know anything about this incident?"

"It doesn't sound like something the FBI would be interested in. More like a standard police investigation."

"The police are at the scene of the crime now. But it struck us as curious you were present at the scene of *all* these crimes. Don't you find that curious?"

"Not really."

The man with the beard is about to say something I expect to be rude when there's a disturbance and the door to the room flies open. A man I haven't seen before sticks his head in and gestures urgently for one of my interrogators to come out. Gene goes out the door. In less than ten seconds, he's back in the room whispering urgently into the ear of the man with the beard. They both look agitated, and the beard guy jumps to his feet, almost knocking over his chair. Together they rush from the room without even saying goodbye.

"I want my gun back," I say. They pay no attention to me.

I sit in the room as patiently as I can, shifting position from time to time, but nothing I do makes the chair comfortable. I find myself checking my watch every minute or so. I'm getting anxious. I need to get out of here and get to the theater.

After almost half an hour, the door opens and a woman walks into the interrogation room. "Your assignment, Detective Zorn," she says, "was to protect Prime Minister Nina Voychek, not get yourself arrested by the FBI. Did I not make myself clear?"

Carla Lowry looks around the little room with profound distaste. She's not often reduced to spending time in places like this. "Why aren't you looking after Nina Voychek?"

"I think I'm being held by the FBI."

"Not any longer, you're not." She sits at the table across from me. "You can go. But before you do, I have to warn you—Goran Drach is now here in the States."

I feel my heart beat faster. I lean forward. "Where is he?"

Carla looks a bit abashed. "We don't know. I wish I did. All we know is he's here in the country."

"How can you not know where he is? What's the point of having a domestic spy agency if you can't find master criminals wandering around doing nasty things? A man you said was acting as the agent of the Russians . . . and you lost him?"

"You don't have to be offensive, Marko."

"You told me Goran Drach was working with the Russians to organize the assassination of Nina Voychek. That would suggest some priority."

"We know he's here through the CIA source in Montenegro. That's sensitive information from the CIA and is strictly close hold. They get into a snit if anyone talks about their secrets."

"I promise to be discreet."

"The CIA is very put out that the Bureau has lost their guy. I've already been lectured to once today. Don't you pile on."

"How do you know he's here?"

"Goran confirmed his arrival to his co-conspirators back in Montenegro by coded message. He told them he arrived here and was in place and they should prepare for the final act. Meaning the assassination of Nina Voychek and a counterrevolution back in Montenegro."

"When did he arrive?"

"A few days ago."

"And we're just hearing about it now?"

"He's traveling under an assumed name and we therefore have no record of a legal entry. The FBI's Counterterrorism Division has an alert out to all field offices to find Goran Drach, but that's going to be nearly impossible. We have no pictures of Goran and no good description."

"How can you have no pictures?"

"Goran Drach always stayed behind the scenes while his brother ran the country. When the Drach regime was about to collapse, Goran had all his pictures and TV film of him purged. Once he arrived on US territory, he simply vanished and is presumably operating under a false identity."

"No description?"

"Goran has no notable distinguishing characteristics or features: medium height, medium build. Speaks English with an accent."

"That's half the population of the United States."

I steal a glance at my watch trying to be discreet. Carla sees me. She sees everything.

"The CIA's source in Montenegro saw him as recently as three weeks ago. The agent asked him for a description. Not much help there. The source described Goran as having a black beard and a large Slavic nose."

"That's it?"

"One little detail. The source told the agent that Goran recently had surgery done secretly by a doctor who is loyal to the old regime."

"Why would Goran do that?" I ask.

"We have no idea."

"How do you expect me to protect Prime Minister Voychek if you don't know what the prime conspirator looks like or where he is?"

"I've told you all I know. But you haven't told me all you know. You haven't told me what the Greek said."

"The Greek admitted he was the middleman who recruited the assassin."

"Who is the assassin?"

"Domino."

"You're certain it's Domino?" Carla asks.

"I'm certain."

"According to our sources, the New York mob families are searching for this man Domino. Why would the mob be interested in Domino?"

"Beats me."

Carla looks at me suspiciously. "If they find him, that might save us all a lot of trouble. How did the Greek communicate with Domino?"

"He claimed his contacts were always through intermediaries and never in person. His principal go-between was a man in Paris who tragically fell into the Seine a week or so ago. The Greek said Goran Drach ran the operation locally to assassinate Nina Voychek."

"The CIA knows Goran has close ties to Vladimir Putin," Carla says. "They're pretty sure Putin and his intelligence agencies are financing this assassination. I assume Goran and the Greek worked together and that Goran had Domino take the Greek out before he was able to tell anyone about who else was involved in the plot."

"That doesn't get us anywhere," I say.

"The man in Chicago you asked me to protect . . . what's his connection?"

"He was one of three men, along with a bunch of friends and neighbors, who organized what amounted to a lynch mob and killed Mykhayl Drach, Goran's brother."

"Why did they do that?"

"They're from Montenegro and their families and friends back home suffered horribly in the massacres General Drach unleashed. In that part of the world, a crime like that must not go unpunished."

"Why do you keep looking at your watch?"

"I have an appointment at the Capitol Theater."

"You're supposed to be keeping Nina Voychek safe. Leave the Victoria West investigation to your partner, at least until the prime minister is out of the country. Keep your focus on the main issue: the safety of the prime minister."

"Vickie's murder and the plot to assassinate Nina Voychek are linked," I tell Carla. "Trust me. When I have the answer to one, I'll have the answer to both."

"Take care of your theater business, then get to the embassy. I want you in that car with Nina Voychek when she goes to the airport."

"I want my gun back. Your guys stole it."

Carla looks at me thoughtfully. "I thought you never carried a gun."

"This situation is different. Nina Voychek is in danger. I need my gun."

Carla bites her lower lip. "That might be difficult. I believe my guys, as you call them, have confiscated your weapon and sent it to the FBI lab for inspection. I don't think they trust you with a loaded gun. I'm not sure I trust you."

"Carla, I must have that gun."

"I'll get it back for you. It may take an hour or so. I'll send it to the Montenegro Embassy. You can pick it up from the ambassador when you get there."

CHAPTER THIRTY-SEVEN

THE ACTORS ARTHUR Cantwell, Natalie Esmond, and Tim Collins; the director, Garland Taylor; Lily, the props girl; and Michael Toland, the stage manager, are standing on the stage when I arrive. Cynthia Fletcher is here, too. Their expressions range from unhappy to enraged. In addition, Hanna Forbes and two bored DC homicide detectives have been added: one is Roy Hunt. Lucy corralled them to stand in for the stagehands who were backstage the night of the murder and as backup for what I hope will be closure to the Victoria West murder investigation and the exposure of the identity of Domino.

For this occasion, Hanna wears a bright yellow scarf along with her usual somber outfit and her Orioles cap. I thought it would be a treat for her to be at the scene before the crime takes place instead of, as usual, afterward.

Lucy is still deeply shaken by last night's experience at the reception, and she doesn't look like she's slept for days.

The set is as it was on the night of the murder. With the help of Lily and Michael Toland, everything is back in its place.

"Thank you for coming here today," I announce, trying to sound positive. "I know this is an inconvenience to many of you."

"You're damn right this is an inconvenience!" Garland Taylor yells at me. "It's more than an inconvenience, it's an outrage."

I'm spared having to reply by Arthur Cantwell demanding: "How long are we supposed to hang around this place? We've answered all your questions. I've had it! I'm leaving. If you want to stop me, you'll have to arrest me! And if you do, I'll sue your ass."

"We have jobs," Michael Toland says. "We have families and I'm losing money."

Even Cynthia Fletcher raises her voice above the tumult, soon to become yelling at me.

"A friend and colleague of yours—Victoria West—was murdered," I announce loudly, over their voices. "Right here in this theater. I don't give a damn about the inconvenience this causes you. Or your clients."

That shuts them up, at least for a moment.

"Hanna Forbes," I go on, "our crime scene specialist, is here to stand in for Victoria West and walk through the action as it was on the night of her murder. I want everyone to take their places where they were just before Victoria West entered the drawing room."

The group grumbles and mills around until everyone finds their places, some on the set, some backstage behind the double doors.

Hanna crosses the stage to the fireplace and Michael Toland gives her the play script.

"*How am I going to get through the evenings, here in this house?*" Hanna reads, a bit uncertainly.

"*I'm sure Judge Brack will be kind enough to drop in occasionally even though I will be away,*" Garland Taylor reads from the script.

"*Oh, every evening, Hedda,*" Arthur Cantwell calls out from his place. "*Every evening. And with the greatest of pleasure. We two will get along famously, I'm sure.*"

"Then Hedda crosses to the drawing room door," Taylor directs.

Hanna removes one of the prop guns from its bracket, crosses the stage to the drawing room door, stops uncertainly, looking first at Taylor, then at me.

"Your line, Hanna," I say encouragingly.

Hanna finds her place in the script and reads, *"I'm sure you flatter yourself that we will, Judge. Now that you are the only cock on the walk."*

Hanna opens the door and goes inside.

"Hedda steps into the drawing room," Taylor reads. "And closes the door behind her."

"Bang!" I say loudly. "That's supposed to be a gunshot. Drop your prop gun, Hanna. As close as you can to where you found the gun when you first inspected the crime scene."

There's a thud from inside the drawing room.

"The actors on stage are supposed to jump to their feet," Taylor says. "They open the door to the drawing room."

"What has she done?" Natalie calls out.

"Blackout!" Garland Taylor says, then to me. "Why are we doing this?" he asks me.

"Because I'm telling you to."

As Hanna emerges from the drawing room, I say to Taylor. "You came onto the stage at that point. How long would that have been after the shot?"

"Almost immediately. Ten seconds at most. I told Michael Toland to douse the stage lights and I went directly to the drawing room. I told everyone on stage to leave and I said something to the audience."

Taylor walks to the double doors, turns, and returns to the drawing room and peers in, then looks back at me. "Okay? Satisfied?"

"What was supposed to happen after Miss West entered the drawing room?" I ask.

"There's supposed to be a few seconds of silence. Then the shot. The actors do their thing, open the door to the drawing room, say their lines, the stage lights go out. End of play."

"Lucy," I say, "stand backstage behind the double doors. When I tell you, walk around the exterior wall of the drawing room and stand for a count of five at the far wall, then return to the double doors. Don't run: Just steady pace. Got it?"

"Got it."

I silently count as Lucy disappears around the corner of the outer wall of the set. After fourteen beats, she reappears, passes by the props table, and joins the group at the double doors.

"What does that prove," Garland Taylor demands.

"It proves there had to be two people involved in the killing," Tim Collins says.

"Very good," I say. "There had to be two people. When Vickie got into place in the drawing room, the killer simply opened the door to the backstage area and fired. It would have been a difficult shot. It was dark in the drawing room and the shooter, we calculate, was twenty feet away. The killer had to know exactly where she would be standing. The killer then passed the murder weapon to someone else, who went to the drawing room from the stage set, placed the gun in Vickie's hand, and then made a speech to the audience. Have I got that about right, Mr. Taylor?"

"Are you saying I put the gun in Vickie's hand? That I planned Vickie's murder? Why should I kill Victoria West?" His hands are shaking. "She was my leading lady in an important production. I had everything to lose by her death."

"Good question: why would you want to kill your leading lady? And why did Victoria West forget her last line?" I ask.

After a long, uncomfortable silence, while I wait for someone to speak up, I say, "Maybe I can help answer that. She didn't forget her lines. She was making a statement."

"That makes no sense," Arthur Cantwell says. "She said I was evil and would be exposed. Why would she say that to me? We were about to announce our engagement."

"She wasn't talking to you," I say. "She was talking to Garland Taylor, who was standing just behind the double door. This was all about a young actress named Valerie Crane. Remember her, Garland? Remember Valerie?"

"I have no idea what you're talking about," Taylor shouts at me.

"She was in your show *Blue Remembered Hills*. Halfway through the run, she quit. She just walked off the show. Why would she do that? Something that would ruin her career? While she was performing in your show, you invited her to your apartment to give her notes. You molested her. She resisted. You wouldn't stop until finally, not to put a fine point on it, you raped Valerie Crane."

"This is absurd! Nothing like that happened."

"What's this got to do with Vickie's death?" Michael Toland asks.

"After you were finished with her, you threatened to blackball her if she said anything to anyone about what happened. You said you'd see she'd never be cast in a play in New York again. You said you'd end her career."

"Jesus!" Garland yells. "You're making this up. You have no evidence of anything."

"That's true. But, like you, I've read the emails between Vickie and Cynthia I found on Vickie's laptop. I've seen Vickie's message saying she planned to denounce you on opening night of *Hedda Gabler*."

"What evidence do you have that I ever looked at Vickie's computer?"

"I have no evidence. But I know you did read her emails."

"You've got nothing."

"You knew the secret names Vickie used in her correspondence with Cynthia. No one else knew the names they used for each other. But you knew that Vickie used the name 'Ariel' when we talked that first night. The only way you could have known is if you'd read Vickie's emails. You got hold of her computer, searched her personal emails, and learned she signed herself 'Ariel.'"

"That kind of 'evidence' would never stand up in court."

"Maybe not in a court of law, but it will have great weight in the court of public opinion. I expect, once the word gets out, many women will come forward with their own stories."

Garland Taylor scans the faces of those around him to find support.

"You thought you were in the clear," I say. "No one saw you put the gun in the drawing room and into Vickie's hand. And then this stranger appears: this funny little man who wrote mystery novels shows up asking questions, and you realized he's figured how you did it. How you must have contracted with someone to kill Vickie, then have him pass you the gun so you could place it in her hand to make it look like suicide."

"You can't prove any of this fantasy."

"The murder weapon wasn't in the drawing room before the performance, so our writer figures someone had to put it there after the murder. And that had to be you, Mr. Taylor. You were the only one to go inside that room. If you are not the killer, you are the accessory. So then you arranged to have the detective–story writer murdered. By the same person who killed Victoria West."

Roy Hunt steps behind Garland Taylor and grabs him by the right arm. The second man from homicide takes Taylor by the left arm.

My cell phone rings. It's Rick Talbot, Janet Cliff's deputy. "The prime minister has disappeared!" he says, not waiting for me to say anything. "Come to the embassy. Now."

There were seven men and women from the cast and crew of *Hedda Gabler* standing on stage when I arrived at the theater.

Now there are six.

Then I remember what the mystery book writer told me about creating a plot. The obvious motive is never the right one. It's the motive you miss.

"Lucy," I say. "I've made a mistake. Vickie's murder was not about exposing Garland Taylor. It was a peasant curse from the Black Mountain."

CHAPTER THIRTY-EIGHT

I GRAB LUCY by the arm and lead her urgently offstage.

"What about Garland Taylor?" she protests as we rush through the auditorium. "I have enough to arrest him."

"Leave him to Roy."

"Roy! This is *my* case! This should be my collar."

We're in the lobby and Lucy tries to free herself from my grip.

"There won't be any charges against Taylor." I won't let her go.

"How can you say that? He must have hired someone to kill Victoria West. He arranged to have that mystery book writer killed. And maybe even the man you call the Greek."

We're out of the lobby and onto the street, standing under the marquee.

"He didn't kill any of them. He probably *did* pay to have Vickie killed, but he didn't pull the trigger. You proved that when you retraced the killer's steps."

Lieutenant Bonifacio is sitting in a police cruiser waiting for me.

"That's not fair," Lucy says. "We could have gotten the son of a bitch on something. This is my last case. I want to leave the force with something positive on my record. Not my miserable performance from last night."

"Not worth it. Leave him to his fate."

"What fate?"

"The word is now out about what he did to Valerie Crane. And there are probably others like her. He's ruined. And he'll go to jail."

I yank open the rear door of the cruiser.

"In you go," I say to Lucy.

"Where are we going?"

"To find the man who really killed Vickie West. Take us to the Montenegro embassy," I call to Bonifacio. "Use sirens and flashers. This is an emergency."

The police cruiser pulls away with squealing tires, and Lucy and I are slammed back into the rear seat.

"What's going on?" Lucy demands angrily. "Did you know all along there was a second man?"

"I never believed that either Arthur Cantwell or Garland Taylor had the expertise or the nerve to shoot Vickie at that distance and in the dark."

"Who was it then?"

"Aubrey Sands gave us the key. He said it was never a 'locked room' murder: it was always misdirection. I didn't take him seriously at first and didn't think through what he told me. Finally, I realized Aubrey meant that there had to be two people involved: one to shoot Vickie, then pass the murder weapon unnoticed to somebody else to place the gun in Vickie's hand to make it look like suicide. We know it had to be Garland because he was the only one to go into that drawing room."

"But Taylor had everything to lose with the death of his leading lady."

"He had even more to lose if she lived. Vickie was going to out him for raping Valarie Crane. And there were probably others victims. Garland had to silence Vickie. Permanently. But he didn't have the skill or the nerve to do the job himself. So he hired someone who does these things for a living."

"How could Garland have arranged for a hit man? His circle of friends and acquaintances are actors, directors. Not gangsters."

"That's not difficult if you know the right people. Garland Taylor has connections with the mob. His mother comes from Naples and has close family ties with several of the Mafia families. If you have the connections and the money, it's not hard to find someone to do your dirty work."

"You haven't told me who the murderer is."

"It's not just Vickie's killer we're after. It's the man who planned the whole thing. A man named Goran Drach."

"How is he involved?"

"This was never just about Vickie. It was always about me."

"Why you?"

"Goran Drach wants to punish me for the death of his brother, Mykhayl Drach, in Chicago at the hands of an angry mob a few weeks ago."

"What's your connection?"

"I was in Chicago to locate Mykhayl Drach. I was supposed to turn him over to the International Court of Justice for Crimes against Humanity. I informed certain individuals in Chicago where Mykhayl Drach was hiding. Drach was brutally murdered and Goran Drach holds me responsible. He's from the valleys of the Black Mountain, where personal vengeance is a matter of honor. He wanted to hurt me in the most painful way he could imagine. He must have learned that Vickie West was a woman I once deeply loved, and he was determined to hurt me through her violent death, just as he was hurt through his brother's death. That made her his target. After which I'm to be taken out."

"Was the man you shot last night at the reception the assassin?"

"The real assassin wouldn't show his hand so publicly. The real assassin is also in hiding now. He wouldn't dare expose himself like that. Last night was a dress rehearsal by a second-string team hired from the Brooklyn Russian Mafia."

"Do you know the name of the assassin?"

"He calls himself Domino. I don't know his real name."

"How do we find this man?"

"He'll find me."

"Are you going to take him on unarmed?"

"I'll be armed. The FBI confiscated my weapon, but I'll get it back."

"Why would they confiscate your gun?"

"It's a long story. My gun is waiting for me at the embassy. Besides, I'll have you as backup."

I speak encouragingly. I need for Lucy to feel confident and assured. She better be. My life depends on it.

CHAPTER THIRTY-NINE

BONIFACIO PULLS UP to the front of the Montenegro embassy, and Lucy and I rush up the steps to the front door. "Follow us," I tell Bonifacio.

The iron gate to the embassy is locked. I press the brass doorbell hard, then call Rick Talbot on my cell phone and tell him we're waiting at the front door. He tells me Nina is still missing.

The short man with the steel-rimmed glasses appears on the far side of the inner door and shakes his head and blinks his eyes. Rick Talbot appears on the inside and argues with the short man, who reluctantly unlocks first the iron gate and then the glass doors. Lucy and I push in, followed by Bonifacio. The chubby receptionist stares at us in panicked outrage.

"You are not allowed in," the man in the glasses expostulates.

"These people are here to help find the Prime Minister," Talbot says. "Let them do their job."

The man in glasses is blocking our way.

Ambassador Lukshich and Viktor Savich appear, on a run. "What is the meaning of this?" the ambassador demands angrily. "This is the official soil of the Republic of Montenegro. You have no authority here. You must leave immediately."

"We're here to search for the prime minister," I say.

"That is our affair. We will take care of that matter."

"Are you taking care of that matter?" I demand.

"There is no danger to Madame Voychek here," the ambassador says. "Viktor has assured me the assassin was killed at the reception at the Lincoln Memorial. Is that not true, Viktor?"

"Yes, Excellency."

"We will find her," the ambassador announces. "The prime minister's absence is of no concern to the government of the United States."

"It is of great concern to my government," Rick Talbot almost shouts. "I insist you let us search the embassy."

"Permission denied. Your presence here," the ambassador says, "is a violation of our nation's territorial sovereignty under international law and the terms of the Brussels Convention and the Treaty of Vienna. My government will protest to your government in the strongest possible terms this violation of our sovereignty."

"Have you forgotten the Helsinki protocol of 1869?" I demand. "Paragraph three?'

The ambassador hesitates. He suspects I'm making this up, which of course I am, but so is he, and, in the heat of the moment, he can't remember whether there is such a thing as the Helsinki protocol or, if there is, what it says. In hesitating, he loses the initiative. Never hesitate.

"I cannot allow uniformed and armed members of your police into the chancery of our embassy" is the best he can come up with.

"My officer will stay here in the reception area."

I tell Bonifacio to wait there but on no account be bullied into leaving the building.

"I will not allow you to search the Chancery." the ambassador is almost shouting. "That is off-limits."

"We'll search the residence only," I say.

"The residence only."

"Agreed."

"And remember, we leave for Dulles Airport in less than an hour."

"At 4:10 exactly," Savich adds. "We must not be late."

"Before you go," the ambassador says to me, "I have something for you. A package was hand-delivered to the embassy just a short while ago."

The ambassador takes a small package wrapped in brown paper from the reception desk and hands it to me. The sender is listed as the Federal Bureau of Investigation, 935 Pennsylvania Avenue, Washington, DC, but there is no name. The address reads: Detective Marko Zorn, care of His Excellency the Ambassador of Montenegro, followed by the embassy's address. A note follows saying this must be delivered to Detective Zorn by hand and must not be opened by anyone else.

The package is wrapped in heavy tape and feels substantial.

"Thank you, Mr. Ambassador. I'll take it from here."

I grab the package and Rick Talbot, Lucy, and I head upstairs at a run into the residential area. Savich follows.

"We can't allow them to exclude us from the embassy itself," Talbot protests. "She could be anywhere in the building. Maybe even in the ambassador's office."

"You're overreacting." Savich says.

"There'll be another attempt on her life," I say. "Goran Drach will try again before she can get on that plane."

I take Savich to one side. "I suggest you and your security team search the offices in the chancery. Rick, Lucy, and I will search the residential parts of the embassy."

"Very well. I'll organize search parties for the chancery area." Savich hurries away.

"Wait here," I say to Lucy and Talbot. I go downstairs to the door leading to the embassy garage. No one's guarding the entrance. The interior door to the garage is open. The two limousines sit side by side, washed, polished, and gleaming, ready for the trip to Dulles Airport. The American and Montenegro flags are secured onto the front fenders of the lead car.

I yank the two flags from their brackets, cross to the number two car, and secure the flags into the brackets on its fenders: the US flag on the right fender, the Montenegrin on the left. I hope I remember the flag protocol correctly: Too late now to find out. I open the lockbox and switch the tags identifying the two limousines.

I inspect the package the ambassador gave me, and I sense something is wrong. There's a slight tear on one of the pieces of tape that seal the package. I can see that somebody has opened the package and probably inspected its contents. Then resealed it.

I tear open the package. Inside rests my Ruger nestled in bubble wrap. I inspect the gun. The clip is loaded, with two rounds gone. I rack the slide and the action is smooth.

But then I touch the firing pin and it feels rough, as if it had been abraded. I hold the weapon up to the light and can see the firing pin's been filed short. The Ruger has been effectively disabled. If I have to use it, it will misfire. I replace the gun in my holster and hope for the best.

Back upstairs, I find Lucy with Rick Talbot waiting for me.

"I have no idea where that woman has got to," Talbot says. "My teams are working through the residence, floor by floor." He looks at his watch. "We're supposed to leave in twenty minutes."

"We'll have a better chance if we split up," I say. "I'll start in the basement. Rick, you take this floor. Lucy, you come with me."

I lead Lucy into the prime minister's private suite and take her down a back corridor. We stop at a small door next to a wardrobe. I open the door. Beyond is a flight of narrow wooden stairs.

"What's this?" Lucy asks.

"People staying in places like this aren't supposed to be inconvenienced by servants emptying wastebaskets or carryings dirty linen. This is the back door to the servants' quarters. Nina told me there's always a back door."

We rush down the narrow staircase to the basement and through the storage rooms I remember from the last time I came this way: a room stacked with boxes, another filled with metal filing cabinets. We blunder through a room with no lights, then into a small conference room.

"I'll search the conference room," Lucy tells me.

"Will you be all right on your own?" I ask.

She draws her Glock. "I'll be fine." She sounds confident, but I'm not so sure.

I go along another corridor, past a room with recycle containers, open a door, and step into the embassy kitchen. It's as I remember: the stainless steel cabinets, worktables, several large gas stoves, a walk-in refrigerator, and three deep iron sinks. The room is spotless, the surfaces gleam.

Nina Voychek stands at one of the steel tables. She smiles a bit shamefacedly. "Sorry, Marko. I had to be by myself for a few minutes. Have I caused problems once again?"

"Your security teams are looking everywhere for you."

"Viktor Savich said the danger is over. He suggested I come here and get a bite to eat before the trip to the airport." She studies me intently. "Was Viktor wrong?"

"Let's go." I take Nina by the arm and start to lead her gently but quickly to the kitchen door.

"Not yet. We have unfinished business."

A man stands across the kitchen from us. He wears dark clothes and an open-neck shirt and has long blond hair. He smiles at us sweetly. In his hand he holds a Walther automatic. The voice sounds familiar, but I can't place it.

I can't make my mind work: I can't process who this man is.

He speaks not in the soft whispers I've been accustomed to. It's strong and deep and confident. Lily, or Props, as I've come to know this person, is no longer a shy, fragile woman—he's now a man—calm and deadly.

Nina Voychek looks at me. "Who is this man? What does he want?"

"I am Domino," he says, pulling the blond wig from his head. I see the red scar on his forehead. A lasting reminder of a pot of boiling tomato sauce thrown at him many years ago.

"This is not a prop." Domino points his weapon directly at Nina.

My heart is pounding. Standing before me is the most dangerous killer I've ever faced. My Ruger is useless. Domino must know that.

I step forward to stand between Nina and Domino.

"Very gallant." Domino smiles, almost a sweet smile. "Gallant. But stupid." He holds the Walther automatic rock-steady, aimed directly at my forehead only a few feet away. He can't miss at this distance.

"Time's up," he murmurs. I force myself to stay cool and concentrate despite the fear pulsing through my veins. I look for a weapon— for anything. There is nothing.

"Don't move." Lucy stands at the door to the kitchen, her Glock pointed steadily at Domino. Lucy's voice is calm. "You're under arrest," Lucy commands.

Domino is stunned. He doesn't expect this and he hesitates as he turns to Lucy. A fatal mistake.

Lucy is pointing the gun at Domino's chest. I can see the rage in her eyes as she raises her Glock and points at Domino's head. I want to scream: *No, Lucy. Not a head shot. You'll miss.* Domino smiles at her.

"Drop the gun, bitch," Lucy commands.

Lucy fires. A single head shot between the eyes, not far from the scar. A single red circle like a third eye appears on the forehead of the person I knew as Props.

I let my breath out. She did what I told her not to do. She aimed for the T-Box. And she made the shot.

She'll make a great cop.

CHAPTER FORTY

LUCY'S GUN DROPS to the floor from her nerveless hand. "Dead?" she asks, almost a whisper.

"Get out!" I yell. "Out now!" I kick the Walther far from Domino's dead fingers.

Nina grabs Lucy firmly by the arm. "I'll take care of her," she says to me as she rushes Lucy out of the kitchen.

I pick up Lucy's Glock and the spent cartridge from the floor and place them in my pocket.

We return the way we came, through basement rooms and up the narrow stairs to Nina's private suite, Nina holding tight to Lucy's trembling arm.

Talbot is waiting for us, so mad he can barely speak.

"Don't ask," I say. "You don't want to know. Stay with Nina."

"We leave for the airport in ten minutes," he says.

"Don't say a word about what happened," I whisper to Nina. "Not to anyone until you're on board your plane and well out of US air space."

I need to get Nina away as soon as possible. I can't have an investigation into Domino's death delay Nina getting on that plane. There's somebody else, even more dangerous than Domino, waiting for her.

I lead Lucy through the waiting room and down the steps to the embassy's front entrance, where Bonifacio waits for us at the reception desk. "Call Frank Townsend," I tell him. "Tell him to come to the Montenegro embassy and take care of Lucy. Now."

Bonifacio is on his cell phone immediately.

"It was a clean kill, Lucy," I say. "It was by the book."

"Fuck the book. Who *was* that man?" Lucy asks, her voice hoarse.

"He was a hired killer who called himself Domino. He killed Victoria West and, later, Aubrey Sands. There are other victims. Stay here until Frank arrives."

I return to Nina's reception area, where Nina and Rick Talbot are waiting.

"Was that man the assassin?" Nina asks. "Was he going to kill me?"

"He's no longer a threat to you. The assassin is dead, but the person who hired him is very much alive."

"Let's get out of here," Talbot says urgently.

Viktor Savich appears when we get into the garage. "Where did you find her?"

"In the kitchen."

"Did you have any problems?"

"Nothing I couldn't handle."

"We must leave now," Savich says.

"We must get on the road. I'll drive the lead car," Talbot says. "And my man will ride shotgun in front with me. Madame Prime Minister—" Talbot gestures as he opens the right passenger door of the limousine with the American and Montenegro flags on the front fenders. "If you please. We're behind schedule."

Nina starts to get into the back seat of the limousine, then hesitates. "Marko?"

"Detective Zorn will go with you to the airport," Talbot says. Nina nods and slips into the car. "Ambassador Lukshich and Mr. Savich will take the follow car, as arranged."

"We will be right behind you," Savich says. "We will stay in touch by cell phone and see that there are no problems."

I get into the limousine with the official flags and take the seat next to Nina. Savich, followed by the ambassador, gets into the second limousine: Savich at the wheel, the ambassador next to him on the front passenger seat. Talbot's men open the garage doors and in front of us two DC police cruisers are waiting.

Talbot speaks on his radio, then turns and looks at Nina in the back seat. "We're good to go, Madame Prime Minister. The route has been cleared. We should have you at the airport in forty minutes."

Talbot turns back, starts the ignition, and we glide out of the garage, the follow limousine right behind us.

"The young woman with you," Nina asks. "Is she your partner? Will she be all right?"

"I'll see that she'll be all right."

"It's not over, is it?" Nina asks. "Goran Drach failed this time, but he'll be waiting for me when I return home to Montenegro."

"Let's find out." I punch in the number of Viktor's cell phone on my phone. It rings once and the ambassador answers. We're a block from the embassy now. Traffic is light and what few cars there are have been pulled over to the side of Massachusetts Avenue by our motorcycle police escort.

"Yes?" Lukshich says. "What is it?"

I turn in my seat. The limousine with the ambassador and Savich is four or five car lengths behind us. The space between us growing.

"I wanted to check how you're doing," I say.

"We are doing fine," the ambassador says impatiently.

"You seem to be some distance from us," I say. "Aren't you supposed to be immediately behind our vehicle?"

"Just keep moving."

"There's something you should know, Excellency," I say. "Before we left the embassy, I took the liberty of switching the diplomatic flags from one vehicle to the other. We're riding in the limousine meant for you. You're riding in the limousine intended for the prime minister. There's no problem unless Viktor put a bomb in the prime minister's car."

I hear a wild shriek.

"This is for Vickie," I say. "See you in hell!"

Savich screams as his limousine disintegrates in a white fireball.

Talbot floors the accelerator hard and we surge ahead. The police cruisers and motorcycles have turned on their flashers and sirens. I catch one final glimpse of the limousine we were supposed to be riding in, now engulfed in flames. Two police cruisers have pulled over to inspect the remains of the exploding car and its passengers.

"What just happened, Marko?" Nina demands, her voice shaking. "Was that Viktor? The Ambassador?" She holds my hand in a fierce grip.

"I'm afraid they blew themselves up."

"Tell me . . ."

"The assassin planted a bomb in the vehicle we were supposed to take to the airport. We were supposed to leave the embassy at 4:10 and it looks like it was designed to explode at 4:20. It went off like clockwork."

"What happened to Viktor?"

"Viktor Savich planned your assassination and hired the assassin Domino."

"Viktor was my protector. Why would he harm me? Or you?"

"The man you knew as Viktor . . . His real name was Goran Drach."

"I don't believe you."

"Drach assumed the identity of someone named Viktor Savich, a policeman. Probably somebody he'd murdered. Then he had himself assigned to your security team. Did you notice the bruises on his face?"

"Of course. He told me he was beaten in a brawl."

"Those weren't bruises from a fight. Those were from plastic surgery. Probably done several weeks ago. That way no one in your entourage would recognize him. And traveling with your team on your aircraft allowed him to get into this country without going through normal passport control."

"He was with me every day. He could have killed me at any time. I understand why Goran Drach wanted to get rid of me. But why you?"

"He was under the impression I was responsible for the death of his brother, Mykhayl Drach."

Nina studies my face intently. "Were you?"

I decide not to answer.

"And the actress. She had nothing to do with my country's politics."

"Victoria West was a woman I once loved a long time ago. She was killed to punish me."

"And Yulia, the code clerk?"

"She read the messages to the embassy arranging for your assassination. Your ambassador was part of the plot. He was the one who saw to it that I was assigned to your protection detail. He was the one who let the assassin into the embassy to trap you in the basement kitchen. Yulia read the messages. That's why she had to die."

Nina covers her face with her hands. "That poor girl. That poor, poor girl."

When we reach the Dulles airport terminal, there's no lengthy departure ceremony. Talbot wants to get Nina and her entourage out of the country. He and his men hustle the crowd out onto the tarmac and into the waiting aircraft.

I stand to one side. My job here is done.

The crowd thins. Nina Voychek speaks with several men and women who, I assume, are US officials, then she breaks away and strides quickly across the asphalt floor to me.

She rises on her toes and, without a word, gives me a kiss on the mouth, warm and hard, then turns and disappears through the large doors and out onto the tarmac and into the waiting plane.

PUBLISHER'S NOTE

We hope that you enjoyed *Head Shot*, the second novel in the Marko Zorn Thriller Series.

Book 1 is *The Reflecting Pool*.

Washington, DC politics at its most savage and brutal—with Marko Zorn in the crosshairs of the White House and competing DC gangs

"In *The Reflecting Pool*, Eskin has created the best crime hero this side of Michael Connelly's Harry Bosch."

—Jon Land,
USA Today best-selling author

If you have not already read *The Reflecting Pool*, we hope that you will—and that you look forward to more Marko Zorn novels to come.

For more information, please visit the author's website:
othoeskin.com

Happy reading,
Oceanview Publishing